D0991273

ST JOSEPH PUB LIBRARY
0801 9100 038 216 3

Lad
OF SUNNYBANK

ALBERT PAYSON TERHUNE

Lad

OF SUNNYBANK

Grosset & Dunlap
PUBLISHERS
NEW YORK

BY ARRANGEMENT WITH HARPER & BROTHERS

PRINTED IN THE UNITED STATES OF AMERICA

To

Lad's Many Thousand Friends,

Young and Old, Everywhere,

My Book Is Dedicated

CONTENTS

Lad
OF SUNNYBANK

Chapter One

THE WHISPERER

DOWN the winding and oak-shaded furlong of driveway between Sunnybank House and the main road trotted the huge mahogany-and-snow collie. He was mighty of chest and shoulder, heavy of coat, and with deepset dark eyes in whose depths lurked a Soul.

Sunnybank Lad was returning home after a galloping hunt for rabbits in the forests beyond The Place.

On the veranda of the gray old house sat the Mistress and the Master, at the end of the day's work. At the Mistress's feet, as always, lay Wolf, the fiery little son of Lad. Gigantic Bruce —dog without a flaw—sprawled asleep near him. Behind the Master's chair snoozed Bruce's big young auburn son, Bobbie.

Ordinarily these collies would have fared forth with their king, Lad, on his rabbit hunt. But, this afternoon, one and all of them had been through the dreaded ordeal of a scrubbing at the

hands of Robert Friend, The Place's English superintendent, and one of the other men.

Lad had recognized the preparations for this loathly flea-destroying scrub and had seen the disinfectant mixed in the bath-barrel. So he trotted off, alone, to the woods, unseen by the other dogs or by the men.

Lad loved his swims in the lake at the foot of the oak-starred lawn. But he abhorred the evil-smelling barrel-dip—a dip designed to free him of the fleas which begin to infest every outdoor long-haired dog with the full advent of spring.

When the Master chanced to be at hand to supervise the dipping, Lad remained, always, martyr-like, to take his own share of the ordeal. But today the Master had been shut up in his study all afternoon. Lad ever refused to recognize any authority save only his and the Mistress's. Wherefore his truant excursion to the woods.

Wolf glanced up from his drowse before Lad had traveled halfway down the driveway, on his homeward journey. Wolf was The Place's official watch-dog. Asleep or awake, his senses were keen. It was he that had heard or scented his returning sire before any of the rest. The Mistress saw him raise his head from the mat at her feet, and she followed the direction of his inquiring glance.

"Here comes Laddie," she said. "Robert was looking all over for him when he dipped the other dogs. He came and asked me if ——"

"Trust Lad to know when dipping-day comes around!" laughed the Master. "Unless you or I happen to be on hand, he always gives the men the slip. He ——"

"He's carrying something in his mouth!" interposed the Mistress—"something gray and little and squirmy. Look!"

The great collie had caught sight of his two human deities on the veranda. He changed his trot to a hand gallop. His plumed tail waved gay welcome as he came toward them. Between his powerful jaws he carried with infinite care and tenderness a morsel of tawny-gray fluff which twitched and struggled to get free.

Up to the veranda ran Lad. At the Mistress's feet he deposited gently his squirming burden. Then, his tail waving, he gazed up at her face, to note her joy in the reception of his gift.

Forever, Lad was bringing things home to the Mistress from his woodland or highroad walks. Once the gift had been an exquisite lace parasol, with an ivory handle made from an antique Chinese sword—a treasure which apparently had fallen from some passing motorcar.

Again, he had deposited at her feet a very dead

and very much flattened chicken, run over by some careless motorist and flung into a wayside ditch, whence Lad had recovered it.

Of old, a run-over chicken or dog or cat was all but unknown in the sweet North Jersey hinterland. Horses and horse drivers gave such road-crossers a fair chance to get out of the way; nor did horses approach at such breakneck pace that too often there could be no hope of escape.

Today, throughout that same hinterland, as everywhere else in America—though practically never in Great Britain—pitiful little wayside corpses mark the tearing passage of the twentieth-century juggernaut.

The slain creatures' owners pay for the smooth roads which permit speed to the invading motorists, thus becoming in a measure the motorists' hosts. The intruders reward the hospitality not only by murderously reckless speed, but by stripping roadside woods and dells of their flowering trees—usually leaving the fragrantly beautiful trophies to wilt and die in the cars' tonneaus and then throwing away the worthless trash before reaching their day's destination.

Where once there were miles of flowery dogwood and mountain laurel and field blossoms bordering the roads, there are now desolation and the stumps of wrenched-off branches and uprooted sod, which mingle picturesquely with chicken bones and greasy paper and egg shells and other pretty remnants of motor-picnickers' roadside lunches.

In one or two states an effort has been made to curb reckless driving by erecting white crosses at spots where some luckless pedestrian has been murdered by a speeding car. In these states the motorists have protested vigorously to the courts; begging that the grim reminders be removed, as the constant sight of them mars the fun of a jolly ride.

But nowhere have crosses or other warnings been raised over the death-places of car-smashed livestock; nor to mark the wastes where once bloomed glorious flowers. There would not be enough crosses to go around, if all craftsmen toiled night and day to turn them out.

It used to be said that grass never again grew where Attila, the raiding Hun, had ridden. Attila was a humane and tenderly considerate old chap; compared to the brainless and heartless and speed-delirious driver of a present-day instalment-payment car.

Lad had shown deep chagrin when the Mistress recoiled from the long-dead and much-flattened chicken he had brought home to her and when the Master ordered it taken away and buried. Carefully the dog had dug it up again, evidently thinking it had been interred by mistake. With wistful affection he had deposited it on the floor close beside the Mistress's chair in the dining-room, and he had been still more grieved at the dearth of welcome which had greeted its return from the grave.

The Mistress looked with dubious curiosity at today's offering he had just brought her. Even before he laid it down on the floor the other dogs were pressing around in stark excitement. Lad stood over his find, baring his teeth and growling deep down in his furry throat. At such a threat from their acknowledged king, not one of the other collies—not even fiery Wolf—dared to come closer.

The Mistress stooped to touch the grayish creature her chum and worshiper had brought home to her from the forests.

It was a baby raccoon.

Unhurt, but fussily angry and much confused by its new surroundings, was the forest waif. It snarled at the Mistress and sought peevishly to dig its tiny milk-teeth into her caressing fingers. Instantly Lad caught it up again, holding it deftly by the nape of its neck, as if to show the

Mistress how the feeble infant might be handled without danger of a bite.

As she did not avail herself of the hint, he laid the baby raccoon down again and began solicitously to lick it all over.

How he had chanced upon the creature, back there in the woods, nobody was ever to know. Perhaps its mother had been shot or trapped and the hungry and helpless orphan's plight had touched the big collie's heart—a heart always ridiculously soft toward anything young and defenseless.

In any event, he had brought it home with him and had borne it at once to the Mistress as if begging her protection for it.

"What are we to do with the wretched thing?" demanded the Master. "It ——"

"First of all," suggested the Mistress, "I think we'd better feed it. It looks half starved. I'll get some warm milk. I wonder if it has learned how to eat."

It had not. But it learned with almost instant ease, lapping up the milk ravenously and with a tongue which every minute spilled less and swallowed more. Its appetite seemed insatiable. All the while it was eating, Lad stood guard over the saucer, inordinately proud and happy that his forest refugee had been rescued from starvation.

"He's taken the little fellow under his protection," said the Mistress. "I suppose that means we must keep the raccoon. At least till it can fend for itself. Then we can turn it loose in the woods again."

"To be killed by the first pot hunter or the first stray cur that comes along?" queried the Master. "That is the penalty for turning loose woodland creatures that have been tamed. When you tame a wild animal or a wild bird and then let it go free, you're signing its death warrant. You take away from it the fear that is its only safeguard. No; let's send it to a zoo as soon as it can live there comfortably. That's the better solution."

The Mistress's gaze roved over the placid sunset lawns, to the fire-blue lake and then to the rolling miles of hills and of springtime forest. She said, half to herself:

"If I had my choice, whether to leave all this for a cramped cage and to spend my life there, behind bars, with people staring at me or poking at me—or to go to sleep forever—I should choose the sleep. It's pitiful to think of any forest creature changing its outdoor heritage for a zoo. I hate to visit such places. It always gives me a heartache to see wild things jailed for life, like that."

"All of which," growled the Master, "means you've made up your mind you want to keep the measly little cuss here, for always. But ——"

"Lots of people have told me a tame raccoon makes a wonderful pet," observed the Mistress, with elaborate dearth of interest. "And I've always wanted one, ever so much. So—so, we'll do exactly whatever you think best."

"Sheer hypocrisy!" groaned the master. " 'Whatever I think best!' That means you and Lad have decided to give this forlorn brute a home at The Place. All right. Only, when it eats up all our chickens and then gets killed by the dogs, or when it murders one of our best collies (they say a raccoon is a terrible fighter), don't blame *me*."

"If you'd rather we didn't keep it," said the Mistress, demurely, as she stroked the fuzzy gray fur of the food-stupefied wisp at her feet, "why, of course we won't. You know that. . . What shall we call it? I—I think Rameses is a wonderful name for a pet raccoon. Don't you?"

"Why Rameses?" argued the Master, glumly.

"Why *not* Rameses?" demanded the Mistress, in polite surprise.

"I don't know the answer," grouchily admitted

the defeated Master. "Rameses it is. Or rather *he* is. I—I think it's a hideous name, especially for a coon. Let's hope he'll die. Lad, next time you go into the woods, I'll muzzle you. You've just let us in for a mort of bother."

Lad wriggled self-consciously, and stooped again to lick smooth the ruffled fur of Rameses. This time the little raccoon did not resent the attention. Instead, he peered up at his adopters with a queerly shrewd friendliness in his beady black eyes. His comedy mask of a face seemed set in a perpetual grin. The food had done wonders to reconcile him to his new home.

He reared on his short hind legs and clasped Lad's lowered neck with his fuzzy arms, his sharp snout pressed to the collie's ear, as if whispering to him.

The Master snapped his fingers, summoning the other dogs. They had been standing inquisitively at a respectful distance, while the feeding went on, being warned by Lad's growl not to molest his protégé.

Now, at the Master's signal, they pressed again around the newcomer, while Lad looked up at the man in worried appeal.

The Master pointed down at the suddenly pot-bellied baby, attracting the collies' attention to him. Then he said, very slowly and distinctly to them:

"Let him alone! Understand? *Let him* ALONE!"

The Law had been laid down—the simple dictum, "Let him alone!" which every Sunnybank dog had learned to understand and to obey, from earliest puppyhood. Henceforth, there was no danger that any one of that group of collies would harm the intruder.

"Sometimes," said the Master, casually, "I wish we hadn't taught these dogs to obey so well. If one of them happens to forget, and breaks Rameses' back, I'll forgive him. . . . I hope they all understand that. But I know they don't."

So it was that The Place's population was increased by one tame raccoon, Rameses by name. And so it was that the raccoon's education began.

The Mistress was delighted with the way in which her new pet responded to the simple training she gave him. She "had a way" with animals and was a born trainer. Under her care and tutelage Rameses not only grew with amazing rapidity, but he developed as fast, mentally, as had Lad himself in puppy days. There seemed almost nothing the raccoon wouldn't and couldn't learn—when he chose to.

He had the run of The Place and he obeyed the Mistress's whistle as readily as did any of the dogs. Even the Master conceded, after a time, with some reluctance, that the coon was an engaging pet, except for his habit of being asleep somewhere in a tree top at the very moment his owners wanted to show him off to guests.

The collies, all except Lad, gave somewhat cold reception to Rameses. They did not transgress the Master's command to "let him alone." But they regarded him for the first few months with cold disapproval, and they slunk away when he tried to romp with them.

Little by little this aversion wore off, and—if with reservations—they accepted him as one of the household, even as they accepted the Mistress's temperamental gray Persian kitten, Tippy. All of them except Wolf. Wolf made no secret of his lofty aversion to the foreigner.

Lad, from the start, had constituted himself the coon's sponsor and guardian. It was pretty to see him in a lawn-romp with the fuzzy baby; enduring unflinchingly the sharp play-bites of Rameses, and unbending as never had he unbent toward any of the grown dogs.

One of Rameses' quaintest tricks was to rise on his hind legs, as on that first day, and to thrust his pointed nose against Lad's ear, as if whispering to the dog. Again and again he used to do this. Lad seemed to enjoy it, for he would stand at grave attention, as though listening to something the coon was confiding to him.

"I'm sure he's telling Laddie a secret when he does that," said the Mistress.

"Nonsense!" scoffed the Master. "We're not living in fable-land. More likely the pesky coon is hunting Lad's ear for fleas. Likelier still, it's just a senseless game they've invented."

"No," insisted the Mistress. "I'm certain he really whispers. He——"

"The only worthwhile thing Rameses ever does, so far as I can see," continued the Master, refusing to argue, "is his washing of everything we give him to eat, before he'll taste it. They say that's just as much a coon trait as the 'whispering.' But it shows a grain of intelligence and a funny love for cleanness. He tried to wash a lump of sugar I gave him today. By the time he had rinsed it in his water dish and scrubbed it between his black palms till he thought it was clean enough, there wasn't any of it left."

The affection between their huge collie and the ever-growing Rameses amused the two humans, even while it astonished them.

They watched laughingly the many absolutely pointless games played by the dog and his queer chum—Lad's blank expression when the coon interrupted one of their romps by climbing—or rather by flowing—up the side of a giant oak, with entire ease, whither the dog did not know in the least how to follow; their gay swims together in the lake, and Lad's consternation at first when the coon would sink at will deep under the water and remain there for a whole minute at a time before sticking his pointed nose and beady little eyes above the surface again.

Nourishing food, and plenty of it, was causing Rameses to take on size and strength at an unbelievable rate; the more since he eked out his hearty meals by daily fishing excursions along the lake-edge, whence he scooped up and devoured scores of crayfish and innumerable minnows.

His little black fore claws were as dexterous as hands and tenfold swifter and more accurate. They could feel out a crayfish or mussel from under submerged rocks at will. They could clutch and hold the fastest-swimming minnow which flashed within their prehensile reach.

By the time he was a year old Rameses weighed nearly thirty pounds. At about this time, too, he showed his capacity to take care of himself against any ordinary foe.

One day his fishing trip, along the lake-edge,

carried him around the water end of a high fence which divided The Place from an adjoining strip of land. Through the underbrush of this strip a mongrel hound was nosing for rabbits. The hound caught sight of the raccoon, and rushed him. Rameses stood up on his hind legs, the water above his haunches, and grinningly awaited his charging foe.

As the mongrel leaped upon him, Rameses shifted his own position with seeming clumsiness, but with incredible speed. He shifted just far enough for the cur's snapping teeth to miss him.

In the same instant he clasped both his bear-like little arms with strangling tightness around his enemy's neck, and suffered the momentum of the hound's forward plunge to carry him backward and far under water, not once relaxing his death clasp from about the dog's neck.

Under the surface vanished coon and mongrel together, with a resounding splash. The water eddied and swirled unceasingly above them, for what seemed several minutes to the Master who witnessed the battle from a fishing-boat a quarter-mile distant, and who rowed with futile haste to the spot.

The Master arrived above the seething tumble of deep offshore water just in time to see Rameses' sharp nose and grinning mask emerge merrily from the depths.

The mongrel did not rise. The coon's bear-like strangle-hold had done its work.

Aware of an unbidden qualm of nausea at the grinningly matter-of-fact slayer, the Master picked Rameses out of the water by the nape of his neck and deposited him in the bottom of the boat.

Unconcernedly, Rameses shook himself dry. Then, spying a slice of bacon-rind bait lying on the gunwale, he reached for it, washed it with meticulous care in the bait-well, and proceeded to eat it with mincing relish. Apparently the mere matter of a canine-killing had passed out of his mind.

But a man clumping fast through the underbrush of the sloping bit of wasteland was not so philosophical about the hound's fate. The man was one Horace Dilver, a ne'er-do-well small farmer who lived a bare mile from The Place.

Dilver had taken his mongrel hound out, in this non-hunting season, to teach him to course rabbits. From the highroad above the lake the man had marked the patch of brushy slope as a promising hiding-place for rabbits, and had sent his dog into it. Thus, from the road, he had seen the sharply brief battle with the raccoon.

Down the slope he ran, yelling as he advanced:

"I seen that coon of yourn tackle my pore Tige and kill him!" he bellowed to the Master. "If I had my gun with me——"

"If you had your gun with you," rejoined the Master, "you wouldn't be breaking the game laws any worse than you did by making your hound course rabbits in September. I'm sorry for what happened, but it was the dog's fault. He pitched into an inoffensive animal, half his size, and he got what was coming to him."

"I wouldn't of took fifteen dollars for Tige!" the man was lamenting as he glowered vengefully at the placidly grinning and bacon-munching Rameses. "I loved that dog like——"

"Yes," put in the Master, bending again to his oars, "I've noticed your love for him. My superintendent tells me your neighbors complained because you used to beat him so brutally when you came home drunk, that his screaming kept them awake at night. Last week I saw you kick him half across the road, when I was driving by. Couldn't you find any easier way of showing your inferiority to a dumb animal than treating him like that? He's lucky to be free from an owner like you. You have no case against me for what my coon has done, and you know you haven't. You and your dog were both trespassing."

He rowed on homeward, leaving Dilver splitting the noonday hush by a really brilliant exhibition of howled blasphemy.

Rameses perched, squirrel-like, high on the boat's stern seat. He grinned sardonically back at the fist-shaking and cursing farmer. Then the raccoon fell to nibbling in epicurean fashion at what was left of the bacon rind.

As the boat drew in at its dock, the Mistress came down from the lawn above. With her was Lad, who had just come home with her from a walk to the village.

The big dog ran joyously to the boat, to greet its two passengers. As the keel grounded, Rameses stood up on his hind legs. As ever, after even a brief absence, he flung his hairy arms around Lad's hairier throat, his mouth close to the collie's ear, with the odd semblance of whispering secrets to his chum. He seemed to be telling the interested Lad all about his exploit.

The Mistress smiled at sight of the clinging arms and the earnest "whispering," and at Lad's usual grave attention to it.

The Master did not smile. That gently embracing gesture of the coon's brought keenly back to him a nauseous memory of the arms' strangling strength, and of Rameses' grinning unconcern at the slaughter of Tige.

Briefly the Master told his wife what had happened.

"Horrible!" she exclaimed with an involuntary little shudder. With her hand rubbing the slayer's head, as if in compunction for her momentary distaste, she continued: "But it wasn't Rameses' fault. You say yourself he didn't start it; and he would have been killed by the hound if he hadn't been just an instant quicker. He isn't to blame."

"Maybe not," assented the Master. "But just the same, it was an uncanny thing to do—to drown the antagonist he couldn't thrash with his teeth! Nothing but a raccoon would have thought of such a trick. I read, long ago, of a wild raccoon killing a dog that way. . . . I wish Horace Dilver hadn't been the man who owned the mongrel, though."

"Why not? Is he ——?"

"I've heard queer things about Dilver. For instance, Titus Romaine's four cows got into Dilver's corn and spoiled most of it. Romaine wouldn't pay damages. A week later all four of his cows were found dead in their stalls one morning. Slosson's police dog bit one of Dilver's children in the ankle. It was only a scratch. But the dog was dead a few days later. The vet thought he had eaten meat with powdered glass in it."

"Oh!"

"Dilver is a sweet soul to have as an enemy! I hope he won't decide to kill Rameses, as he just threatened to. If he does, we're likely to have a squabble on our hands. More neighborhood feuds start over livestock killings than over everything else put together. We ——"

The Master broke off, to make a futile grab at Rameses. The raccoon had finished his whispered colloquy with Lad. Then he had thrust his arm into the fish-creel the Master had laid down on the boat-house bench. Drawing thence a two-pound black bass, Rameses was washing it scrupulously in the lake-edge water, preparatory to eating it.

On an evening less than a week after the killing of the mongrel the Master and the Mistress went to an early dinner given by some friends of theirs at the Paradise Inn, at the foot of the lake. The maids were at the movies, over in the village. Bruce was asleep in the Master's study, where his nights were spent. Wolf, vigilant as always, lay on a porch door mat outside the front door, alertly on duty.

Through the early dusk Wolf saw two shapes making their way in leisurely fashion down the dim lawn and toward the lake. One was Wolf's bronze-and-white sire, Lad. The other was a low and shambling creature, less than half the big collie's height.

Well did Wolf recognize Lad and Rameses, and well did he know his sire was accompanying the raccoon on one of the latter's frequent nocturnal fishing expeditions along the shore.

Yet he forbore to leave his mat and trot along with them, not only because he was officially on guard, but because he still had a sullen dislike for the raccoon.

The other dogs had learned to tolerate Rameses comfortably enough. But Wolf's hotly vehement prejudices could not brook any acquaintance at all with the outsider. Wherefore, having long ago been bidden to "let him alone," Wolf kept out of Rameses' way as much as possible.

These fishing jaunts of his coon chum were always of mild interest to Lad. He himself did not understand the art of fishing; nor did he eat raw fish. But manifestly he enjoyed strolling along the bank and watching Rameses, stomach deep in the water, feel for crayfish under stones or dart beneath the surface with paws and nose together and emerge in triumph with a tiny and wiggling minnow tight gripped.

There was something about this coonlike form of hunting which seemed to appeal to Lad's ever-vivid imagination and to his sense of fun. Head on one side and tulip ears pricked, he would spend hours at a time, an amused spectator at Rameses' minnow-and-crayfish-catching antics.

Tonight the coon worked his way northward, along the shore of The Place, toward the bridge. As on the day when he fought Tige, he swam around the water-jutting end of the fence which divided The Place's north boundary from the strip of bush-slope that ran from the lake to the highway.

Lad swam at his side. When they had rounded the fence end, the collie waded ashore, shaking the water from his vast coat. The coon began, as before, to crawl, stomach-deep, in the shallows, in quest of fish.

Presently Lad raised his head and growled softly. He heard and scented an alien human presence moving furtively toward him from the highway above. This was no human of Lad's acquaintance. Moreover, the collie was no longer on his master's land. Wherefore, he felt no need or duty to bar this stranger's way or otherwise to stop his advance.

Lad knew every foot of The Place's forty acres, and he had been taught from puppyhood that humans were not to be interfered with unless they should trespass thereon. This bushy slope was no part of The Place. Thus the furtively approaching human's presence was no concern of Lad's.

The growl was not a threat or a menace. Rather was it a mode of notifying his coon chum of the man's approach; or else it was a mere reaction on meeting a human, at dusk, in so isolated a spot.

Horace Dilver did not descend by mere coincidence or accident through the impeding thickets toward the lake's margin, this September evening. He was a patient man. Half a dozen times, during the summer, when he was passing along the shore, he had happened to see the dog and the coon on one of their evening fishing tours. He had noted that this stretch of bank was one of their favorite haunts at such times.

Thus, with deadly patience, he had repaired to the highroad every evening at sunset, since the day when his hound had been strangled by Rameses.

Time meant little to Dilver, and revenge meant much. Soon or late, he was certain, the two chums would fish in that direction again. The time had come sooner than he had dared hope. And Dilver was ready. Dilver had a habit of being ready—except perhaps for work.

Under one arm he held a right formidable and nail-studded club, tucked there ready for use in case of necessity. But he did not expect to be called upon to use it. There were better and safer ways.

Were the dog and the raccoon to be found with their skulls smashed, the Master might get to remembering Dilver's blasphemy-fringed threats and there might be trouble. But if both animals should be taken agonizingly and fatally ill, soon after their return home, who could prove anything against anybody? Nobody had been able to prove anything in the cases of the poisoned cows and of the police dog.

Besides, Dilver had heard neighborhood brags of big Laddie's prowess, and he did not care to attack so formidable a dog, unless as a last resort. He knew—everyone knew—how devoted were the Mistress and the Master to the great mahogany collie. To kill him at the same time he killed the raccoon,—that would be double payment for the drowning of Tige and for the Master's unloving remarks to himself.

The man drew near and nearer, among the lakeside bushes. After the first involuntary growl,

Lad paid no further attention to him. Naturally, having a collie's miraculous sense of smell and of hearing, Lad knew to the inch whither each stealthy step was leading the ever-nearer human.

At an instant's notice Lad could have located and sprung at him as Dilver skulked closer with awkward attempt at soundlessness and concealment. But it was none of Lad's business to assail men who chose to slink along on neutral territory. As to the thought of possible danger to himself—fear was one emotion the great dog never had known.

Rameses was equally aware of the man's approach, and he was equally indifferent to it. Humans—except the friendly folk of The Place who had tamed and trained and brought him up—meant nothing and less than nothing in the raccoon's self-centered life. Besides, he was nearing a most seductive school of minnows which took up all his spare attention.

Then the rank human smell augmented by a far more seductive odor—the scent of fresh raw meat. Dilver had drawn from a pocket a greasy parcel and was unwrapping it.

Something sped through the air, close to Lad's head. The collie, with wolflike swiftness, darted to one side, growling savagely and baring his fangs. If this human were going to throw things at him, the aloof neutrality was at an end.

But, even as he snarled, Lad saw and smelled what the missile was, and his new-born anger died. This was no rock. It was a gift.

It struck the very edge of the lake, midway between the dog and Rameses, and it lay there in the dusk; a chunk of raw red beef, perhaps three ounces in weight, and rarely fascinating to any normal four-legged meat-eater. Rameses saw it at the same time.

Strong as was the temptation, Lad drew back from the luscious morsel, after the first instinctive advance. Had the meat been found lying there, he might or might not have eaten it. But he had heard the man throw it to him and it bore the scent of Dilver's hand.

Always Lad had been taught, as had others of the Sunnybank collies, to accept no food from an outsider.

This is a needful precaution for dogs that go to shows—at which more than one fine animal has been poisoned—or for dogs that have a home to guard and must be prevented from accepting drugged or poisoned meat. Lad had learned the rule, from his earliest days.

He halted in his advance toward the chunk of beef, reluctantly turning away from its lure and thereby saving himself from a peculiarly hideous form of death.

But Rameses had had no such teachings, and probably would not have profited by them if he had. After a second of polite waiting, to see if Lad intended to share the feast with him, the coon picked up the meat, holding it squirrelwise between his palms. Horace Dilver grinned almost as broadly as did Rameses himself.

Daintily the coon dipped the meat deep into the water; washing his food, as always, before eating it. Thoroughly he scrubbed the chunk between his handlike claws. In the midst of this rubbing process he paused, allowing the beef to fall uneaten into the shallows.

Blinkingly, the raccoon peered down at his black paws. The palm of one was cut. A drop of blood was oozing from it. The other palm was scratched lightly in two or three places.

The vehement washing and kneading and rubbing had pulled open the carefully interfolded envelope of meat. Its contents—a half-teaspoonful of powdered glass—had excoriated the washer's hands.

Rameses let the meat sink out of sight in the water, while he stared grinningly at his scored palms. Something was wrong here. A hundred times he had washed meat, and never before had it turned on him and scratched him like this. Irritant stuff which will tear the hands will hurt the mouth and stomach, too. Experience with sharp fish fins had taught that simple fact to Rameses, long ago.

Horace Dilver ceased to gloat pleasantly over his ruse. For some unexplained reason these two creatures were rejecting a lure to which other victims had yielded without a moment's hesitation. Disappointment and an hour of mosquito-bites and a naturally filthy temper combined to sweep away the man's hard-held patience.

Even if it were not safe to tackle that great brute of a collie, yet it would be easy enough to brain a silly pet raccoon and then to tie a stone to it and toss it far out into the lake.

Dilver pounced suddenly from behind the screen of bushes and caught Rameses by the nape of the neck, lifting him aloft with one hand while in the other he poised his studded club. Thus had he brained unwanted puppies and kittens.

But his knowledge of raccoons was rudimentary.

For one thing, he did not know that the loose skin of a grown coon's neck enables him to twist about, when held thus, as easily as if the skin were an overlarge collar.

Rameses never had liked handling; though he endured it, when necessary, from the folk of The Place. Now, at this alien and roughly painful grip, the coon twisted himself sharply.

Into the fleshy part of Horace Dilver's thumb flashed Rameses' double set of buzz-saw teeth. The upper and lower teeth met and ground together in the flesh.

With an echoing screech of torment, Dilver let fall the raccoon and danced about, sucking his mangled hand. The flung Rameses landed as lightly on the ground as might any cat. He crouched there, snarling up at the dancing man in utter hate.

Lad, too, turned back from his homeward journey, at the sound of strife. Teeth bared, he faced the anguished Dilver, starkly ready to resent any further possible attack upon his loved protégé.

Out through the death-still night rolled that initial pain-screech of Dilver's, and the less piercing but equally agonized yells which followed upon it. These latter were muffled by reason of an alternate sucking of the hurt; but they carried far.

The Mistress and the Master had returned early from Paradise Inn. They were just getting out of the car at their own door when Dilver's first bellow was wafted to them.

"Some one is drowning out there—close offshore—just a little way to the north!" exclaimed the Mistress.

The Master did not wait to hear her out. He broke into a run, making his stumblingly rapid way northward along the bank as fast as he could cover the dusky and uneven and wooded ground.

He had not gone ten steps when Wolf raced past him, travelling at windspeed in the same direction. His deities safely at home, Wolf could afford to abandon his post as watchdog and to gratify his ever-keen curiosity as to what all the fuss was about.

Wholly unaware that his cries had started human and canine investigation, Horace Dilver ceased presently from sucking his bleeding hand and groped for the studded club he had dropped. Pain had changed his wrath into maniac rage. The creature which had bitten him should pay full and immediate penalty.

Mouthing and cursing, he swung the club upward and rushed at the snarling Rameses.

The coon had been more than a little entertained, through all his own indignation, by the noisy and saltatory antics of this human. Even Lad had ceased his menacing advance and had paused to behold and listen to the strange performance.

When the club whizzed aloft, Rameses did not dodge out of the way. Never had he been struck. His year on The Place, as the Master had foreseen, had deprived him of the precautionary fear which has saved the lives of so many wild things.

But Lad was wiser. The collie sensed the awful peril to his little chum and he launched himself at the club's wielder. He was a fraction of a second too late.

Down crashed the nail-bossed club, impelled by all the fury-strength of a strong man. It smote the grinningly unflinching Rameses full athwart the furry shoulders—a blow which would have killed an animal of double his size.

Before the club could be raised for a second blow—before it had fairly struck the first—Dilver felt himself hurled forward by a smashing weight of eighty pounds which flung itself full upon the middle of his broad back.

Before the forward-plunging man's body could hit the stony ground of the lake margin, a double set of teeth were at work at the back of his neck and the base of his skull, accompanied by a ferocious growling that sounded like a rabid beast worrying its prey.

Over and over rolled the bawling man, down

the remaining yard or so of the steep slope and into the water itself. On him and all over him ravened Lad, striving ever to reach the jugular.

The dog knew well what must have been the result of such a smashing blow as his little friend, Rameses, had received from this human brute. The dog's mighty heart was hot and sick and raging within him at the loss of the pal he had found and had brought up so lovingly.

Again and again Lad drove for the throat, Dilver shoving him away as best he could and striving vainly to rise or to recover the club which had flown from his hand as he fell.

Once, with hammering forearms he thrust back the avid jaws. Through coat and shirt sleeve and deep into the arm the terrible teeth clove their way. But Lad abandoned this non-lethal hold and drove afresh for the throat.

It was then that a red-gold meteor-like thing burst through the bushes.

Wolf did not know what it was all about. On the ground he saw a writhing and tortured mass that so lately had been the merrily grinning Rameses. On the ground, too, a few yards away, half in and half out of the water, he beheld another writhing and tortured mass—a human, this time—with Sunnybank Lad seeking industriously to throttle him.

That was all Wolf saw. That was all Wolf cared or needed to see. Gleefully he whizzed forward to the fray; gripping the nearest part of Dilver's anatomy, then changing his grip for a better. Under the irresistible onslaught of the two furious dogs, Dilver gave himself up for lost.

With all his remaining strength he sought to roll himself—since they would not let him rise—into deeper water, in an attempt to dive, and thus to escape them. But, as if they caught the meaning of his plan, both collies assailed him together from the lakeward side, blocking this one sorry hope of safety.

It was then that the Master came up. The flashlight which he had jerked from his fall-overcoat pocket revealed a gruesome scene, there at the water's edge. His horrified shout of command made the two dogs draw back in fierce unwillingness from their victim.

By the Master's aid, Dilver got to his feet. The man was all but naked. His body was scored by an alarming patchwork of bites. He was blubbering, gasping, praying, half dead with panic terror. He staggered a step or two, then sat down drunkenly on a rock, chattering and sobbing in violent hysterics.

The Master turned from him and stared about

in stupid wonder, trying to discover what might have been the reason for the turmoil.

His flashlight fell on a piteous tableau. On the ground Rameses was huddled. He lay in a posture which Nature never intended nor permits. Above him stood Lad, his deep-set eyes infinitely sad, his whole statue-like body adroop.

There was a crashing through the bushes. Lad did not stir or glance up as the Mistress and The Place's superintendent hurried forward. They came to a halt, of wonder, at the picture disclosed by the flashlight's white ray.

The crushed body of Rameses stirred. The beady black eyes opened. The grinning little comedy mask of a face was raised slowly toward the sorrowing dog that bent above it.

Then, inch by inch, Rameses lifted his stricken body. By sheer effort of torment he reared himself waveringly on his haunches.

His arms went around Lad's neck. His pointed nose was buried against the collie's listening ear. Once more he was "whispering." Lad seemed to listen, as with heartsore attention, and to understand.

The clinging arms relaxed. The furry gray body slumped lifeless to the ground at his collie's chum's feet.

Lad stooped and picked it up, holding its dead weight between his powerful jaws as tenderly as when he had brought the baby Rameses to The Place so long ago.

Then, moving unswervingly, and carrying his dead playmate with that same mother-like gentleness, he made his way up the slope and onward toward the very heart of the far-off forest—the forest whence once he had brought his little comrade.

The superintendent took a step, to follow. The Mistress intervened.

"No," she whispered. "Let him go. Lad knows. Lad always knows. I—I think Rameses told him what to do, and he is doing it. Let him go. The—the Wild is going home to the Wild."

Chapter Two

THE GUEST

SHE came to The Place on the strength of a sheaf of letters of introduction which would have gained admittance for Benedict Arnold into the Sons of the Revolution. The letters were from European friends to whom the Mistress and the Master owed much in the way of courtesies and hospitality.

Wherefore Mrs. Héloïse Lejeune was invited to spend a week at The Place, on her arrival in America on a tour which was to serve as basis for a series of lectures in her own Latin country. She accepted the invitation with much alacrity.

"Everything in life has to be paid for," grumbled the Master as he and the Mistress sat in their car at the rural railroad station, waiting for the guest's belated train. "And always it has to be paid for at the most inconvenient times and in the most inconvenient way. Debts that can be settled in cash are the easiest to wipe out. The others are the really tough ones. They make me wish there were a moral bankruptcy court I could go through."

"But we ——"

"We didn't want to visit at any of those houses in England and Scotland and France," said the Master. "We'd have had a better time and a less expensive time at hotels or village inns. And now, of course, three of our loving hosts are 'collecting,' by sawing off this Lejeune woman on us as a guest—at a time when I ought to be working twelve hours a day and when you want to get those songs of yours finished. Why couldn't she ——"

A reassuring pat on his shoulder made the Master turn in annoyance toward his wife.

The Mistress was not a shoulder-patter, and he wondered glumly why she should choose this irritating mode of trying to dispel his crankiness. But her gloved hands were resting lightly on the car's steering-wheel—even as the pat was repeated with insistent vehemence.

Not a hand, but an absurdly small and very white paw, was tapping the man's shoulder.

A huge collie had been lying lazily on the rear seat. At the peevish note in the Master's voice the dog had risen in sudden worry, and had shown quick sympathy for his god's unknown trouble by patting eagerly at the nearest part of the man's anatomy.

The Master's scowl changed to a reluctant grin as he leaned back and rumpled the collie's classic head.

"Lie down, Laddie," he said. "It's all right. Or if it isn't, you can't make it so by swatting my shoulders with your dusty feet. This is the only clean white suit I have left."

The dog stretched out again on the seat, his plumed tail wagging. Lad was well content. The tone of annoyance was gone from the Master's voice. Apparently everything was all right again. That was all Lad wanted to make certain of.

"Mrs. Lejeune wrote that beautiful essay in verse, on dogs, for one of the English magazines," the Mistress was saying. "So she must like them. I wouldn't have brought Lad over to meet her unless her essay had shown such a splendid understanding of ——"

"Mrs. Lejeune didn't write it," was the Master's morbid contradiction. "Maeterlinck wrote it. She took most of the best things in his 'My Friend the Dog,' and rhymed them and put them into her own words. Just the same, she wouldn't have done it if she hadn't liked dogs. That's the one bright spot—or the least *un*bright spot—in the thought of having her at Sunnybank with us for a whole interminable week. She ——"

The behind-time train hooted dismally as it neared the station. The Master left the car and strode along the platform to meet the guest.

A minute later he returned, convoying a large and grenadier-like woman whose walk and demeanor gave somehow the impression that she was leading a ceremonial parade of ancient Egyptian priests.

The Mistress had signaled Lad to jump over to the front seat at her side, leaving the tonneau to Mrs. Lejeune and the Master and to an extensively labeled array of hand-luggage which a station porter distributed as best he could between and around their feet.

With lofty graciousness and with an ever-so-slight foreign accent, Mrs. Lejeune acknowledged the Mistress's greeting. Then she stiffened at sight of the great mahogany-and-snow collie that nestled at her hostess's side on the front seat.

Lad returned her unloving look with an icy gaze of aloofness. Then, with his tulip ears flattened close to his head, he turned his back on her.

There was chill insult in the collie's manner. He did not like this newcomer. One glance had been enough to settle that fact in his uncannily psychic mind. He did not like her, and he saw she did not like him.

The Mistress and the Master, in the order named—these two were Sunnybank Lad's deities. To them, from puppyhood, he had given eager and worshiping service. The rest of mankind did not interest him. But to most of The Place's guests he accorded a cold courtesy. Toward none of them had he showed the affronting and affronted distaste which he bestowed on the large Mrs. Lejeune.

"This is Laddie," the Mistress was explaining to her visitor, speaking fast and trying to ignore the collie's rudeness. "I know how fond of dogs you are, so I ——"

"I am *not!*" denied Mrs. Lejeune with charming frankness. "I detest them. I find them either gleesome or fleasome. When they are gleesome they smear their muddy paws on people's white dresses. When they are fleasome, they ——"

Laddie created a diversion at this point in the guest's harangue. A right alluring and thrilling scent had assailed his keen nostrils so potently as to banish momentarily his disgust at this noxious stranger. The scent exhaled from a square black satchel the porter was lifting into the car from the heap of luggage on the platform edge.

Lad leaned far over the back of the seat, sniffing at the satchel with pleased interest. From a tiny wire grillwork at one end of the bag a sharp hiss rewarded the poke of his exploring nose. The hiss was followed by a fretful yowl which rose in timbre and volume until it merged into a second and more irate hiss.

Instantly Mrs. Lejeune's lofty manner changed to solicitous tenderness. She bent over the satchel, lifting a corner of its lid and crooning softly into the interior:

"There, there, Massoud darling! The filthy brute sha'n't bother you. He——"

Mrs. Lejeune's promise was broken well-nigh before it was made. The inch-wide opening of the bag's top was vastly entertaining to the inquisitive Lad. In merry expectation he nosed at the crack, to widen it for better inspection. Mrs. Lejeune aimed a corrective slap at him. The slap did not reach its target.

For the joggled lid flew wide, by reason of sudden internal pressure. A shapeless gray paw flashed forth—a paw equipped with a set of pin-like claws. Lad shrank back instinctively, with his nose tip adorned by three red furrows. At the same instant Massoud, a large and gray and frantically spitting Persian cat, whizzed forth from the satchel into a new and unfriendly world.

"Kittykittykitty!" wailed Mrs. Lejeune, imploringly, as she grabbed for the escaping cat.

But Kittykittykitty rewarded the effort at capture by side-swiping virulently her owner's large, fat hand as it sought to seize her flying gray form. The same leap carried Massoud clear of the car and onto the station platform. Thence, without breaking her stride, she made a dash for the far side of the tracks.

Elated at the jolly adventure which had come so opportunely into his staid life, Lad gave chase. Before either the Mistress or the Master could guess at his intent, he was out of the car and galloping in mischievous pursuit. The whole thing happened in a fraction of a second.

Now, Massoud was in about as much danger of harm from Lad as would be a duck from immersion into a pond. The great collie had the fighting pluck and prowess of a tiger. But never had he harmed any creature smaller and weaker than himself. His meeting with the suddenly abhorred Mrs. Lejeune had somehow aroused in him the perverse imp of mischief that never sleeps any too soundly at the bottom of a collie's nature.

He could not wreak his dislike on Mrs. Lejeune herself. Not only was she a woman, but also she was very evidently a guest.

And from babyhood Lad had understood and

obeyed the rigidly simple guest-law of The Place. But he could and would pester her and at the same time add to his own fund of amusement, by chasing harmlessly the cat she had crooned to so lovingly.

Toward the tracks catapulted the fugitive, ears flat, tail enormous, the shapeless gray legs carrying her over the ground at an amazing pace. Close behind galloped the big collie, mischief in every inch of his giant body and in his deep-set eyes. Lad was having a beautiful time.

The Mistress was first to find voice.

"Laddie!" she called. "*Lad!*"

Almost in midair the charging collie checked his run. Always had he obeyed that soft voice. Nearly always, hitherto, he had rejoiced to obey it. But now his obedience was solely a matter of lifelong duty. Humans had such a silly way of interrupting, just when sport was at its height!

He halted disgruntledly, and made as though to come back to the car. Then, changing his purpose, he stood stockstill for an instant, while the mischief and even the reluctance went out of his eyes, leaving them troubled and alert.

Massoud had sped across the nearer of the two railroad tracks beyond the side platform. But as she struck the farther track she was aware of a sinister buzzing of the rail beneath her galloping paws and of a dismaying roar that ripped at her temperamental nerves.

Glancing sidewise as she ran, she beheld a gigantic black bulk rushing down at her.

The New York express was thundering southward, making no stop at this unimportant country station.

Massoud saw it looming above her. Strength and sense deserted her at the sight. She had reached the far rail of the express track. On it she crouched—helpless, shuddering, her glazed green eyes fixed on the onrushing locomotive.

It was this which had caused Lad to check his leisurely return toward the car and to the Mistress who had summoned him thither. Seated beside the Mistress in that same car, not a month agone, he had seen a stray kitten cut in two as it meandered across a railroad track in front of a train. Well did the dog realize Massoud's sickening peril.

The Master saw also. Even as the cat came to a paralyzed standstill on the rail, the man moved the bulk of his shoulders between his guest and her pet's impending slaughter.

Mrs. Lejeune thus missed seeing Massoud's terrified pause, though, nursing her scratched hand, she sought to follow the chase by peering around the Master's interfering shoulders.

She filled the air with denunciatory lamentations and with shrill demands that the murderous dog be recalled from his pursuit. Neither of her hearers gave heed.

For, as the express bore down upon the cat, a swirl of sunlit orange-tinted mahogany fur flashed across the track, under the very prow of the engine's cowcatcher. Sunnybank Lad had gone into action.

Seemingly bent on a hideous form of suicide, the mighty collie hurled himself at lightning speed in front of the roaring train. Across the track he sped at the incredible pace known to no dog but collie and greyhound. As he sprang, he dipped his head earthward, without abating one jot of his fiery speed.

Then the express, traveling at nearly sixty miles an hour, cut off the onlookers' view of the scene.

The guest continued to whicker forth her wild commands. The Mistress stared at the obstructing train's spinning wheels with bone-white face and hard-set mouth. Unconscious of what he did, the Master swore softly and venomously, as an accompaniment to Mrs. Lejeune's screeched prattle.

A million centuries crawled by. Then the express was gone, leaving a blinding eddy of cinders and dust and smoke in its wake. Through the murk stared the Mistress and the Master, their gaze studying the gleaming rails, with sick horror for signs of what they dreaded.

On the far side of the track, perhaps twenty feet beyond the rails, stood Lad. From between his mighty jaws dangled and squirmed and writhed and yowled a mass of gray fur. He was holding the rescued Massoud deftly and gently by the nape of her furry neck, even as he had snatched her up during his shrewdly judged dash across the track.

Through the maze of dust and cinders Mrs. Lejeune caught her first semi-distinct view of the situation. She saw her adored cat twisting futilely in the grip of a huge dog—a dog seemingly bent upon breaking her neck.

With a dexterity foreign to women of her size, she darted across the track and grabbed her imperiled and indignant cat, holding the squalling and spitting and scratching feline hysterically to her breast—and at the same time aiming a fervent kick at Lad.

The kick caught the dog full in the ribs, painfully and humiliatingly. In all Laddie's three years of life, never before had he been kicked. At The Place dogs were not punished in that way, the Master believing that man can find better ways of showing his inferiority to dumb brutes than by kicking them. The unprecedented assault staggered the collie. He whirled on the assailant, his curved white eyeteeth agleam from under his upcurled lip.

Had a man other than the Master done this foul thing to him, Lad would have been all over the aggressor before the punitive foot could have touched ground again. But this was a woman, and Lad contented himself with snarling loathingly up into her rage-purpled face. Then, majestically, he strode back to where the Mistress and the Master stood.

He thrust his muzzle into the Mistress's cupped hand for comfort and for praise. He got both.

With difficulty the Master swallowed words which would have shamed The Place's hospitality. Then he said to his wife:

"Drive home with her. Try to explain what really happened. *I* can't explain it to her. If I tried to speak to her now, I'd say things I could be jailed for. I'm going to walk. Come along, Laddie."

Thus began a visit which to this day is remembered at The Place as might be an epidemic of smallpox. On Lad it bore harder than on the humans. Always, from farther back than he could remember, the collie had been as free throughout the house at any and all times as were his owners. But now everything was different.

In the first place, the obese guest with the faint Continental accent, and the temperamental Persian cat, was ubiquitously present, and the presence shattered for Lad the sweet peace of the home he loved.

They hated him, these two intruders; they made no secret of their hate. Moreover, an hour after their arrival, the Mistress had led the collie to a kennel down near the stables, and very gently had made him understand this was to be his abiding-place for the time. He was forbidden the house—he who had been the house's guard and honored inmate from puppyhood!

Worse, his queerly sensitive mind told him the Mistress was wretchedly unhappy and that the Master was in a continuously villainous temper.

The great dog grieved bewilderedly over these manifestations of malaise in the two humans he worshiped. True, both of them contrived to hide their state of mind from the guest, but no slightest shade of human mood can be hidden from a chum collie.

Exiled and worriedly sad, the dog moped miserably around The Place, welcoming with pathetic eagerness his very few chances to romp or walk with the Mistress or the Master, during such times as one of them was free from the entertaining of their guest.

Also there were dinners, and at least one tea and a garden party, in Mrs. Lejeune's honor. Such functions implied the presence of many outsiders. Lad hated crowds.

Mrs. Lejeune did not scruple to tell all and sundry the story of Lad's supposed attempt to kill her darling Massoud. Nor did she hesitate to reiterate to everyone that the very sight of a dog nauseated her. In that dog-loving hinterland community—especially among The Place's intimates, who were fond of Lad—she won scant popularity.

"Why did you write that essay poem, praising dogs, if you hate them so?" asked the Master once, when she had been holding forth on this chronic dislike of hers.

"Why did your American poet, Fergus Ager, write exquisite child-poems, when he abominated brats?" she countered. "Why did the English poet, Brunning, write that deathlessly beautiful horse-ballad of his, when he shuddered at the sight of a horse?"

"I don't know," said the Master. "Why?"

"Children and dogs and horses are popular themes with the masses," explained Mrs. Lejeune.

"Anything written about them is certain of popularity, if it is well done. For that matter, it is common knowledge that the most inspired dog-book ever written was by a Britisher who not only did not own dogs, but who was afraid of them. He told me that when he came to America to lecture, people used to insist on bringing their horrible dogs for him to see, and it was the worst ordeal that he ever went through. Now, cats—especially Persian cats ——"

"Yes," vaguely assented the Master, "now, cats. Especially Persian cats ——"

He broke off to watch Massoud craftily stalking an oriole that was singing its heart out from the summit of a tiny veranda-side shrub. At The Place, song birds of every kind were as much at home as was Lad himself. No cat or other animal was allowed to molest them. As a result they were as tame as chickens and they nested by scores among the thick veranda vines.

Now, for the first time, a Sunnybank song bird was annoyed by a Sunnybank human. The Master flung his pudgy tobacco-pouch at the oriole. The bird, in fluttering surprise, broke off its song and flew away—just as Massoud completed her stalking preliminaries and sprang for her escaped victim.

"Yes," repeated the Master, apropos of nothing at all, "especially Persian cats. We have two cats of our own. One of them is a Persian. Tippy, you know. We are fond of them both. We've had them for years, and they're part of our household. They leave the birds alone, and the dogs leave our cats alone. It's all a matter of simple early training."

Gloomily he watched the mincing progress of Massoud across the lawn toward the lake edge. Along the bank were bushes where nested innumerable small birds.

Lad also noted the progress of the detested Massoud, from the kennel where he lay in unhappy solitude. The Mistress's early command of "*Leave her alone, Laddie!*" had rendered the Persian cat immune from further jocose harrying by the law-abiding collie.

But now, as she made her dainty way over the sward in the direction of the lakeside bushes, the command seemed harshly difficult to obey. There was a full hundred yards of lawn between the cat and the lake, and an increasingly wide space between her and the protection of the house.

It would be glorious fun to whiz out in chase of her. Of course, he would not harm a fuzzy hair of her when at last he should overhaul her. But the chase would be a delight.

Then, sighing, Lad resigned himself to the dull

cheerlessness of lying inert in his kennel while a million attractive things waited to be done.

The Mistress and the Master—they were with that odious big woman who loathed him and whom he loathed. The house, with his cool "cave" under the piano—that too was denied him while Mrs. Lejeune should remain at The Place.

This peculiarly teasable alien cat—she must be left alone. His human deities were distressingly unhappy about something. That was the worst phase of all, to Lad, in this period of interminable unpleasantness.

Drowsily his eyes continued to follow the lake-bound cat.

No longer was the Master watching Massoud's progress from the veranda and speculating surlily on the probable killing of one or more of the trustful birds whose nests dotted the shore bushes. He had just been called indoors, to the telephone. The Mistress also had gone into the house a minute earlier to give orders for dinner. Mrs. Lejeune was left alone on the shaded porch.

The air was lazily warm and athrob with bird songs. The lake lay fire-blue at the foot of the emerald lawn and amid its circle of softly protecting hills. From the rose-garden drifted faintly a myriad sweet odors. Mrs. Lejeune's poetic soul expanded under the loveliness of it all—as might the soul of an elephant at scent of a ton of circus peanuts.

She smiled as she saw Massoud draw near to the first of the lakeside bushes, and saw the mincing gait of the cat merge into a tigerish crawl. The dear little pet had discovered an unsuspecting bird somewhere in the bush. That was evident. She was creeping up on her prey with that lithe grace which her owner so admired in her.

Better to see the stalking process, Mrs. Lejeune left her veranda chair and started down the lawn amid the ancient oak trees, toward the water's edge. She moved slowly and on tiptoe, lest sound of her approach disturb the absorbedly creeping cat.

She came into the line of Lad's vision. The dog's upper lip curled instinctively, showing once more a glint of the terrible white eyeteeth. Then, in chill contempt, he looked once more at the craftily moving cat—the cat he had been bidden to leave alone.

As Mrs. Lejeune neared the bank, Massoud halted, crouching low and swishing her great feathery tail. The cat's jaws chattered. Her whole body was aquiver.

Then, gauging her distance, she launched herself at a slate-hued catbird that was singing on a twig midway up the bush.

Of the infinite variety of birds which made Sunnybank their summer abiding-place—a cloud of them staying all winter to feast on the ample daily rations of suet and crumbs doled out to them—the catbirds were loved by the Mistress and the Master better than all the rest combined.

As a result, catbirds nested in the big lilac clump near the house and in even nearer shrubbery, and were as tame as canaries. One or two of them even used to alight close beside the Mistress's feet on the veranda floor during breakfast and lunch, sometimes singing gloriously, sometimes pertly demanding food. They seemed to know of these two humans' protective fondness for them.

Nearly all singing birds have but a single song —two or three or four notes which they repeat over and over in changeless iteration. But a catbird has a repertory. His song lasts sometimes for several minutes; soft, divinely sweet, shifting from one theme to another without repeating itself.

Even more beautiful and varied than the mocking-bird's is the catbird's changeful song. (Both of them excel, by far, the nightingale, as singers.) The catbird seems to be making up his music, afresh, as he goes on in his song, and to be improvising with conscious skill.

True, once in a way, he seems to be making fun of his own poetic chant by breaking it off with a half-disdainful and wholly mischievous catcall. But this startling contrast only intensifies his song's beauty.

As a mimic he has no equal. For hours he will try to imitate the oriole's four-note call, until he has learned it so perfectly that human ears cannot detect the difference between it and the original (and indignant) oriole's. It is the same with his deftness in catching and copying the songs of two or three other varieties of birds.

It is not a chance repetition. As I have said, he will try for hours, sometimes, before he has reproduced another bird's song flawlessly and to his own satisfaction. Nor will he cease until he has achieved the task. About him, too, is found a strain of elfin mischief, a true and keen sense of fun. And he is gaily fearless. I have seen him drive a five-foot black snake from his babies' nest, and chase the squirming monster for more than a hundred yards; pecking in punitive rage at the shining black head, yet clever enough to elude the snake's jaws or his coils.

So much for a digression, which perhaps is not so much of a digression, after all; as it explains the tameness of the catbird which Massoud was stalking and the affectionate welcome it and its kind had always found at The Place.

Massoud sprang upward and outward, toward the bush. It was a good pounce—powerful and well judged. But a scud of rain had fallen during the night. The lakeside grass was damp and slippery.

In the take-off, Massoud's driving hind feet slipped ever so little. Not enough to spoil her leap, but enough to make it fall short of its goal by some three or four inches.

Thus, instead of digging deep into the feathers and flesh of a luckless songster, Massoud's fore-claws found themselves scrabbling desperately for a purchase hold amid a mesh of brittle twigs.

Away flew the bird, in wrathful amaze at such treatment. The cat clawed with all four feet to keep from falling through the interlacing little branches into the deep water below.

There she hung, squalling and clawing, unable to move forward or back, and hard put to it to avert a tumble into the lake.

Lad lifted his head from his white paws and gazed with new and genuine interest. This promised to be very entertaining indeed.

Mrs. Lejeune was running forward in an agony of apprehension, calling shrilly for some one or anyone to help her in extricating her cat from this peril of a ducking. The lake bottom shelved down at that part of the bank, with no intermediate shallows. Massoud must needs swim if she should fall into the water. And Mrs. Lejeune did not know whether or not cats could swim.

Panting, she hurried to the rescue of her pet. Gripping a handful of the bush twigs and bracing her slippered feet against the steep edge of the bank, she reached far out over the water, grasping for any seizable part of Massoud.

The impulse was laudable, but several laws of nature rendered it a failure.

One of these laws concerned gravitation and the tendency of unbalanced heavy bodies to topple. Another was the aforesaid slipperiness of the lakeside grass. A third was the inability of a handful of thin witch-elm twigs to withstand a sudden tugging weight of two hundred pounds.

The still summer air was shattered by a calliope-like shriek. Lad saw Mrs. Lejeune's body shoot forward through space as if it had been shoved violently from behind. Through the unimpeding bush it drove its way and for some short distance farther.

Then once more the abused law of gravitation asserted itself and the unfortunate woman fell with an echoing splash into the smooth blue water.

Massoud was jarred loose from her own precarious hold on the crackling twigs by her owner's dramatic passage through the bush. The cat landed well out in the lake, whence she swam with entire ease, if with much discomfort, to the safety of the shore.

Mrs. Lejeune was less fortunate. She went clean under. The air billowed her clothes. Her own fat aided in bringing her to the surface like some obese cork.

Spraddled out and making desperate efforts to swim—an art she never had troubled to learn—she gurgled and gasped, seeking to clear her lungs and mouth of water in order to scream afresh for help.

Her shriek, as she fell, had changed Lad's academic interest in the scene into immediate concern. There was terror in that yell. There was peril in the water.

The dog tore forward at top speed, racing for the lake. He was following the instinct of his kind, heedless of whether the imperiled human were friend or foe.

Mrs. Lejeune's aimless struggles carried her head under again. With a frantic twist she brought it to the surface. As she did so, her water-bleared eyes, staring in panic glassiness, beheld a mahogany-and-snow body leap from the bank and hit the lake resoundingly, close beside her.

As her head was about to go down again, from the mad uselessness of her own struggles, she felt something grip her shoulder, bearing her up and easing momentarily the mysterious force which was tugging to draw her under.

"*Lad!*" she gabbled, deliriously, wrenching her body around so as to fling both thick arms about the dog's throat.

Now, Lad was having enough trouble, without this added handicap. It was no light matter for even so powerful a dog to hold above the surface the head and shoulders of a crazily writhing woman of Mrs. Lejeune's weight.

When that weight was shifted so as to bear down on his battling forequarters and when convulsive arms squeezed shut his breathing apparatus, and when the woman's impeding bulk pressed against his chest and pinioned his front legs—the situation waxed acute.

Woman and dog went under water together, both of them helpless. The strangling pain in her nostrils and throat made Mrs. Lejeune loosen her grip on the collie, in order to beat uselessly with her hands in an effort to rise. Freed of the dead weight that was choking and drowning him Lad came to the surface.

A five seconds' swim would have brought him comfortably to shore. But he was not minded to accept life at the expense of the woman who had half-smothered him. A blur of whitish cloth appeared just below the surface. Lad struck for it and seized it, pulling it upward with all his might.

Luckily his teeth had found the victim's shoulder once more. A mighty heave brought her head above the water.

Lad churned the lake to foam as he swung the heavy and twisting body sidewise in an attempt to tow it ashore. This time Mrs. Lejeune's arms missed their clutch for him. Straining every splendid muscle, the dog dragged her shoreward. Faint with fright, she relaxed. Thus, her feet sank and her tall body became almost perpendicular. As a result, she felt the shelving lake bottom beneath her soles.

The solid touch revived her. With a last scrambling summoning of all her strength, she floundered landward. For perhaps three steps she waddled; then her legs gave way and she sat down hard, in some eighteen inches of water. Lad had let go of her shoulder and had splashed ashore. His work was done.

It was then that the Master and the Mistress,

drawn by their guest's first calliope shriek, came running to the edge of the lake.

"It's worse than when she hated Lad!" sighed the Mistress that evening when, for a minute, she and her husband were alone. "Worse for Laddie, I mean. He was happier out in his lonely kennel than with Mrs. Lejeune trying to kiss him every five minutes, and ——"

"Dogs aren't meant to be kissed," said the Master. "And when it comes to being kissed by Mrs. Lejeune, the term 'a dog's life' takes on a new and horrible meaning. She says she is going to get the Humane Society to give him a medal—he'd lots rather have a steak bone—and she is going to bring him into her new lecture on 'Real Life Heroes.' Poor old Lad!"

"He behaves beautifully about it, though," declared the Mistress. "And she doesn't know enough about dogs to see how he detests being pawed and cooed to by her. It's an awful reward for saving her life."

"He didn't," contradicted the Master.

"Didn't what?"

"Didn't save her life. I know every inch of the lake, all along our shore. The water isn't more than five feet deep, anywhere, at that part of the bank. If she had had sense enough to try to stand up, instead of spread-eagling, when she fell in, she could have walked ashore. The water wasn't above her chin."

"Oh!"

"Don't tell her that, of course. Lad saved her cat's life, and she hated him. He *didn't* save her own life—and she is daft about him. That's how it goes. But ——"

"She has a wonderful idea," interrupted the Mistress. "I know you'll appreciate it. She wants us to give Lad to her and to accept her heavenly cat, Massoud, in exchange."

The Master's mouth flew ajar from the force of a torrent of words that sizzled for utterance. Before they could be spoken, Lad came pacing solemnly past them as they stood on the veranda.

From the house he emerged. He paid no heed to either of his deities as he strode by. In his jaws he was carrying a spangled purple satin girdle which the grateful Mrs. Lejeune had taken from her own ample meridian and had knotted artistically around the disgusted dog's throat.

Twice Lad had managed to wriggle free of the undesired gift. Twice Mrs. Lejeune had retied it lovingly about his neck.

A third time he had freed himself of it; and now he was bearing it forth into the night. Every line and every motion of his shaggy body was vibrant with grim resolve to be made ridiculous by it no more.

Solemnly he made his way to the nearest flower border. There his white little forepaws wrought vehemently in the soft loam until he had dug a hole nearly a foot deep.

Into this cavity he dropped the garish purple satin ornament. With his nose for a shovel he pushed the loose earth over it until the hole was filled.

Then, with a last disgusted look toward the house whence Mrs. Lejeune's voice could be heard calling tenderly to him, he slunk away to the Lejeuneless sanctity of his own kennel.

Chapter Three

THE VARMINT

THE Master came up from the direction of the stables, a gun in the crook of his arm, his eyes bleared, and his hair tumbled. He looked as if he had been up all night, as indeed he had.

At his side paced majestically the huge bronze-and-snow collie, big Sunnybank Lad.

The Mistress had just come downstairs to breakfast. Catching sight of her husband, she went forth to meet him. Dainty and well groomed and gaily fresh of aspect from her night's sleep, she formed a stark contrast to the dishev-eled man.

"What luck?" she hailed him; adding, "But if you had fired it would have waked me, I suppose. So ——"

"So we drew blank, Laddie and I," answered the Master. "It wasn't Lad's fault. He didn't know what we were there for. But it was mine," he continued, shamefacedly, "because I must have gone dead asleep out there on that rottenly uncomfortable stump. One minute it was pitch dark. The next minute the east was all gray. I'm a grand sentinel! It happened while I was asleep. Three more of them gone, this time. And it's all my fault, for drowsing. Next time I'll ——"

Down the driveway plodded the rural delivery postman. He was an oldster who had been one of the Master's fishing and swimming and hunting companions when the two were boys, there in the North Jersey hinterland.

"Special-deliv'ry letter for you, Boss," said the postman as he came up to the group. "I —— Hello! What's the gun for? They must have changed the game laws hereabouts since yesterday, if there's anything that's legal to shoot in June."

"There *is* something 'legal to shoot,' " returned the Master. "And I spent the night trying to shoot it. But I'm getting old. Remember how you and I used to sit up all night waiting for the bass to strike at daybreak? Well, this time I fell asleep. I was watching for something or some one that has been looting my chicken-yard and taking from one to three of my best prize fowls every few nights. It was a 'something,' though, not a 'some one.' Lad would have nailed any human prowler. It ——"

"Sure," assented the postman. "And that means it was a varmint."

"Whatever it was, it was clever enough to outwit Laddie and me."

"Don't go smearing half the blame onto the Big Dog, Boss," expostulated the postman. "'Twasn't up to *him*. He's a watchdog. That means he's on the watch for folks, not for varmints. Where was you watching from?"

"That chestnut stump down yonder," said the Master. "It's fifty yards from the main hencoop, but it's nearer the small one. I figured that was the best position to watch both coops from. I thought I could surely hear the faintest sound from either roost. But——"

"Well," argued the postman, still firm on clearing Lad, who was dear to him from years of daily meeting, "like I said, you can't blame the Big Dog. So please don't either of you go misjudging him wrong. If one of your hens had let out a bunch of squawks and had flapped around, Lad would have knowed there was something wrong with the things he was set to guard. But some kinds of varmints are as cute as sin. They can clean out a hen-roost without a single one of the birds getting a chance to make a sound. Foxes is like that, and——"

"This isn't a fox," said the Master. "I've been

all around every corner of the chicken-yards and the coops. There's no hole dug anywhere and no opening big enough in the boards or the wire for so much as a squirrel to wriggle through."

"Varmints has funny ways—some of 'em," declared the postman, cryptically, "and this is one of 'em. If Laddie saw or scented some critter moving along quiet and minding its own business, he'd likely not give another thought to it. That's how he didn't go for the varmint that stole your hens. If the hen would of squawked or flapped or if he'd achally saw the critter carrying it, he'd of got busy, quick enough. Don't be blaming him. As for there not being any way for anything to get into the hen-houses—well, maybe you're mistook in your judgments of that."

"Just the same," said the Master as the postman climbed the driveway to the highroad above, leaving his skeptical dictum for the others to ponder over—"just the same, I'm *not* 'mistook in my judgments' about there being no way for any marauder to get into either of the henhouses. I can swear to that. I've been over every inch of them, first alone and then with Robert. There's no hole or tunnel. No board or slat has fallen off. But—something *did* get in there, last night and other nights. Shall we go to breakfast?"

"You'll try to get a nap this afternoon, won't

you?" asked the Mistress, as they made their way to the veranda-corner breakfast table. "Don't forget the dinner this evening. If you don't get some rest, after your wakeful night, you'll be dreadfully sleepy by the time the people get here. They ——"

"Lord!" snorted the Master. "I was consoling myself with the idea of getting to bed early. I'd forgotten all about that crowd coming here for dinner. What can be more delightful than a dinner party? And the most blissfully delightful thing about it is a valid excuse for staying away. I suppose I couldn't quite do that, though, in my own house? Same old crowd. Same old food. Same old talk. Same old everything!"

The Master was wholly mistaken. There was not to be the "same old everything." There was to be a somewhat striking innovation.

In those days, Lad was the only Sunnybank collie permitted in the dining-room. Whether the family were eating alone or with a roomful of guests, the great collie's place was always on the floor, close to the left of the Master's chair, during meals.

This to the stumbling discomfort of the servants, in passing things; but as the servants idolized the dog, there was no complaint.

On this evening, a few minutes before the arrival of the first guest, the Mistress fluffed up Lad's burnished mahogany coat and then roused his vanity to a climax by tying to his collar an enormous scarlet satin bow.

The dog always thrilled to this form of adornment, on the rare times it was lavished on him. He was absurdly vain, as is the average collie. And, though strangers bored and bothered him, he was not above enjoying the admiration and the wholesale greetings of such guests as he knew and liked. He began to look forward with real interest to the evening's familiar preparations.

When Lad was brushed and his bow was becomingly in place, the Mistress busied herself with last touches to the flower-bowls, here and there. The Master had not come down from his dressing-room. The maids were busy. Nobody had time to admire Lad's finery or even to speak to him.

Perhaps seeking admiration, the collie strolled out through the open front door and toward the stables and other outbuildings.

Dusk was settling down—the warm and scented dusk of early summer. From the stables came the sound of drowsy champing of hay and an occasional hoof-stamp. Somewhere a whip-poorwill was complaining. An occasional muffled cluck or a ruffle of feathers from the larger and nearer henroost told of fowls going to sleep. But there was no human in sight to exclaim over the strutting dog and his flaring scarlet satin bow.

Lad was turning back again toward the house, at the sound of the first carful of guests coming down the drive. Then a faintly unpleasant odor tingled in his sensitive nostrils.

The smell was not new to him. A score of times he had encountered it, in strong or in scarce-perceptible degree, on his woodland rambles. Once or twice recently—last night, for instance—he had smelled it close at hand here.

There was nothing disturbing or alien about it. He had been familiar with this acrid reek, off and on, since puppyhood. Human nostrils could not have detected it at the several rods' distance whence Lad had now sniffed it.

Thus, the dog was moving on, with no further heed to the scent. Nor did he pay much more attention to an equally familiar black-and-white and furry creature which moved noiselessly toward the henhouse in full view of him, from the direction of the woods behind the stables.

The oncoming animal showed no terror of the dog. It was the least timid of all woodland things. Experience and ancestral instinct had taught it that few dogs cared to try conclusions with it, be they thrice or five times its size. Thus it approached the hencoop with not the slightest dread of Lad and with a surety born of various earlier visits.

Lad would have continued his way to the house without further thought of the intruder, but for a rather odd proceeding which quickened his ever-alert collie curiosity.

The black-and-white animal had advanced to one side of the coop. There, unerringly, it had wriggled its pointed nose and its forepaws under the lower edge of a seemingly firm perpendicular board.

At the slight pressure, the bottom of the board swung outward. Through the narrow slit thus made, the invader slithered into the coop.

Thus has many a marauder entered henhouses, since first those unlovely structures were built. Most coops are ill-constructed and without foundations. Often their nails are driven carelessly. The floors sag and settle, with wet and dry weather and with alternate frosts and thaws, until sometimes, at one end, the bottom nails of the vertical boarding tear loose, from sheer pressure, while the nails at the topmost end of the board may still be strong enough to hold it crazily in place.

Any rightly directed outward pressure from below will cause the board to move more or less easily outward for a few inches, as on a hinge. Gravity makes it fall back in place when the pressure is removed. Carnivorous woodland creatures seem to have a genius for discovering such boards in coops they want to break into.

Small wonder the Master's cursory inspection had failed to find a hole for ingress! There was no need for such a hole.

The furry thief had but to seize his prey and then to butt his way out to freedom with it, leaving the board to swing back into place.

Some night, of course, the crazy and rusted nails at the top might give away under these oft-repeated wabblings and might let the whole board fall off, leaving a gap that the first human could not fail to see in the morning.

That would be a signal for the complete renovation of the coop and a sealing of the secret mode of entrance and exit. But in the meantime the pickings were monstrous easy for the shrewd creature that had discovered the loose-bottomed board.

The vanishing of the furtively bold animal through the apparently solid side wall of the coop puzzled and interested Lad. He paused; then he turned back to investigate.

He approached the coop and, by scent, nosed until he found the precise place where the entry had been made. At the same time another and more sinister scent smote his keen nostrils. It was the smell of blood.

The robber, hungry after his long day's fast and sleep, was sating his appetite before dragging forth another victim and traveling, thus laden, back to the lair where his mate and six blind black babies waited for the feast.

Silently as a serpent he had struck. Silently he had slain. Not a sound had marked the fowl's death. So skillful was the killer that the other chickens were not disturbed.

But the blood-reek had gushed forth to the sniffing dog, and it had told a story which changed his half-amused curiosity into vigilance. Blood tells its own tale to every animal that smells it. The tale is of death.

One of the chickens in there, beyond this sagging board wall, had just been killed. Lad knew that much. The chickens, like all other things at Sunnybank, were under the guard of The Place's official watchdog.

The watchdog was responsible. Well did Lad realize that, even as a million other natural watchdogs have realized the same kind of thing without its being taught to them.

The collie snarled savagely, deep down in his throat, and strove to find a way to get in at the slayer. He ran around the coop to its door, and scratched imperatively at it. The noise disturbed the slumbering chickens. One of them began to cackle loudly. The cackling was taken up.

The door shook under the collie's angry impact, but its lock held. The din from inside the coop waxed louder.

The killer crouched in one corner, waiting for the turmoil to die down, so that he could seize another silly hen as she slept. Failing to get in at the door, Lad trotted around the coop to where he had seen the intruder get in.

Again he nosed futilely at the boards. Then he sat down to wait until the slaughterer of his feathered charges should emerge.

Car after car had come down the drive by this time, but Lad did not notice them. Forgotten even was his gorgeous and prideful bow of red satin. He had work to do—professional watchdog work—punitive work. There was no scope, until after that, for parading his bow before admiring humans.

Thus he sat, tense and waiting.

But if supernatural scenting powers are given to many collies, so were they given in equal measure to the killer in the henhouse. He could scent the great dog watching there in silence for him to come out. He could hear the collie breathe.

From the rage-snarl and from the futile assault on the loud-creaking door, he knew Lad was waiting for him in no friendly welcoming spirit.

Yet, calmly and with no shadow of fear, the creature crouched there, biding his time until the chickens should be asleep again. He was familiar —by ancestry and by experience—with the ways of fowls. He knew that a whole coopful of them may be in wild excitement through panic, after nightfall, and yet that in an incredibly short time they will settle down to roost as if nothing has disturbed or warned them. He could wait.

His forecast was justified. Presently the clamor died to somnolent flaps and cluckings.

(Years ago, I saw four fowls tossed into a den which held two hungry pythons. At first the birds were in screeching terror, the more especially as the pythons caught and crushed and swallowed two of them in most revolting fashion. But in a very few minutes the two survivors had quieted down as for sleep. One of them flapped to a perch on the larger python's back, and dozed there —until the other snake grabbed her. Chickens are perhaps the most insensately foolish of all birds.)

Lad, keen of ear as of nostrils, heard at last the all but imperceptible seizure of a sleeping pullet, and the subsequent soft patter of padding feet across the floor of the coop toward the loose board.

The slayer had eaten his fill, and was carrying home this second victim to his lair in the nearer woods. The dog tensed himself for a spring.

The bottom of the board was pushed outward. Through the slit the killer wriggled, with his booty. Lad made a savage dive at him as he emerged into the open. Then ——

Gasping, sneezing, staggering in sick discomfort, the collie rolled on the grass, striving to get rid of a Horror that encompassed him, and to overcome a sudden blindness.

Unruffled, the killer picked up the dead chicken and proceeded mincingly toward the woods, without so much as a backward glance toward the discomfited Lad. By no means was this the first rashly attacking dog he had put to rout.

Presently, Lad recovered his shattered self-control. His sight was coming back, though his eyes stung. He did not know what had befallen him. But he did know he felt most miserable and that he had been bested and that he had been unable to avert the killing and theft of one of the Little People of The Place, whose safety it was his life-duty to protect.

As ever, in moments of stress, he sought out the Mistress and the Master. In their company he was happiest. Perhaps they could console him in some way for the indignity he had just suffered and which had cut, knifelike, into his abnormally sensitive feelings. To them he turned now for comfort.

He trotted to the house. Dinner had begun. Gone was Lad's vanity and with it his wish to show off his satin bow and his new-brushed coat to the guests. It would be enough for him, in his present chastened mood, to slip quietly into the dining-room and to lie there on the floor in his wonted place close to the left of the Master's chair.

Thither he hurried.

The soup course was under way. The candle-lit room buzzed with talk and with soft laughter. A mass of crimson roses in the center of the table filled the air with soft fragrance.

"I don't know where he can be," the Mistress was saying, in reply to a question from the man at her right. "He is almost never late for a meal. He never begs. He just lies there, at my husband's left, and he doesn't expect anything to eat. I put a red satin bow on him, a little while ago, to match those roses. He ——"

She broke off in her idle speech. No longer did the delicate perfume of the roses permeate the dining-room. As well might the whisper of an æolian harp seek to drown the shell-fire at the battle of the Marne, as could any normal fragrance cope with the awesome and hideous odor which all at once seemed to fill the whole world.

The Mistress gasped. The guests laid down their soup-spoons—there was no further desire to eat—and tried to look as if they were not in nasal agony.

For a fraction of a second no word was spoken, while that unspeakable stench seeped into every nostril and made the sweet candle-lit room a place of abomination.

It was the Master who found his voice. Glancing down beside him, to his left, he beheld a forlorn clump of mahogany-and-white fur from whose neck dangled a once-gay satin ribbon. Lad had stolen into the room and to his wonted place, unnoted. But now anyone within fifty feet of him would have known he was there.

"Out!" thundered the Master. "*Out*, Lad!"

At the command, Lad departed at top speed, through the open long French windows behind the Master's chair. In mental anguish he heard the note of horrified disgust in the loved voice, and its reiteration in the Mistress's ever-gentle tones as she echoed the Master's command of dismissal.

In the presence of all mankind he had been

humiliated—he had been ordered from the room in angry disgust by the two people to whom he had fled for comfort.

Out into the early summer twilight he slunk, hating himself and the world at large and grieving as only a sensitive collie can grieve at unmerited disgrace. Did these humans think he enjoyed the awful odor that clung to him? Wasn't that bad enough, by itself, without his being driven forth like some unbroken puppy?

Nor did he smell any worse, even now, to these humans, than many humans had smelled to Lad's tormented senses, again and again, with their sickening perfumes and tobacco and booze! Lad had borne all that—though he loathed it—for the sake of being near those he loved. Yet when, through no desire of his own, he chanced to be malodorous, they ordered him from them in disgust!

A dog's sense of smell, like a dog's hearing, is infinitely stronger and more intelligent than is any human's. Nature seems to have tried to make up to him for his nearsightedness by giving him abnormal powers of scent and of ear.

An odor, wholly imperceptible to the most acute human, can not only be detected, but can be read aright by the average dog. An evil smell is positive torture to him.

The high notes of a violin sometimes pierce his delicate ear-drums agonizingly and make him scream with pain or a piteous sound of protest which his owners often mistake for an attempt on his part to sing and which they delight in showing off to chance visitors.

The only difference, except in degree, between a canine's sense of smell and a human's is that certain odors which disgust a man or woman are a joy to dogs. Carrion is the chief of these.

A dog does not eat the semi-liquescent carcass of an excessively dead animal that he finds in the woods. Instead, he rolls in it, digging one shoulder after the other into the awful stuff—then trots proudly home to share the divine fragrance with his human friends. Probably he wonders why his presence, for the next day or two, is a horror to them.

In like manner, the subtlest form of sachet is sickening to a dog. The stronger and more pervasive the costly perfume, the more he detests it. Of his own accord, your dog will not pick up a handkerchief if there is the slightest taint of perfume on it.

It is the same with tobacco. No dog likes its reek. To many sensitive dogs it is positive agony to sniff it.

In former times I encountered several dogs

which would make friends with women only and would not go near any man. The tobacco smell, strong or faint, made them avoid men, even as men might avoid the odor which now pervaded Lad.

(I do not know what such ultra-fastidious dogs would do in this era of "double-standard" smoking. Probably their only human friends would be children who were too young to have learned to smoke.)

Not that Lad, sensibly, was conscious of any such mode of reasoning. Yet it was true.

Again and again the tobacco smell on the Master's breath and clothes had sickened the collie; so had the supposedly delicate perfumes used by the Mistress. Yet blithely had Lad endured these affronts to his tortured nostrils, in order to remain close beside these two humans who were his gods.

At an odor to him much less sickening they had just exiled him in disgrace from their presence and from the presence of their gasping friends.

"What—what is it?" faintly panted a woman halfway down the table—a woman whose knowledge of the country was less than limited. "I never knew of anything so—so ——!"

"The polite word for it, in fur circles," expounded the Master, "is 'Alaska sable.' The naturalist name for it is '*Mephitis mephitica.*' We plain folk call it a 'skunk.' It is one of the most beautiful animals in the world. And it is one of the most odorless and harmless, except when it is scared or attacked. Lad has just scared or attacked one. You know the result. I'm sorry. I thought the old dog had too much sense to tackle a skunk. It's instinctive with most grown dogs, that live in the country, to leave them severely alone. . . . There are five windows in this dining-room, and they're all wide open. My only criticism of my father, in building the house, is that he didn't have five thousand windows in the dining-room and a hundred-mile-an-hour draught blowing through every one of them. I wonder if the odor will *ever* get out!"

The dinner was a ghastly failure. The Mistress had prided herself on the menu. But a starving man could scarcely have partaken of food in that vile atmosphere.

The night was windless. The scent lay everywhere like a pall. Scientists claim that, on still air, the skunk-reek can be noted for the distance of a mile. Lad had been 5,280 feet less than a mile from the dining-room of Sunnybank.

When the last guest had gone—and all of them departed at an unprecedentedly early hour—the Master wound a muffler around his nose and mouth and sent for a pail of hot water and for many cloths. Then he whistled for Lad.

Out of the summer darkness reluctantly appeared the collie. For a solid hour the Master wrought over the miserably uncomfortable Lad, scrubbing with all his strength and to the dog's infinite malaise, until he was exhausted.

"In another week or two, Laddie," he said, wearily, as he finished his wholesale task, "you may be fit to come into the house again. If I could have gotten to work at you the minute this happened—as I did with Bobby when he was a puppy—the time would be shorter. But it's had a chance to 'set.' So it has 'hurt me worse than it has hurt you'—and in exactly the same place. Where's my pipe?"

"Don't scold him," exhorted the Mistress. "I've been thinking, dear. And I believe we know now what kind of 'varmint' has been killing your prize chickens. Laddie would never have been foolish enough to go for a skunk for his own amusement. He remembered how you guarded the henhouses all last night, so he did some guarding on his own account, early this evening. And this is the result."

Without answering, the Master strode down to the out-buildings. Presently he returned.

"A killed and half-eaten rooster in the bottom

of the bigger coop," he reported. "And a Buff Orpington pullet gone. Perhaps you're right. Laddie, I'm sorry I ordered you out of the room tonight. I—I apologize. But—well, you were pretty fearful, and you made us score the first dinner-failure in Sunnybank's history. Shall we call it square, Lad?"

But Lad was far from willing to call it square. He had been shamed—publicly shamed. He had been ordered from the dining-room in the presence of more than a dozen people. He had heard a laugh—a tremulously unconvincing laugh, but still a laugh of derision—as he slunk from that room.

Then, after an evening of lonely unhappiness, he had been scrubbed in agonizingly rough fashion, till his tender skin was sore and tingling.

All this—as any mongrel puppy could have deduced—was due directly to the foul black animal which had belittled Lad's worth as a watchdog and had slain chickens whose safeguarding was part of his sacred watchdog duty. A hate for the fearless black-and-white killer throbbed in the collie's supersensitive heart. There was a debt to pay.

Lad slept ever in the house—either in his "cave" under the piano in the music-room or else (as did Gray Dawn in much later years until the glorious old gray collie's death on Decoration Day, 1929) on a rug at the foot of the main stairway.

The French windows of the downstairs rooms stood wide open all night, in summer-time; for the house was as safe from thieves, with Lad on guard inside it and with his fiery young son, Wolf, on the front porch mat, as if a machine-gun company were on duty there.

Tonight, as soon as the house was quiet, the big mahogany-and-snow collie crept out through the first open window he came to. At sight of his sire, Wolf sprang up from his mat on the porch. A low growl, far down in Lad's furry throat, checked his onward progress.

Lad passed on, unaccompanied, to the larger of the two hencoops. There he lay down, wide awake, his deep-set sorrowful eyes fixed on the board under which the skunk had crawled.

Scent and sound told him his enemy was not there. He turned his gaze toward the black line of woodland whence he had seen the skunk approach. And there, wide awake and vengefully watching, he remained until sunrise, before going back into the house and to his piano cave.

And so the next night and the next. Lad had something to do—a blot on his watchdog escutcheon to wipe clean.

Meantime, on the day after the slaying of the two chickens, the Master and Robert Friend, his English superintendent, and one of the other men, made a careful inspection of the supposedly holeless henhouse. There, more by chance than by skill, they happened upon the swinging wallboard. It and two other almost as badly damaged planks were replaced, and the whole structure was strengthened, pending an early succession of the old coop by a new one.

The mystery of the skunk's predatory entrance was solved.

But Lad's grievance was no whit abated. In his memory rankled the tinge of blood that had come to his nostrils from the chicken which had been part of his guard duty at The Place; recollection of the other chicken stolen under his very eyes, of the rank defeat that had been his, and of the crowning humiliation in the dining-room, which it all had led up to.

He ached at the thought, and he yearned morbidly and cravingly to wipe out the splotch on his watchdog honor and housedog prestige.

Wherefore, at odd times, by day, and every night, he took to haunting the region of the mended chickencoops.

It was on the eighth evening, early, that his long vigil was rewarded. By this time, thanks to the Master's scrubbing and to other administrations, the frightful reek had departed from Lad's heavy coat, except in rainy weather, when it had the same elusively unpleasant aura of an old-time wet Alaska-sable muff.

Once more he was welcome in the dining-room at meals. Yet, in the depths of his bruised heart he grieved.

Yes, it was early on the eighth evening that his patient watching was repaid. Dinner was over. The humans were sitting on the veranda in the dusk. At the Mistress's feet on the porch lay Lad. Then to him came the very faintest hint of the skunk's presence somewhere within a few hundred yards of him.

No human could have caught that all but imperceptible animal odor, so vastly different from the scent associated with a skunk. But Lad caught it, and it stirred him to instant and vengeful activity.

Unnoted, he arose from his sprawling-place at the feet of the Mistress. Down the steps he went, noiselessly, and around the house corner and toward the group of stable-buildings.

No longer was he a sedate house collie. Subtly he had become a beast of prey. With soundless pads he sped along, every sense strained, every faculty ready.

Thus, ten thousand years ago, had sped his wolf-ancestors to the chase.

Lad might well have spared his instinctive precautions. The skunk both heard and scented him almost by the time the collie began his progress. Yet, the knowledge that the avenging dog was at large and was coming toward him did not check the invader, nor even make him move more warily.

Once before he had encountered the collie, and had come off triumphant. There was no reason to cringe from him this second time.

Moreover the skunk was hungry. So were his brood. He had steered clear of this particular chicken-coop for some nights now. Not for any fear of Laddie, but because the scent of new boards and of human touch and fresh human footsteps was vaguely distasteful to him. But now these undesirable signs were wearing away.

Wherefore, he was making another pilgrimage to what had hitherto been an unfailing source of food-supply to him and his.

Across the patch of open grass between the woods and the stables came the skunk. He was a slow and clumsy traveler, as are all his kind. As he neared the chicken-yard a furry avalanche dashed out from the shadows and bore down on him.

The skunk was in no way taken by surprise. He

had seen the dog in ambush there in the dark and had even heard Lad's quick breaths. He checked his own leisurely advance, but he did not give ground.

Instead, he braced all four of his feet and awaited in grim confidence the onslaught of the opponent he felt so certain he could put to rout.

Full at the braced and deadlily-prepared foe Sunnybank Lad launched himself. But Lad had a brain which did not let him make the same kind of fool of himself twice. Moreover, Lad was descended from the wolf-folk that had made many a meal, unscathed, upon skunks.

As he came within perhaps twelve feet of the waiting skunk Lad shifted far to one side, in a single bound, without slackening his lightning-swift speed. In what seemed like practically the same motion he flashed in at the skunk from the left.

Before the wily enemy could brace himself again, or so much as turn to meet the flank attack, two mighty jaws had caught him in mid-spine—jaws that could crack a beef bone, jaws whose snap was instantaneous in its swiftness.

The recently formidable black-and-white pest lay stone-dead on the grass, his back broken by that one terrific snap. Lad had paid his debt. The account was squared.

"I would have made my dinner call sooner," a woman was saying to the Mistress and the Master, on the veranda. "But I thought Sunnybank would seem more like its lovely old self if I waited till Lad could be thoroughly fumigated or even buried. You poor people! What a way to spoil a jolly dinner!"

"It is past history now," answered the Master, uncomfortable at her raillery. "Lad is back to normal, and we've fixed the chicken-houses in a way to discourage any further visits from his malodorous enemy. The incident is closed at last We ——"

His mouth fell slack. A waft of breeze bore to the porch's occupants a right conclusive proof that the incident was still wide open.

During the pause of horrified revulsion that followed, a bulky Shape advanced from the twilight and mounted the steps with majestically proud stride. With it and in advance of it came the odor which had checked the Master's boast that the incident was closed.

Lad advanced toward the Master's chair. At the man's feet he laid something indistinct and limp and furry. Then he stepped back, wagging his plumed tail and eagerly awaiting a chorus of approval for his valiant deed in destroying the destroyer.

Dim as was the night, the humans knew well what trophy it was that Lad had brought along. In utter darkness they would have known.

The Master sent the dead thing flying out onto the lawn with a furious kick, then called to one of the men to carry it away and bury it. The guest made babbling excuse for her call's abruptly early ending.

Lad gazed with hurt amazement at this reception to his triumph-gift. His plume of a tail ceased to wave, and it drooped pathetically.

It was the Mistress, as ever, who divined her collie chum's unhappiness and who hastened to lighten it. Interrupting the Master's scarce-begun scolding, she took the dog's classic head between her little palms.

"*Good* old Laddie!" she applauded. "It was fine of you! And it was a splendid present to bring us. Nobody's going to scold you for ridding The Place of such a horrible creature. You're a dear old dog. Only—next time you play St. George and come home from a dragon-slaying expedition, I hope it will be on some evening when we all have frightfully bad colds in the head."

As she stooped over the comforted dog, Lad caught a whiff of the delicate French perfume she used so sparingly. The same puff of breeze brought him the rank smoke of the Master's pipe. Both odors were not only abhorrent to Lad, as I have said, but were actively painful to his nostrils' tender nerves.

But willingly and even joyously did Lad endure this dual torment, as a very petty price to pay for being near these two deities of his.

Chapter Four

OLD MAN TROUBLE

"THE average family dog," Twinch was declaiming—accusingly, "the average family dog has privileges and pleasures that are denied to the average child."

"Quite," agreed the Master. "For example, not one child in a million gets a chance to bite the iceman or to forage in ash-cans. You are right. But ——"

"There are children starving, in the gutter, all over this broad land," continued Twinch, nettled into fresh vehemence by the Master's mild flippancy, "so that dogs may be pampered on costly food that ought to go to them."

This time there was no hint of banter in the Master's reply.

"I don't agree with you," he said. "Fifty years ago there were homeless and hungry children by the hundreds in every big city. There were sixty thousand of them in New York alone. It was a dirty smear on civilization. But now there are scores of wise and efficient societies all over the country, for children's welfare, and mighty stringent laws for that same welfare. No child need starve. If what you say were true, I'd never own a dog. For all the dogs on earth aren't worth as much as one child."

"I ——"

"In the meantime," finished the Master, "if you can find me one child that needs dog biscuits and table scraps, such as we feed to our collies, the child is welcome to them and to anything else I can give it. But, till you can prove that claim, I am going to keep on owning dogs. Especially Lad, here."

The great collie lifted his head at sound of his name. His plumed tail smote resoundingly upon the boards of the veranda; as he lay there, happily, at the Master's feet.

Lad did not like this loud-voiced visitor who had invaded The Place, uninvited, today. Strangers, in general, were distasteful to Lad. Indeed, the big dog cared for nobody except the Mistress and the Master—in the order named. Toward the rest of mankind, as a rule—always excepting small children, whom he loved with all his protecting heart and soul—he held himself more or less courteously aloof.

This particular visitor aroused more than usual

distaste in Laddie, by dint of a harsh voice and an altogether jarring personality. But for the fact that it was pleasant to drowse on the veranda mat at the Master's feet, Lad would have vanished promptly and unobstrusively, when first he saw the newcomer. As it was, he blinked in icy disapproval at the man.

The Master had little more fondness for his harsh-voiced, hectoring guest than had the dog. With a collie's odd psychology, Lad sensed this.

Peter K. Twinch had telephoned, on the Master's busy work-morning, to say he was about to call at The Place in behalf of an Orphan Home for which he was trying to raise funds. His voice over the wire had not been prepossessing, but his mission was sacred. Wherefore the Master had consented to see him.

He found the man's face and general manner to be wholly in keeping with his voice. Yet, he listened with what civility he could, to the preamble of the caller's fund-raising mission—until Laddie chanced to saunter up from his morning swim in the lake and to lie down on the sunny veranda to dry himself.

This was the signal for Twinch to break into violent invective against dogs in general, declaring he hated them all. Thence he drifted raucously into a diatribe on the sin of spending money on mere canines when so many children were in dire need.

The Master's hard-held patience began to fray. It all but snapped when Twinch declared that children, everywhere, were starving, in order that dogs might eat. Yet he thought he had replied with studied politeness. Twinch thought otherwise.

"You are like all dog-owners!" he snorted. "Bigoted and prejudiced, and with no vision beyond your own wretched pets. I am not an animal-hater. I love horses. Horses do a grand work in the world. I admire them all. But dogs and cats are filthy parasites. If I had known you keep dogs, I might have spared myself this useless visit. I won't detain you any longer."

"Dogs and cats are 'filthy parasites,' you think?" rejoined the Master, "and yet you call *me* bigoted! Look over the British War Office archives, if you haven't heard the tremendous work that was done by dogs in the war. War Office records are made up of facts and not of mushy sentiment. If dogs had never before earned their right to live, their war service would have won them that right. They ——"

"The war is over," coldly answered Twinch. "In the meantime ——"

"If all dogs were wiped out," insisted the Master, "much of the civilized world would be overrun by beasts of prey within ten years. That is not my own statement. It's a computation made by professional forestry men. If all cats are destroyed, how long will it be before rats and mice and plenty of other vermin eat us out of house and home and spread disease everywhere? No. Both dogs and cats earn their way. And even if they didn't—well, there's got to be something in this old world besides grim utility. There's a chumship in ——"

"Rot!" grunted Twinch with his usual exquisite courtesy. "You're a fanatic. I'm sorry I wasted my time in coming here to try to interest an animal-crank in anything so sublime as child welfare. I ——"

"Leave a subscription blank with me," suggested the Master, rising, "or tell me where to have a check sent. My wife attends to our charity subscriptions; and she isn't at home this morning. You may be sure that if this orphanage project of yours is all you say it is, we shall be glad to give whatever we can to it."

"If it is all I *say* it is!" flared Twinch. "Just what do you mean by that? I insist on knowing."

"I meant no more than I said," answered the Master, "and very certainly I meant no less. Send us any pamphlets or prospectus you may have.

And—may I suggest something to you in the way of easing your job? I know what a rotten task it is to have to go around and ask for subscriptions. But you'll get much more cash out of people by stating your case civilly and not stamping on their pet hobbies. Courtesy costs very little, and sometimes it pays good dividends. I suggest it not as a criticism of you, but because you'll get more funds that way."

Twinch sputtered forth an inarticulate word or two. Then, controlling himself with difficulty, he said, abruptly:

"You can make the check out to me, *now*, please, and save me the trouble of hunting up all our orphanage literature and sending it to you. Make it out to ——"

"I have just told you my wife always decides how much we shall give to charities. She is wiser about such things than I am. As soon as she comes home I ——"

Peevishly Mr. Peter K. Twinch glowered at his host. It was then that Lad created a diversion.

There is ever an imp of mischief lurking somewhere in the background of a collie's queer brain. Lad had paid more and more attention to the talk between the two men. Naturally, he could not understand at all what it was about. But he sensed that the Master was growing keenly averse to his raucous-voiced visitor. Also that the visitor's voice was waxing more strident and that he was making uncouth and perhaps threatening gestures as he spoke.

Quietly Lad arose from the warm veranda floor on which he had been drying some of the volume of lake water which still adhered to his mighty coat.

Over to Twinch strolled the dog. When he was six inches away from the angry guest, Laddie shook himself violently all over. As a result, a shower of muddy water flew from fifty parts of his drenched coat and sprayed Twinch's pale fawn suit from ankle to chest.

With a veritable yell of wrath, the man swung aloft his furled umbrella and smote fiercely at the shaggy brute that had marred the freshness of his new clothes.

In practically the same gesture Twinch was reeling backward, clawing the air in quest of his lost balance, and screeching in fright.

Lad had dodged the clumsy blow and was ravening madly at his wizened assailant. In a trice the elfin mischief was gone from the collie's deep-set dark eyes. His eyes were flaming and he was ablaze with homicidal fury. It was not on the free list to strike at Sunnybank Lad.

He sprang snarlingly on Twinch, his impact

knocking the man backward to the floor, while Lad tore in to finish his punitive work.

"*Lad!*" shouted the Master.

The collie checked his furious charge, turning instantly, if sulkily, from his foe, and ranging himself alongside the Master.

Well did Laddie know the simple Guest Law of The Place. Only under intolerable provocation could he have forgotten that an accredited visitor was sacred from molestation.

Aware how black was his fault, he looked up into the Master's face to learn his doom. Something which his uncanny powers of perception read there reassured the dog. The white tip of his tail began to twitch. Then, casting his eyes once more upon Twinch, he snarled loathingly, far down in his furry throat.

The Master was helping the infuriated and terrified man to his feet. The soft spring air was shattered by Twinch's gabbled sputterings. The man was beside himself with anger—anger tinged with a very wholesome terror of the big collie that eyed him so balefully.

"I'll swear out a warrant and have your vicious dog shot!" he screamed with his first articulate breath. "If there's a law in the land ——"

"There is," affirmed the Master. "There's a law against property damage. Here on my grounds, you have wantonly sought to injure this dog which is my property. Then you got what was coming to you, and nothing more. If I hadn't called him off when I did, you'd be one hundred per cent eligible to the hospital by this time. Bring your damage suit, if you like. In the meantime I suggest that it'll be pleasanter for everyone if you clear out of here."

Twinch's bellowings had subsided to snarled mutterings. He took off his coat, examined ruefully a furrow in its lapel made by one of Lad's slashing eyeteeth, then laid it on the floor while he felt his tie and collar for further possible damage.

Solemnly Lad crossed over to where the coat lay. He rubbed one of his muscular shoulders against its fawn-hued surface, then the other shoulder. Then he rolled luxuriously on it.

"Lad!" again rebuked the Master, but this time in a voice choked with ill-held laughter.

As the dog reluctantly got up from rolling on the coat and as Twinch's furious denunciations burst forth afresh, the Master pointed sternly to the open hall-door.

"Inside!" he commanded. "And stay there."

Head and tail adroop, Lad obeyed. He had been ordered away like an undisciplined puppy. This too in the loathed presence of the stranger.

All the fun and all the rage were gone from him. Indoors he plodded and sought refuge in his "cave" under the music-room piano.

Not being a dog-man, Twinch had missed the true meaning of the double shoulder-rubbing and the rolling on his cherished coat. To him it had been only an act of senseless mischief.

But the Master understood. Lad had perpetrated the most abominable insult possible, upon this man who had tried to strike him. For only into carrion does a dog thus shove one shoulder after another, following up the action by a luxurious roll.

It was no fault of Laddie's if Twinch's mind failed to grasp the full horrible significance of the collie's prank.

The Master picked up the misused and crumpled coat and handed it back to its owner.

"Send me the bill for pressing and repairing it," he said. "And now please go."

"You haven't heard the last of this!" sputtered Twinch. "You'll hear more from me, plenty soon."

"I'm afraid so," assented the Master. "And the next house you visit, to raise funds for your orphanage, you'll get more money by not orating against dogs, and assuredly by not hitting at them. We North Jerseymen look on our dogs as friends. Send me your subscription blank. Good-by."

When the Mistress came home, a half-hour later, the Master told her the whole annoying story.

"I called up Vanderslice," he finished, "and I asked him about this Twinch pest. I had a morbid hope the man might be an impostor. But he isn't. Vanderslice says he's on the level and that the orphanage deserves all support. So, if you like, we'll send it a check."

"But ——"

"Vanderslice says two charity organizations have fired Twinch for his tactlessness and his nasty temper and his altogether rotten personality," went on the Master; "but that he's a good man, just the same, and that he spends his own time and money in raising funds for such things. So I can't even feel smug about the way he was treated here today. I can't even hate the fellow, as I'd like to. But Laddie can. Lad will never forget that blow."

Two days later, in a morning paper, the Master read a lurid account of the injuring of Peter K. Twinch, a noted charity worker, by a vicious collie dog. Names and details were given in full.

Twinch, it seemed, had gone to The Place in

quest of a subscription for an orphanage. There he not only had been repelled by the Master in most discourteous fashion, but the Master had encouraged his savage brute of a dog to attack the defenseless philanthropist. He had then ordered Twinch off his land.

So ran the newspaper's version.

"If I were ever fool enough to look for trouble by going to law over anything at all," fumed the Master, "I'd have grounds here for a swell criminal-libel suit! Nice name it'll give us and our kennels, all over the country! From this newspaper yarn, I seem to be a Simon Legree who has no ambition in life except to sic his murderous dogs onto holy charity workers. At that, Twinch probably thought he was telling the truth."

"Don't let it worry you," soothed the Mistress. "Nobody who knows you or Laddie will believe it. All we have to do is to say nothing at all. That's always best. There won't be any more bother about it, I'm sure."

For once, the wise Mistress was mistaken. There was infinitely "more bother about it."

A little later in the day a noncommittally gloomy person called at The Place and served upon the Master a formal document in a civil suit for damages, in the sum of $10,000, brought against him by one Peter K. Twinch, who sought that amount as balm for "abrasions and contusions and mental and physical anguish" wrought by the defendant's dog.

"Old Man Trouble seems to be paying us one of his jolly little visits," commented the Master when the process-server had gone. "Well, we know the worst now, anyway. I was dead certain there'd be something like this."

But it was not a good year for prophecies at The Place. The Master's boast that he "knew the worst" was as ill-justified as had been the Mistress's belief that there would be "no more bother about it."

At noon next day, a roadster came down the oak-bordered driveway. A comfortable-looking, round-faced man rolled obesely therefrom. Smilingly he accosted the Master, on the porch; flicking one thumb athwart his own coat lapel to display a silvery badge.

He introduced himself as the county marshal, from Ramsey, and said he came armed with a court order to shoot the "incurably vicious dog" which had so fearsomely bitten and manhandled Peter K. Twinch.

"If there's any shooting to be done here," flamed the Master, stung to sudden wrath at this threat to his loved collie, "I can——!"

"One moment, dear!" quietly interposed the Mistress. "*Please!*"

Stepping between the two men, she addressed the professionally smiling marshal.

"May I look at that court order of yours?" she asked.

Her brows furrowing, she scanned the paper, then handed it back to the marshal.

"But this order doesn't mention the dog's name or even say what breed he is," she demurred, gently. "And we have five dogs on The Place. Which one of the five are you going to shoot?"

"Why, the one that bitten poor Mr. Twinch, of course, lady!" explained the moon-faced marshal, wondering at such stupidity. "It says here on this paper that——"

"Yes," interposed the Mistress, her pleasant voice unruffled, her face calm, "I just read it. But still that doesn't answer my question. You say you're going to shoot the dog that bit Mr. Twinch. (Not that we admit that any of our five dogs bit him.) But how are you going to find out which of the five it is?"

"Hey?"

"Two or three of the dogs are valuable, from a money standpoint," continued the Mistress. "So you can't very well shoot all five. You would be letting yourself in for a terrifically large damage suit. You might even lose that very becoming badge you just showed us. How are you going to find out which dog it was?"

Her sweet voice was courteously quizzical. There was a half-smile on her lips. The Master knew she was sick with fear. He gave mental homage to her perfect acting, as well as to her quick resourcefulness.

The marshal looked puzzled, scratching his head, then reading the court order through.

"Yes," resumed the Mistress, "we have five dogs here. The order calls for the shooting of only one dog. You realize you have no right to kill them all and you wouldn't do such an insane thing. More than that, you can't kill any one of them at random, on the chance that he may be the dog you were told to kill, because the odds would be five to one against your killing the right dog. And if you should kill the wrong one, you would be in all sorts of trouble with the law. What are you going to do about it?"

The marshal scowled, his round pink face puckering like a cross baby's.

"Did Mr. Twinch describe the dog that he says bit him?" asked the Mistress, with the air of one who seeks to encourage a defective child. "Perhaps that might give you a clue."

"Yes, he did!" snapped the marshal. "I heard

him tell the judge it was as big as a yearling calf and had great big glaring eyes and a blackish curly coat and tusks like a wild boar's and ——"

"Good!" applauded the Mistress. "That gives you something to go on. Suppose you take a look around the kennels and the house. And when you find a dog as big as a yearling calf and with great big glaring eyes and a curly black coat and wild-boar tusks, all you have to do is to shoot him. Unless you're afraid of getting the wrong dog and standing a heavy damage suit."

"Ma'am—and you, too, Mister!" roared the marshal, in sudden arrogance. "In the name of the law I call on you to tell me which of your dogs bitten Mr. Twinch!"

The Mistress's laugh was infuriating to the official as she answered:

"I didn't read anything in your court order directing either my husband or myself to point out the dog to you. Pick out the right one, if you can. You can hardly expect us to do it for you."

"Ma'am!" growled the marshal, after glaring furiously into her smiling face for a full half-minute, "it'd give me a lot of pleasure to see you in jail for the way you've hornswaggled me! But —if ever you run for office, you've got my vote."

"That's ever so good of you! I ——"

"Only—say, the both of you, I like this job of dog-killing about as much as I like the toothache. I got a grand little collie of my own, at home. Fetches my slippers when I come in, and brings me the noospaper off'n the stoop, and all that. Cute little cuss. I got to go back now and report. That'll mean the judge will make me bring my noble next-door neighbor, Twinch, over here to identify the dog, which same he will sure be able to do. If I was you, I'd hide that dog somewheres before neighbor Twinch gets here. He's due to get here mighty soon, too. So long, Lady! You'd ought to be in politics."

As the marshal's roadster wheeled out of the grounds into the highroad, a furlong beyond, the Mistress turned to her husband. The half-smile was gone from her face, leaving it white and pitifully anxious.

"He was right!" she exclaimed. "And we haven't any time to lose. After lunch let's drive over to Doctor Byrd's kennels and tell him all about it, and have him keep Laddie there till this blows over. We can trust him to do it. I hate to send Lad into banishment, but it's better than having the dear old dog shot."

"Doctor Byrd!" gasped the Master. "Why, he lives in Ramsey! And Ramsey is where Twinch lives. It says so on that ten-thousand-dollar-damage-suit paper. And that fat marshal, too. He told us he lives next door to Twinch. We'd be taking Lad into the enemy's camp."

"And the enemy's camp is the one spot where Mr. Twinch will never think of looking for him," explained his wife. "It's the very safest hiding-place we could find. Besides, Laddie likes Doctor Byrd—as much as he likes anyone except you and me. I'll telephone, now, and we'll drive over there as soon as we've had lunch."

There was much traffic on the road to Ramsey, that afternoon. It was the first day of the yearly horse-show; a mixture of modern equine exhibit and of old-time county horse-fair. Not only were there to be trotting races and ring exploits, but the breeders of that horse-breeding region brought for exhibition their steeds of all types, from mammoth Percherons to Shetland ponies. Polished until they shone like veneered chestnuts or slabs of ebony, the best horses of the county were to be judged, even as cattle are judged at county fairs.

It was a neighborhood institution. The Mistress and the Master had attended it always, in former years. They had planned to attend it today, but the visit of "Old Man Trouble" had put it out of their minds.

As they neared Ramsey, the sight of much motor traffic all headed one way recalled it to them. On the parking space just outside the fair grounds a horde of cars were ranked in close formation.

They drove on to Dr. Byrd's dog hospital, a bare quarter-mile farther. There they told the veterinary of their dilemma.

It was arranged that they should leave Lad in one of Byrd's spacious kennel yards until it might be safe to take the collie home again. The vet. promised utter secrecy as to Lad's presence in his kennels. Gladly he pledged himself to do everything possible for the big dog's comfort.

The Mistress looked genuinely unhappy as she and the Master turned away from the yard after leaving the indignant Lad imprisoned there. To take his wife's mind momentarily from her worry, the Master suggested:

"Let's go to the horse-show for an hour. We were thinking of going there, anyway. We can leave our car here. It's only a little walk, and when we come back for the car we can look in on Laddie again, to cheer the old chap up and let him know we haven't deserted him altogether. How about it?"

With no great enthusiasm the Mistress agreed to the suggestion. She could not dismiss from her memory the amazed and hurt look in her loved collie chum's eyes as she had walked away, leaving him in this alien kennel yard.

Worry and resentment stirred afresh in her heart as the Master recognized Twinch in the group surrounding a fair-ring wherein a half-dozen gigantic Clydesdale stallions were led around for the judge's inspection.

By the hand Twinch was holding a wriggling eight-year-old child. With raucous voice and expansive gestures he was trying to interest her in the ring-parade of the huge shining horses.

"Probably he is telling her how wicked it is to have horse-fairs when there are starving children everywhere," hazarded the Mistress as the Master pointed out the philanthropist to her.

"No," demurred her husband. "Twinch told me he loves horses. He said they're 'splendidly utilitarian' and that he admires 'the great work they are doing for mankind.' Vanderslice told me the same thing about him. He says horses are Twinch's hobby. Says he has fathered two or three bills in the Legislature for their better treatment. Naturally the mangy fanatic would be here at the show, since he lives in Ramsey. The average man who likes horses likes dogs, too. I can't understand the queer twist to Twinch's alleged mind. He ——"

They had come within earshot of Twinch as they neared the ring. The Master ceased speaking.

As the six immense stallions were led from the ring, Twinch caught sight of the Master and scowled blackly. Then, as if to withdraw his child from such contamination, he started across the open field with her toward the next judging-ring, into which four dark-brown Morgans had just been led.

The six Clydesdales were convoyed from their ring and toward their sheds. Five of them went in massively docile fashion. The sixth did not.

This sixth stallion was a shimmering chestnut. More of the whites of his eyes showed than is usual with a decent-tempered horse. His ears were laid back. His teeth showed under his curling upper lip.

Very evidently he was in a fiendish temper; in one of the rages which sometimes obsess an underworked and overfed stallion when he has been forced into the company of others of his sex and species. The groom had had a hard time piloting him around the ring and in keeping him from picking a fight with his competitors.

Now, the groom was having an equally hard time not to be jerked from his feet by the angry brute's curvets and head-tossings.

Twinch's little daughter looked backward, attracted by the sound of passaging hoofs on the turf. Seeing the stallion so unruly, and perhaps seeking to alleviate her own boredom, she let go of her father's hand.

Running a few yards toward the plunging horse, she picked up a sharp pebble and threw it gayly at him. The idly-flung missile chanced to flick the stallion stingingly in the ribs.

Then, all at once, several things happened.

The horse's evilly rolling eye had marked the running child and had seen her throw the stone at him. The sting of the impact on his polished side added the last touch to his ire, turning mere viciousness into ungovernable rage.

In a sidewise leap he tore the halter rope free from his groom's unprepared grasp. Then, neighing shrilly, he charged at the dismayed child.

Twinch turned to see what had become of his adored little daughter. He beheld her some thirty feet away from him. She was standing stockstill, paralyzed with fear, while toward her thundered a gigantic chestnut stallion.

With a gasp of horror, Twinch ran to her rescue.

There was no cowardice in the wizened fanatic, especially where the welfare of this only child of his was concerned. Realizing as he must have realized, the crass futility of his attempt to save her, he dashed, nevertheless, to her aid.

Then, past him, traveling at the speed of light, flashed a furry shape whose mahogany coat gleamed like orange fire in the sun.

Past Twinch and past the terror-stricken child whizzed the flying shape, and straight at the charging stallion.

Laddie had been left in the kennel-yard at Dr. Byrd's, but he had not been bidden to stay there. Thus, when he saw his two human gods departing on foot up the road, he made strenuous efforts to follow them. From side to side of the wired yard he ran, vainly seeking egress, butting the unyielding barrier with his head, striving to leap over its seven-foot height.

Presently Dr. Byrd appeared, carrying a dish of meat and bread for him.

Lad ceased his futile efforts to break through the unbreakable fence and lay lown wearily. Dr. Byrd chirped to him, but the dog paid no heed. Apparently he was almost asleep. The veterinary opened the wire gate of the yard and came into the inclosure.

As he did so the recumbent dog woke to sudden life. He dived between the doctor's legs, too rapidly for his onset to be guarded against.

Through the half-open gate of the yard he bounded to freedom.

In an instant Lad had picked up the trail of the Mistress and the Master and was following it at a hand gallop. In another minute or so he was at the entrance to the fair-grounds.

An attendant grabbed at him as Lad sped through the gateway—grabbed and missed. Nose to earth, Lad followed the trail of his deities with ease, across the field which a thousand other human feet had trod.

As the trail grew so fresh that Lad was about to follow it by sight alone, he heard the fury-neigh of a horse. The stark rage in the sound made him look up in time to see the enormous Clydesdale rip free from his groom and thunder down upon a helplessly cowering little girl.

Lad needed no more than this moment's vision to tell him all he needed to know. From puppyhood he had been slavishly devoted to children, suffering willingly any tail-pulling or other indignities from them. And now a child was in hideous mortal peril.

Lad went into vehement action.

Madly the horse galloped at his helplessly moveless little victim. The Clydesdale's teeth were bared. His eyes were bloodshot and rolling. He was traveling at top speed toward the work of bloody annihilation which his maddened brain craved.

Almost the rending teeth and the crushingly striking forefeet were within reach of their helpless goal when something flung itself at the horse's face—something furry and catapult-like.

A double set of fire-hot teeth met in the stallion's soft muzzle. Eighty pounds of whalebone weight and muscle twisted itself sharply to one side as the teeth gripped the hot nostrils.

The sidewise jerk and the intolerable pain made the charging brute swerve sharply to the left. That narrow swerve from his path of destruction saved the child from the flailing forefeet and the trampling rear hoofs—saved her, if only by inches.

As for the horse's cruelly snapping teeth, they were otherwise engaged in biting furiously and uselessly at the furry catapult that clung to the sensitive muzzle.

Missing his prey by a bare hand's breadth, the Clydesdale thundered past. Instantly he wheeled and returned to the assault.

But Lad had other plans for him.

Even as the stallion missed his mark, Lad loosed his bulldog grip on the nostrils, dropping lightly to earth and shrinking aside to dodge the hammering hoofs.

As the Clydesdale wheeled back to the demolishing of his victim, Lad sprang again.

Before the stallion's tremendous body had made its full turn, the collie was at the Clydesdale's head once more, leaping high, slashing one ear and the side of the dappled jaw with a single sweep of his curved white eyetooth; then fastening his terrible jaws anew in the mangled nostrils, and throwing his own muscular weight sharply to the left.

For the second time the horse was thrown off his stride and his charge was deflected. For a second time the stallion whirled about to finish his crazy mission of bloodshed.

As he wheeled, his forequarters chanced to brush against Twinch, who was running to place himself between the giant murderer and the screaming child. The touch sufficed to knock Twinch clean off his feet and to send him rolling over and over on the turf, the breath knocked out of him.

People were running up, now, from all directions—grooms and spectators. From the far-off sheds ran two men brandishing pitchforks, and a third who gripped a club. But they were none of them near enough to avert the impending Horror.

The Mistress was closest to the fear-palsied child. She darted forward and swung the little girl behind her just as the stallion returned to his charge.

Now, at the joint peril of the Mistress and the child, Lad went quite insane.

No longer bothering to elude the flying hoofs, he sprang at the stallion's face with a wild-beast roar. One of the iron-shod forefeet touched his side, tearing loose a patch of skin and flesh, but not checking an atom of the collie's wild onslaught.

Driving his teeth deep into the Clydesdale's lower jaw, Lad swung sidewise again. This time his weight and strength were eked out doubly by the momentum of his leap.

The horse's head was yanked to one side, and his galloping body with it. His polished fore-hoofs slipped on the greasy turf. Down he crashed, the thud of his fall shaking the earth.

Before the giant foe touched ground, Lad was all over him, slashing his unprotected underbody; ripping the chestnut ears, scoring afresh the bloody and torn face.

A bulldog gets a grip and hangs on. A collie can hang on almost as well as can a bulldog. But ever he is ready to loose his grip for a better one. He can bite effectively in twenty different spots, if need be, in less than a minute. Moreover, almost alone of all breeds of dogs, he has the ancestral wolf-trick of slashing, razor fashion, with his deadly eyeteeth.

He is not a pleasant opponent, whether for other dogs or for horses or for cattle. By instinct he seems to know just what is the most punishing thing to do at every stage of a fight.

So now it was with Sunnybank Lad. Into his kicking and floundering foe he tore with every atom of fierceness and skill and punitive power he possessed.

By a wrenching effort the Clydesdale blundered to his feet. His once shining coat was rumpled and slashed and bleeding. His whole system was jarred by the heavy fall. His dull brain was blindly confused by the bewildering events of the past half-minute.

Trembling and heaving he stood there, head down, all the battle and murder zest knocked out of him, shuddering with fear, and in an agony of multiple pains. For the moment he was as harmless as any worn-out cart horse.

As the stallion lurched scramblingly upward from the ground, Lad crouched for another spring, to launch himself anew at his giant enemy.

Then something seemed to tell him that this enemy was no longer an enemy, but a panic-seared and dazed and beaten mass of torn flesh. The chivalry in the gallant dog's soul—ever gentle to defenseless things—would not let him assail so impotent a creature.

Panting, Lad stood warily on guard, between the Mistress and the huge horse. A groom ran up and seized the sweating and trembling Clydesdale's dangling halter-rope. Another stable attendant passed a running noose about his slashed neck.

The fight was over.

Lad's torn side ached and stung and throbbed. But, apart from that easily curable flesh wound, he was none the worse for his experience.

Yet he stiffened once more, his hackles beginning to bristle, the tip of one white eyetooth showing from beneath his lip. Scent and sight told him of the presence of a new adversary.

Not ten feet away from him was Peter K. Twinch, the objectionably noisy visitor who had struck at him and whom he had been forbidden to punish adequately for the insult. The dog glared in vengeful distaste at the man.

Then, two trembling little arms were flung rapturously about Lad's neck. The dog's silken head was pressed spasmodically against a heaving little breast. Twinch's daughter had recovered from her moveless panic and she was giving hysterical thanks to the dog that had rescued her.

Two or three men had gathered about the fallen Twinch and had helped him to his feet. One of them was his next-door neighbor, the Ramsey marshal.

Dizzy and breathless from his tumble, the philanthropist blinked confusedly. Then his eyes fell upon his little girl.

Not only was she unhurt, but she was embracing tearfully the great dog which had saved her from being trampled to a shapeless pulp under the stallion's iron-shod hoofs and mangled unspeakably by the horse's flaring jaws.

Twinch stood there, mouth agape, staring glassily. The Master took a step toward him, but the Mistress halted her husband by a light touch on his arm. It was the moon-faced marshal who broke the brief silence.

"Well, Neighbor," he observed, with an effort at joviality that failed to mask his own groundswell of reaction from the recent terror, "there's the folks you brought the ten-thousand-dollar suit against. And there's one of their five dogs, too. I'll bet he's the one I got the court order to shoot. Shall I take a chance and put a bullet into him?"

"This is the dog," said the Master—"the 'filthy parasite' that kept a magnificent utilitarian horse from carrying out certain playful yearnings, just now. This is the dog, Marshal."

It was a petty thing to say, and the Master had the grace to be ashamed of the sour words before they were fairly out of his mouth. Nor did he need the Mistress's glance of reproach and the restraining touch of her little hand on his arm to make him still further ashamed of himself.

But his own nerves were not at their best, after what he had just beheld. More than for most of his human friends, the Master cared for the big dog that so blithely had been coquetting with death in the duel with a maniac antagonist twenty times his size and strength.

The marshal grinned, reaching ostentatiously for his pistol holster.

"You hear that, Mr. Twinch?" he gibed. "They admit that that's the dog. I've still got the court order, right here in my pocket. Say the word and I'll put a bullet through the vicious cur. It'll sure be one grand way for you to show your gratitood for what he done for your kid. Shall I shoot?"

Twinch shook all over, as with a palsy. Twice he made as though to speak. His face twisted itself into ludicrous contortions. Then he yanked free from the marshal's shoulder-grip, snarling peevishly:

"*No!* This isn't the same dog. I never saw this dog before. And you're not going to execute that court order. And I'm not going to press that ten-thousand-dollar damage suit. Understand that? The—the incident is closed. *Closed!*" he reiterated, his harsh voice scaling an octave in squealing cadence.

For another moment Twinch glowered upon the Mistress and the Master and then on the contemptuously aloof Lad.

"Just the same," he snorted, swallowing something like a sob, "I never did like dogs, and I don't now! . . . Come on home, Daughter. We've had enough, for one day—enough of a *lot* of things."

As he stamped past Lad, on his progress toward the entrance gates, his unaccustomed hand dropped furtively to the collie's classic head, in a gesture which might have been either an awkward caress or a benediction.

Whichever it was, Lad, for some strange reason, forebore to resent it; but waved his plumed tail in grave friendliness.

Chapter Five

CHANGELINGS

THE little old lady sat primly erect among the window-seat's inviting cushions.

She disdained to loll back. In her own long-vanished youth, gentlewomen were not supposed to loll. She balanced a teacup and saucer deftly in her black silk lap, while she chatted in precise Victorian diction with her hosts—the Mistress and the Master.

She was like a Jane Austen character come back to life; or a demure fashion plate from *Godey's Ladies' Book.* About her was an indefinable hint of antique lace and lavender.

Her pale old eyes behind the trim gold spectacles gazed forth in placid contentment over the sweet sunlit lawns of The Place.

Flower-girt and starred with century-aged oaks, the emerald acres of close-shaven grass rolled billowingly down to meet the fire-blue lake, a furlong below. The fragrant hush of midsummer was in the air.

Suddenly the pale old eyes focused with an unwonted sharpness. Into the placid face came a blank look which merged into grotesque incredulity. Then, as if recalling that a gentlewoman must not give visible sign to violent emotions, the little lady turned to her wondering hosts and said with an apologetic half-smile:

"My dears, if—if we were living in the days of Æsop's fables, I should—well, frankly, my dears, I should—I should *almost* fancy I had just seen a fox walking across the lawn out there—a—a fox with a monkey riding on his back—a monkey that is smoking a pipe. I—I grow old, and my eyes are ——"

"Your eyes are telling you the truth, as usual," the Master reassured her. "But I don't blame you for doubting them. I suppose a pipe-smoking monkey riding on the back of a fox is not to be seen on every lawn in this North Jersey hinterland of ours."

"But," expostulated the old lady, "it is quite impossible that a ——"

"Perhaps you'd like to hear how it all began and then what happened?" suggested the Mistress. "It's a queer story. To this day, part of it is an absolute mystery. At least, it's a mystery to all of us except to dear old Laddie, here," stooping to stroke the classic head of the giant bronze-and-white collie drowsing on the rug at her feet. "Laddie was part of it—a very great part of it. So he knows. But he can't tell. It's a kind of Christmas story, too. Would you like to hear it?"

On a crisp early spring morning the Master strolled down to the brood-nest shed behind the stables. In this blanket-floored pen, for the past week, Sunnybank Lady, the temperamental little gold-white mate of Sunnybank Lad, had been locked every night. Every morning the Master had hurried to the brood nest as soon as he was dressed.

Lad trotted gayly along at his side, as always, and stood dancing impatiently as the Master unfastened the brood-nest door to let the fly-away gold-white collie out. But today Lady did not come rushing out, as usual, to greet the visitors or to lure her sedate bronze-and-white mate into a romp.

Instead, she lay, weary and weak, deep in a scratched-up huddle of torn blankets. Scattered around her were seven limp little creatures of indeterminate hue and scarce as large as rats. Pathetically, Lady was licking an eighth puppy and whimpering soft encouragement to it.

She wagged her tail in feeble welcome to the

Master, peering up at him as if in appeal to his godhead to bring back life to her litter.

Lad stood gravely sniffing at her and her pitiful brood, as though trying to find the reason for his adored mate's keen grief.

There was a step outside the brood-nest door. The Master turned, to see The Place's English superintendent, Robert Friend, who had just come back from the woods, where he had set two men to work at the cutting of dead trees for hearth fuel.

"We're out of luck!" said the Master. "Lady had eight pups during the night. Either they were all born dead or else they died as soon as they were born. That's the way with collie pups! They're either the easiest or the hardest animals on earth to raise. Lady has always had tough luck. Wolf is the only pup of hers and Lad's that ever lived to grow up. We won't breed her again. Take these away and bury them somewhere, before she tries to 'clean the nest' by eating them. The poor old girl is in bad shape and she's heart-broken. I wish we could find a new-born live mongrel pup somewhere for her to foster. She ought—— What have you got there?"

The superintendent was pulling something from under his coat, handling it in gingerly fashion. The thing was rufous red and tiny and shapeless, and was making futile motions with its awkwardly wide-spread paws.

"It's a baby fox," explained Friend. "Sam found it in a tree-stump, back yonder in the woods. The mother wasn't anywhere around. Sam brought it to me. It can't be more than a day old. I'd have put it back in the stump, only I know the dam wouldn't have anything to do with it after she smelled the touch of a human's hand on it. I got remembering how unhappy the Mistress was when her pet coon got killed last fall. I thought maybe she'd like this fox, to take Rameses' place. I could bring it up for her on a bottle. It ——"

"You can do better than that," interrupted the Master. "You can give it to Lady to bring up. It will do just as well as the 'new-born mongrel pup' I was talking about. Wait."

Lady had been sniffing with weary resentment the vulpine scent that began to fill the nest. The fox odor was exotic and vaguely hostile to her, especially at this moment when nature warned her to protect her own brood from any possible enemy.

The Master picked up the dead puppy she had been licking. He picked up another of the dead pups at random.

He held the two inanimate morsels, one on each side of the new-born and helplessly shivering fox cub, softly rubbing them against its sides and back and stomach. For several minutes he did this, Lady watching him worriedly, and Lad vibrant with interest at the odd sight.

Then, when the superintendent had taken the rest of the pups away from the sorrowing mother and out of the nest, the Master knelt down among the torn blankets, holding the fox cub in one palm, while with the other hand he grasped Lady's neck with gentle firmness.

He snuggled the baby fox against her warm underbody. At the touch, Lady shrank back a little. Quieting her with his voice and still holding her from snapping at the infant intruder, he continued to hold the fox against her furry underbody.

With no hesitation at all, the wisp of wilderness babyhood began to nurse. He was starvingly hungry.

Lady growled forbiddingly, straining her firm-held head to get at the ravenous little outlander. Inch by inch the Master allowed her nose to approach the eagerly nursing foxlet.

She sniffed at it in hostile fashion. Then to her inquiring nostrils was borne the scent of her own babies, along with the vulpine taint. She ceased to growl and she nosed the cub doubtfully. This for only the briefest moment.

Then the scarce-silenced growl was followed by a soft crooning as Lady nuzzled the foster-baby closer to her and began industriously to lick smooth its rumpled reddish fur.

The Master nodded approval and got to his feet. His task was done. Henceforth Nature would handle the case, even as Nature has handled such cases since the birth of time.

Back to the house and to his long-delayed breakfast went the Master.

"Lady's pups were born in the night," he reported to his wife. "And they all died—all except one fox."

"One—*what?*"

"One fox. A dog fox. That's her only surviving child. Laddie's stepson. After breakfast, come down there with me and I'll show it to you."

Briefly he explained what had happened. He wound up his recital by saying:

"So you see we're saddled with another denizen of the Wild. What we're to do with him I don't know. If Lady hadn't needed him, I'd have had Robert kill him. You're still grieving over Rameses. And the raccoon was a better pet in every way than any fox ever could be. I know a little about foxes. And I don't know anything good about them."

"They're beautiful, though. And I'd ——"

"But, whatever wild thing may be tamed—coon or fox or bear or deer or bird—remember that one of two things is bound to happen," continued the Master, pessimistically. "Either it will sneak back to the Wild some day, or else it will be tamed into losing the inherited fear that is its only protection and it will be killed by a hunter or by some other animal. You're just storing up heartaches if we keep this fox cub. As soon as Lady doesn't need him any longer we'd better get rid of him, somehow. He ——"

A guest was announced—Harry Steele, an old friend and neighbor. Wondering at so early a call, the Mistress insisted on his coming into the dining-room and joining them at the breakfast table. In one hand Steele was carrying with great care a small basket from which edges of canton flannel bulged.

Lad, as a rule, paid no heed to visitors. But he walked along at Steele's side, into the dining-room, pressing close to the guest and smelling with puzzled interest at the basket.

"I don't know whether I'm going to be welcome this morning, or whether you people will throw me out," said Steele as he faced the Mistress and held the basket toward her. "I've brought you a present. If you don't want it, just say so and I won't be sore. But I remember how fond of Rameses you used to be; and how unhappy you were when he was killed, last September. So I've brought over a successor to him, if you'll accept it. He's barely a week old. Last night his mother was run over by a car that came whizzing into our dooryard when she was scampering across the drive. This poor little chap can be brought up on a bottle, I'm sure. He ——"

Steele finished the presentation speech by lifting the wicker lid from the basket.

In the middle of an expanse of canton flannel and cotton batting crouched something which, at first glance, seemed to be an infinitely small and infinitely wizened human baby. It blinked up dazedly at the Mistress. Then it wound its ten prehensile talons around an exploratory forefinger she held toward it.

The Master had not needed to glance into the basket to guess its contents. Again and again he had guyed Steele upon the latter's one fad—a hobby for the difficult task of breeding monkeys, for his own amusement, in a superheated wing of a rambling country house three miles from The Place.

"Fine!" exclaimed the Master. "I've always

said The Place would seem more homelike if only we had at least one live animal on it. What could harmonize better with a bunch of collies than a nice little fleasome monkey? Now if only some loving friend will bring us a young rattlesnake or a youthful warthog or even a half-grown dinosaur, we'll just be one grand happy family. All except *me*. I'll go somewhere else to do my living."

But he was alone in his annoyance at the new gift. The monkey's queer humanness and the confiding way it gripped the Mistress's forefinger had roused in the woman a protective liking for the squirming atom.

Lad, too, was nosing at it in friendly inquisitive fashion, its helplessness making the same appeal to him as to the Mistress. The Master saw all this and he gave up the hopeless fight.

"To save the bother of bringing it up on a bottle," he ventured in heavy sarcasm, "let's turn it over to Lady. Her only living offspring, at present, is a fox. A monkey can't seem much of a novelty to her, after that."

The Mistress ignored the irony in his suggestion.

"Good!" she cried. "That will be the very thing. I am going to carry it down to her. I'm sure I can get her to believe it's hers. It won't do any harm to try. Walter Peirce had a collie that brought up a baby monkey. Why shouldn't Lady?"

To everyone's amazement, except the Mistress's, Lady was induced to accept the wrig-glingly hungry monkey with little more difficulty than she had been persuaded to adopt the fox. It was not the first nor the thousandth time that a dog had been used as foster-mother to fox or to monkey or even to lion cubs.

Thus set in an odd era at The Place.

The two fosterlings throve apace on the nourishment which Nature had intended for eight greedy puppies. Very evidently, Lady considered them own children. She washed and fed and cared for them after the best methods of a true collie mother.

Faster than would the average collie pup did the two changelings shake off their first impotent clumsiness and learn to move about. Before the end of three weeks they were lapping warm milk with a raw egg beaten up in it. This in addition to the sustenance they derived from Lady.

Presently they were scampering about the largest puppy-yard, gamboling wildly with each other and with their gold-white foster-dam. As the need for day-and-night maternal care slackened, Lady threw off her never-too-strong mother instincts and became her changelings' playmate rather than their nurse.

It was pretty to see the trio at play. The fox was lightning-swift of motion, at an age when collie pups would still have been pudgily awkward. Sure and dexterous was he in every move.

Faster was he, at rollicking maneuvers and at short dashes, than was Lady, herself. Also, when she essayed correction in the way of nip or slap, he would flash his needle-like milk teeth at the nearest point of her anatomy, instead of rolling on his back for mercy as do chastised baby collies.

The monkey was slower of development. But, under the influence of the warmth of early summer and of the dual rations, he waxed strong and agile.

It was amusing to watch Lady's blank expression when, in the course of a romp, he would leap lightly in air and either land on the middle of her furry gold back or on the top of the kennel-house. Or perhaps he would vary this by mounting to the top of the kennel-yard's wide shade tree in less time than Lady could follow him to the foot of it.

"I don't know about the monkey," the Master used to say, "but I'm dead sure the fox thinks he is a collie. I wonder if Lady thinks so, too.

Sometimes I catch her staring at them both with a queer kind of bewilderment, when they're playing. She is beginning to have vague doubts about it, I think. They're amusing enough, those two freaks of hers. I grant that. But I was right, just the same, when I said we sign the death-warrant of any wild thing when we try to domesticate it. Watch and see."

(As it happened, the Master's prophecy was to come true. Two years later, as the fox was wandering through the home woods, a hunter shot and killed the luckless animal that had lost its native instinct to get out of danger's way. At about the same time the monkey died of acute indigestion. But many things were to happen before then. As you shall see.)

Dogs are guided by scent, even as humans are guided by sight. It is by scent, not by sight, that your dog recognizes humans and other animals.

If you doubt that, place your dog in front of a mirror. Nineteen times in twenty he will scarcely glance at his reflection in it. His eyes tell him another dog is there. His nose tells him there is not. He discredits his uncertain eyes, and he believes his nose.

So it was that the inimical fox-reek and the wholly foreign odor of the monkey became soon so familiar to the dogs at The Place that they took the outlanders as a matter of course.

Bruce and Bobby and young Gray Dawn had scant interest in them. These three collies seemed to regard the changelings as something mildly repulsive, and they turned annoyedly away from all play-advances.

Bruce always had disliked puppies. Never would he hurt one of them or even snarl at it. But always he would get out of its way with the ludicrous haste of an elderly bachelor who is pestered by kindergarten children.

Bobby and Dawn growled warningly when the fox or the monkey frisked up to them, and they shook themselves free in disgust when the monkey leaped on their backs in play.

But Wolf's reaction was the oddest of all.

Wolf had looked with cold distaste, from first to last, upon Rameses, the luckless pet raccoon. But a latent impishness in the fiery red-gold collie made him unbend in gay good-fellowship toward these two mischievous youngsters.

He would romp wildly on the lawn with the fox, enduring without a show of his wonted hot temper the occasional pin prick bites inflicted on him. As for the monkey, Wolf willingly would let the frolicking little simian pull his ears and explore his coat for fleas and ride proudly on his back. Some elfin trait in the dog's own strange nature seemed to respond to like traits in theirs.

Lad, from the first, had constituted himself the guardian of the changelings. Not through any love for them—never did he accept either of them as a friend—but because they belonged to his worshiped mate, Lady, and as such were under his protection. The great dog, moreover, had an unbelievable gentleness toward everything small or weak, whether humans or fellow-quadrupeds.

If Bobby or Dawn snarled threateningly when either of the two dared take liberties, Lad ever stepped between and, with icy authority, made them shrink back from the fulfilling of their threats.

The Mistress named the fox "Æsop" and the monkey "Darwin." In a surprisingly short time they learned their names and learned to come at her call.

She it was, too, who, more than once, enacted Lad's chosen rôle of standing between them and punishment. Not from punishment by the dogs, but by her husband. The Master's patience was scraped raw, again and again, by the changelings' antics.

For instance, Æsop's kennel was moved, one morning, to be repainted. Under it the Master discovered a veritable cache—a neatly dug hollow nearly full of the feathers and chewed bones of chickens. The occasional vanishing of some of his best white leghorns had been attributed to rats. Now the mystery was cleared up.

Darwin vaulted in through the open study window the same day, and proceeded to have a really pleasant time. The pleasure was all his.

The Master came in from breakfast to find a nearly completed manuscript torn neatly into a hundred shreds, and the contents of his ink bottle sprinkled artistically all over his best rug and on the room's newly tinted walls.

Incidentally, a stuffed osprey had been plucked naked, and nearly a bushel of feathers drifted the inky floor. The monkey had made golden use of every instant of his time in the desecrated study.

These were but stray samples of the escapades on the part of both Æsop and Darwin which made the Master clamor for their blood and which strained all the Mistress's tact and eloquence to keep the miserable pests alive.

The superintendent had a new pipe, sent to him from England. It was his pride. Darwin filched it from his pocket before ever the man had had a chance to fill and light it.

With true simian mimicry, Darwin proceeded

to stick the pipe stem into his own mouth. Thenceforth it became his favorite possession.

For hours at a time he would pretend to smoke it, especially after he saw the hit his performance made with the guests at The Place. He loved to show off. Therefore, the moment a guest arrived on the grounds, Darwin would fetch forth his treasured pipe from some hiding-place and would go through the motions of smoking it.

The superintendent refused indignantly to touch the pipe again after the monkey had been sucking at it. So the Master had to send to England for another in its place.

Adornment of all kinds was Darwin's delight. He would find and drape himself in any article of wearing apparel that he could make stay in place. As he was little larger than a kitten, this was not always an easy task.

The long lush summer drowsed away and autumn chill tinged the still October nights. Æsop reveled in the cold. His rufous coat waxed thicker and more luxuriant.

But Darwin hated the icy weather. Shiveringly he hung back from going out-of-doors at all as autumn whitened into winter. He spent much of his time cuddled down in the warmest corner of the disreputable fur rug in front of the living-room fireplace.

Christmas drew near. Day after day the express truck would discharge a load of parcels at the back door of Sunnybank House. Some of these were for The Place's people. Some were ordered gifts, to be sent away.

It was these latter parcels that the Mistress enjoyed most—their buying and their arrival and wrapping them up daintily for resending to their various destinations. She reveled in this form of Yuletide preparation.

One of the gifts she spent most time and loving care on was a doll which she had bought and was outfitting for a little niece of hers.

The niece's elder sister had been married, a few weeks earlier, and the child had been thrilled over the wedding arrangements. So the Mistress had bought for her, as a Christmas gift, a "bride doll" with a tiny trunkful of trousseau garments. She herself had made the bridal dress and veil and wreath and the imitation-flowers bouquet.

Some difficulty attended the wrapping and unwrapping of Yule parcels, because of Darwin's almost delirious curiosity as to the contents of each and every one of them.

At last it became necessary to shut him up somewhere when they were opened. This, after he had dragged a shining lace scarf from its tissue-paper bed and had draped it meticulously about his own shoulders—his paws being foul from playing in the hearth-side soot.

On an evening five days before Christmas, the Mistress and the Master were getting up from the dinner table, when one of the maids reported excitedly that there was a great glare of fire beyond the woods to the north.

In the country, especially at night, fire is a thing of horror. News of a burning building is quite enough to make every man, and woman, and child within the radius of a mile drop everything and hurry to the conflagration.

Thus, no country-dweller needs to be told that every soul at Sunnybank House and at the gate lodge bundled into wraps and started at top speed toward the ever-brightening glow.

As they crossed the highroad they saw neighbors converging toward the same goal. All of the Sunnybank collies which were not shut into their kennel-yards galloped gleefully along with the Mistress and the Master, exulting, collie-like, in the prospect of a walk, and grateful to these human deities of theirs for setting out for a stroll at so unusual an hour.

All except old Sunnybank Lad.

The grown dogs, at The Place, had but one meal a day—a big dinner, usually fed to them at dusk. Lad and Bruce were fed by the Master himself, nightly, as soon as he had finished his own dinner.

Lad was the dining-room dog. Always he lay on the floor at the Master's left, during meals. Tonight, when his owners got up so suddenly from the table and sought their outdoor clothing before hurrying into the night, Lad followed the Master, unnoticed, to the study, when the man went there for his thick mackinaw.

In the study, before dinner, Darwin had been imprisoned, to keep him from meddling with the heap of Christmas presents. He slipped out of the room, merrily, as the Master entered it.

The Master found the mackinaw and ran out, shutting the study door behind him—in the indignant Lad's face.

Thus the big dog was left a prisoner, while his fellow-collies could be heard dancing and barking around the fast-hurrying Mistress and Master, outside. In other words, a gay walk was in progress and Lad was left out of it. The abnormally sensitive collie was cut to the heart by this supposed slight on the part of the two humans who were his gods.

Though the Master instinctively had slammed shut his study door behind him—a needful precaution when Darwin was incarcerated there—he had been more careless in shutting the house's outer door. It did not latch, at his inefficient tug. A gust of breeze blew it a few inches open.

Æsop pattered home, a minute later, from a foraging trip in the woods. He had drawn blank in his effort to catch some unwary rabbit or partridge, so he had come back hungry.

He heard and saw the walkers as they neared the gate lodge, but he was of no mind for a longer ramble. He wanted food. As he passed by the house he saw the front door slightly ajar. In the kitchen and elsewhere, before now, Æsop had been able to find delectable titbits.

In through the slightly open doorway he slunk, like a furtive ghost, and on through the house to the deserted kitchen. There he smelled, on a table, the dinner just laid out for the maids. In two minutes he had wolfed all of it that met with his approval. Then, lazily, he strolled back into the larger wing of the house; to be met in the living-room by his congenial little foster-brother, Darwin.

Darwin had been only mildly interested in the tramping of feet and the barking of dogs. He was free—free to get into any form of mischief that might appeal to him.

Looking around for something to amuse him, he had happened upon a daintily wrapped parcel, high on a wall shelf. This he had tucked under his arm and borne back to the hearth. He was just ripping open its wrappings when his dear friend Æsop jogged into the room. A romp seemed in order.

Tully Meed and Gil Yeager were local geniuses who had solved the problem of making the world pay them the living it owed them, without giving any undue amount of manual toil in return.

They were next-door neighbors, in ramshackle cabins just below the so-called "Steel Works District," two miles south of The Place. Here, a half-century agone, had stood the Ludlum Steel Springs factory, long since abandoned. Hereabouts still abode certain villagers, some few of whom saw no sense in searching for hard labor.

Yeager and Meed had hit on a truly brilliant plan for bringing Yule money into their homes this year. From neighborhood talk and from fleeting glimpses, they knew the custom of their several distant neighbors along the lake, of receiving Christmas packages for a week or so before December 25th.

It occurred to the two that a comfortable haul might well be made by visiting these widely scattered houses; locating and pouching such packages, and then carrying the combined plunder to a kindly pawnbroker of their acquaintance in

Paterson, nine miles away. The kindly pawnbroker was always glad to give them cash for such pilfered articles as seemed to him resalable.

There was a grievous flaw in their otherwise simple plan. Almost all of the people who lived on or near the lake owned watchdogs.

At The Place there was Sunnybank Lad, whose keen white teeth had met before now in the flesh of midnight prowlers. At The Place, too, were other collies scarcely less formidable. A nocturnal visit might well be fraught with more lacerations than loot.

It was Yeager who solved the problem. All his life he had lived in the country. Thus he knew the instinct which makes a whole rural neighborhood turn out at first news of a near-by fire.

Behind the woods, to one side, just beyond the highroad, stood a very large and very old and sagging barn in which a Pancake Hollow farmer was wont to store his winter hay. It would furnish a famous blaze and it would be visible for miles.

At nightfall the two men met, carrying big canvas bags folded under their arms. In addition, Tully Meed had brought along an element of pre-Christmas cheer, in the shape of a quart bottle nearly full of "green" moonshine corn whisky—

liquid flame, containing something like seventy per cent of alcohol.

The adventurers drank, in turn, to their enterprise. Then, in turn, they drank to Christmas. Then, as a courteous afterthought, they drank to the kindly pawnbroker.

Then they journeyed, in a cautious backwoods détour, to the fated hay-barn in Pancake Hollow. After one more libation they set fire to the barn in five places. Then, at top speed, they made their unostentatious way to the first of the four houses they planned to bless with their presence.

They knew that all untied dogs would run to the fire with their owners. Tied dogs could only bark the alarm, and there would be nobody at home to hear the bark. The venture was ridiculously safe. Another drink made it seem doubly so.

Scarcely had the occupants of the first house on the chosen route streamed forth across the fields toward the far-off fire when Meed and Yeager entered the deserted house and set to work.

They had scant trouble in locating the downstairs closet where the Christmas packages were kept. Rejecting such parcels as manifestly held non-pawnable toys and the like, they dumped the better-promising plunder into their bags and hustled to the next house, where they repeated their first success.

So on they sped until they reached the third house, laughingly barking an imitation of the furious chained watchdog as they came out with their sacks laden.

In each of the three houses they had paid a cursory visit to the dining-rooms and had tossed into the bags such loose silver as they chanced upon. By way of rebuke to pikers, they had merely twisted or broken any pieces of plated ware they happened across, and left them on the floor. So pleasant had been their experiences, thus far, that they took another drink in honor of their easy success.

The Place was next to be visited.

No clamor of vibrant barks assailed their ears as they ran down the winding oak-bordered driveway from the road. Everything was silent. The front door was even hospitably ajar. Fearlessly the two entered the soft-lit living-room.

The room was cozily warm after the biting chill of the outer December night. It is not always well to come into a warm room, out of zero cold, when one has been drinking heartily of high-proof "green" liquor. It does things to one's brain.

From the study came thunderous barking and

infuriated snarls and the impact of a raging body against an unyielding door.

Lad had heard and Lad had scented. He was struggling mightily to get at the marauders and to fulfill his life-long duty as watchdog.

But, after the first startled jump, the men realized he was shut up somewhere and could not harm them. Also, they could see the piano in the adjoining music-room, piled high with many-shaped boxes and packages. This though the lights were shaded and though the intruders' eyes were still vague and blurred and dazzled after the blackness of the outside night.

They made their dizzy way to the piano. There they set down their heavy and bulging sacks and prepared to gather in the new plunder by the armful. This seemed due to be the richest haul of the night.

Then a faintly pattering sound on the hardwood flooring made Yeager turn his head, in drunken dread lest the noisy dog had managed to get out of prison.

Yeager's gargling snort of amazement caused Meed to cease appraising the prettily tied parcels and to wheel about in the direction of his partner's glassy and droop-jawed gaze.

Across the living-room rug, toward them, was

advancing mincingly a most impossible and horrifying Apparition.

A large and stately red fox was walking up to them. On the fox's back rode haughtily a tiny creature which looked like an incredibly old woman.

On the rider's head was a flowered wreath from which a shimmery bridal veil floated backward over its shoulders and down along the fox's red back. Between its jet-black hands the creature carried a shower-bouquet of artificial flowers. From one corner of its mouth protruded a disreputable tobacco-pipe, on which it sucked with relish.

Darwin, as ever, was rejoicing to show off for the benefit of stranger-guests, the more so since he had just opened the box containing the bride-doll and her trousseau and had been able to find a part of the costume which fitted him to perfection.

Æsop, with all a fox's innate vanity, was entering to the full into the spirit of the masque. Eagerly, both of them awaited the exclamations of surprise and glad amusement with which strangers always greeted their equestrian advent.

But, for once, they were to be disappointed.

It was Meed who emerged first from the brief trance of horror which had stricken the two drunken and superstitiously ignorant men at the dumfounding sight.

With a wild falsetto screech which drowned out Lad's thunderous assault on the study door, Meed leaped high in air, diving straight through the long French window beside the piano.

Yeager emitted a fascinating sound, such as might have issued from the throat of a turkey whose tail is pulled violently just as the bird starts to gobble. He wasted no precious time, as had Meed, in leaping high in air. In a single maniac plunge he crashed through the long window nearest him.

The two panic-scourged men cleared the broad veranda in a single bound. They fell, together, on hands and knees in the icy driveway below.

By the time their abraded knees and glass-cut palms touched ground the thieves were up again, tearing down the long snowy slope of lawn to the thick-frozen lake and across it, slipping, falling, scrambling to their feet again; bleeding at faces and fingers from the cruel glass-edges; moaning and gibbering crazily as they fled.

Midway to the Steel Works, Meed collapsed and sprawled on the ice in a fit. Yeager did not stop to succor him. Indeed, Yeager did not stop until he burst into his own hovel and crawled sobbing and slavering under the bed.

"We never did find out everything that happened that night," the Master concluded his tale to the astounded little old lady in the cushioned window-seat. "We came clumping back through the snow, from the spectacular hay-barn fire, to find Laddie roaring and tearing at the door of the study. We don't know even yet how the old dog happened to be shut in there or how Darwin got out.

"Then we went into the living-room; and we found the bride-doll and her clothes and her wrappings lying scattered everywhere. Then we went into the music-room, and we found two of those French windows broken to pieces.

"There was a trail of spattered blood on the porch and on the snow. And Darwin and Æsop were racing from one end of the house to the other. They'd been mixed up in the rumpus, in some way or other, I know; though I can't figure how.

"Then my wife discovered two enormous canvas sacks on the music-room floor. We opened them. They were stuffed to overflowing with initialed silverware and ornaments and wrapped-up Christmas packages. We studied out some of the initials on the silver and we did some telephoning. Then most of our neighbors trooped down here to sort out their valuables. The state police reported finding a man lying on the ice in a stupor, with foam on his lips and glass-cuts over his face. And there's a story about another man, in the Steel Works District, who wouldn't come out from under his bed for three days.

"We pieced the whole thing together, but a lot of it is still a mystery to us both. Laddie could tell. But Laddie *can't* tell. . . . By the way, want to buy a monkey? I'll sell one, cheap; and I'll throw in a perfectly good English tobacco-pipe and one live red fox. How about it?"

Chapter Six

THE RINGER

SEVERAL magazines formed the base of a heap of mail on the veranda breakfast table at The Place, that morning. The Mistress and the Master glanced over their letters in desultory fashion while they ate and chatted.

Now and then the Master would toss a morsel of buttered toast to Lad, lying on the stone floor beside his chair.

The collie scorned to beg, but when something was given him from the plate of either of these two human deities of his he accepted it with quick relish.

Coming to the end of her handful of letters, the Mistress picked up and opened the topmost of the magazines, riffling its pages with no special interest. It was one of the many illustrated dog-periodicals which keep breeders all over the country in touch with one another and with events in the canine world.

"There's a double-page advertisement of the

Kingcroft show, here," she said, presently. "They seem to be trying to make it a second Tuxedo show. This ad says it is to be 'the biggest and most important of the autumn outdoor shows, with the largest premium list on record' and ——"

"Most of them have 'the largest premium list on record,' " returned the Master, idly, as he tore open another letter. "And I've seldom read of one of them that wasn't due to be 'the biggest and most important,' ever. Anyhow, it won't do us any good. Lad, here, is the only Sunnybank collie that isn't dead out of coat just now. The rest of them look more like picked chickens that have been sleeping in rag-bags than like show dogs. It's funny how a collie's looks are made or ruined by the condition of his coat. In full bloom, he's the handsomest dog on earth. Out of coat, he looks like a scarecrow."

He stooped to toss Lad another crust of buttered toast, his eyes running appraisingly over the dog's massively graceful body with its wealth of burnished fur.

"If I could borrow Lad's coat and put it on Bruce or on Treve or on Gray Dawn," he mused, "I wouldn't be afraid to show any of the three in the stiffest competition anywhere. Lad, old boy, we promised you, two years ago, that we'd never take you to another dog-show, when we found how you hated shows and how hideously wretched it made you to go to one. Well, we're silly enough to keep our word even to a fleasome and toast-crunching collie. But—I believe we could clean up with you at Kingcroft, just the same, Laddie."

The big dog was eyeing the man with head on one side, his tulip ears up, his deep-set dark eyes alight with puzzled eagerness to understand. His plumed tail thumped the veranda floor vehemently at each mention of his own name.

"We can't even go to the show, ourselves, I suppose," went on the master. "We won't be back from our Canada trip by then. It ——"

"Why, here's a picture of Laddie!" broke in the Mistress. "A splendid one! How did they ever get it, I wonder? Look!"

She handed the dog magazine across the table to her husband. Its front cover was adorned by the tinted photograph of a magnificent dark sable collie.

At casual glance, and even on closer inspection, it was a more than tolerable likeness of Sunnybank Lad. It had his coloring and markings and his great shaggy coat and his classically chiseled head and even his elusive expression of blended mischief and sternness.

The Master stared at it, blinking. Many a photograph had been taken of Lad, but none in this particular pose. He opened the magazine and found the table of contents. Then he grinned ruefully.

"No," he said, "it isn't Lad, though it's a better likeness of him than any we've got. Listen: '*Cover Illustration. Brightcliff Bandit, owned by Cassius Malachi Hogan of Delmond, Iowa.*' "

"Oh! It's the best likeness of Lad I've ——"

"I read about Bandit in the *Kennel Gazette*, last month," resumed the Master. "He's been doing a lot of winning in the Middle West this season. He must be within a point or two of his championship by now. And it isn't even queer that he looks so much like Lad. He's Laddie's half-brother. They had the same dam. Lots of times I've seen stronger family resemblance among dogs than ever I've seen among humans. You must remember Hogan, don't you? He ran out here to look at the Sunnybank kennels when he was East last spring. He ——"

"Of course I remember!" said the Mistress. "I was so misguided as to ask him to stay to lunch, and he broke one of the rock-crystal goblets. Indeed I do remember!"

"I had forgotten the broken glass," rejoined the Master. "But I remember he made such funny sounds eating soup that Laddie began to growl at him. Lad thought Hogan was trying to tease him. A sweet guest, as I recall it. Most of the dog crowd who drop in here are mighty good fellows. Perhaps that's why Hogan's visit stands out so in our memories."

"Probably. The dogs didn't like him, either."

"Well, anyhow, he's got a grand dog, if this picture is telling the truth. We need more collies like Lad and Brightcliff Bandit—American breeds with clean strong bodies and clean strong heads. Not spindly imported weaklings with toothpick noses and receding back skulls. Americans breed better collies, today, than all Europe. Lad and Bandit are a proof of it. There's no sense, any longer, in sending to England and paying double rates for a second-rate collie. Some of the imported British collies are first rate, but a lot of them —— Well, since we aren't going to be at the Kingcroft show, we won't meet the soup-gargling and crystal-smashing Hogan. That's one comfort. We'll be safely in Canada before he strikes this part of the country."

But, on the very eve of the Canada motor trip and about a fortnight before the forthcoming Kingcroft show, a visitor dropped in at Sunnybank, early one evening. The Mistress and the Master were sitting on the porch, watching the afterglow's last faint ashes-of-roses fade out from the lake's waters.

A car came around to the front of the house, disgorging a thickset man in the flashiest of sport suits. There was light enough for both host and hostess to recognize him as he ran up the steps toward them. The unexpected guest was Cassius Malachi Hogan.

"Hello, folks!" he hailed, breezily. "I'm showing at Cornwall tomorrow, and I thought I'd run over to say 'Howdy' and have another look at that big dark sable collie of yours—Lad—the one that looks so much like my Bandit."

"Lad was here a minute ago," said the Mistress after she had greeted the visitor with what cordiality she could muster. "He has a way of disappearing when strangers call on us. I'll see if he's still in earshot."

"I liked him when I saw him the other time I was here," explained Hogan. "He made a hit with me. Then, less than a month later, I saw Brightcliff Bandit. He was the image of your Sunnybank Lad. I bought him, and I've been making the round of the summer shows with him in the Middle West. He lacks only another three-point show to win his championship. But three-point shows for collies aren't very common, in summer, out there. So I've brought him East and entered him for Ridgewood and Cornwall and Kingcroft. One of those is dead sure to be a three-pointer."

The Mistress had taken a silver whistle from her girdle. She blew on it. In response, Lad came cantering up from the direction of the lake.

Lad did not like strangers. And, at a glance, this particular semi-stranger had impressed him unfavorably.

(Which had no bearing whatever upon Hogan's character, for either good or bad. There is no more arrant lie than that a dog can size up the nature of any human at first sight. Lad did not happen to care for Hogan's type. That was all.)

He had betaken him toward the lake, in quest of an evening swim. But the Mistress's whistle had recalled him before he could reach the water. Up the porch steps he bounded, and stood, expectant, in front of the woman who had summoned him.

There he posed in the fading daylight, statuesque, magnificent, his burnished coat in fullest bloom. Cassius Malachi Hogan eyed him with keen appraisal, then nodded.

"A grand collie!" he vouchsafed. "I've seen few finer. I don't mind confessing he's even a shade better in coat and head than my Brightcliff Bandit, though the two are alike enough to be twins—ten times as much alike as most dog twins, at that. And they're both in full coat when nearly every other collie is bare. That's another likeness. Are—are you showing him at Kingcroft?"

"No," said the Mistress; "we never show him nowadays. He hates it so. Besides, we'll be in Canada at the time of the Kingcroft show."

"I'm glad," answered Hogan. "Not that I dodge ordinary competition. But I feel easier about Bandit's three points, now that I know Lad won't be against him."

As he spoke, he walked across to the collie and laid a hand on the silken head. Very gravely and very determinedly Lad drew away from the caress.

This man was a guest, and, as such, had the privilege of trying to maul and pet the dog. But Lad's was also the privilege of avoiding the alien's touch. Thus, with what courtesy he might, he turned from Hogan and lay down at the Mistress's feet, his back to the visitor and his tulip ears pressed close to his skull. Lofty disapproval and aloofness were in his every line.

Hogan laughed embarrassedly, but the laughter did not extend to his quizzical eyes. He made no further attempt to touch the unwilling dog, though a dozen times during his brief call he chirped to Lad and spoke to him. To none of these advances did Laddie pay the slightest heed.

"Do you people happen to know Rufus G. Belden, of the Beldencroft collie kennels, at Midwestburg?" asked Hogan, as he got up to take his leave.

"Only by name," replied the Master. "I've seen his dogs, once or twice, when he sent them East to the Westminster show at Madison Square Garden, and to the Interstate. He used to send them by a Scotch kennel manager of his, Jamie Mackellar, a good little chap that I took a liking to. Mackellar used to show a glorious old collie —a dog named Lochinvar Bobby. But I haven't seen any of that outfit in a couple of years. Why did you ask if I know Belden?"

"Because I've got a bet with him," expounded Hogan. "My Bandit beat his Beldencroft Sahib at the Cleveland show; and Sahib beat Bandit at the Cincinnati show the next week, under a bum judge. That started it. Belden and I got to chewing the rag about our two dogs. Presently Belden went up in the air and said Bandit could never beat Sahib except under some judge who liked me and didn't like Belden. I told him that was all rot. Nine-tenths of the collie judges are square, even if not all of them know their job.

But when Belden once gets an idea, it sends roots all through him and stays with him forever."

"Do you mean ——?"

"I mean he thinks the judge was competent and on the level in putting Sahib over Bandit, but that the judge who put Bandit above Sahib was a crook. It wound up by his offering to bet me an even ten thousand dollars that Sahib could beat Bandit under any competent judge who didn't know either of the two dogs by sight and who didn't know either Belden or me. I took the bet—and I know I can win it."

"Ten thousand ——?"

"We decided to bring both dogs East to the Kingcroft show. An Englishman is judging collies there—a rather famous British collie judge who won't land in New York till the week of the show. That means he never heard of Belden or of me, and never heard of either of our dogs. So we're entering both of them in the 'Open, Any Color' class, and we've posted our certified ten-thousand-dollar checks with *The Dog-Fancier.* I brought Bandit along East, a month early, to get him acclimated. Not a bad notion, either. Sometimes a high-strung collie gets to moping and goes off his feed the first few days in a new part of the country."

"I didn't know people made such enormous

bets on a dog-show decision," commented the Mistress. "Ten thousand dollars is ——"

"Is chicken feed, to Rufe Belden," finished Hogan. "It's a bit more than *I* can lose with any great comfort. But I figure I'm not taking any risks. Bandit's the better dog, any way and every way. In Europe there are much bigger wagers, sometimes, on one dog winning over another. And we have had some pretty stiff bets on the same thing, here in the States.... Well, so long, folks! Wish me luck. I'm glad your dog isn't entered against Bandit at Kingcroft. But I wish you could be there to see me clean up over Sahib."

"Laddie," said the Mistress, bending down above the huge collie, when the guest had gone, "I don't blame you for not wanting him to pat you. He's an abhorrent sort of person, isn't he? I don't know why I dislike him, but I do. I'm sorry a beautiful dog like Brightcliff Bandit should have such an unpleasant man for an owner. What a pity great dogs can't have great masters!"

In the preparations for their lazy Canadian motor tour, the Sunnybank people all but forgot Cassius Malachi Hogan, nor did he call again on them at Sunnybank.

In a dog paper they read that Bandit got Winners and Best of Breed at both the Ridgewood and Cornwall dog-shows and that the former exhibition was only a one-point show for collies, while the latter carried two points.

Bandit still lacked his second and final "three-or-more-point show" which the American Kennel Club rules wisely demand for a championship. But Kingcroft promised to bring out at least three points for collies; perhaps four or even five points.

The Mistress and the Master set off for Canada in due course, leaving Lad lonely and miserably unhappy, as always he was during their few absences from The Place.

Meanwhile, Cassius Malachi Hogan was also undergoing a minor quota of unhappiness. He had established himself at a sporting road house near Paterson, where accommodations for dogs were advertised. Every day he groomed and exercised Brightcliff Bandit, and conditioned him for the coming Kingcroft match against Belden's renowned Sahib.

But as time went on, a chronic melancholy began to oppress Hogan's buoyant soul.

Certain stocks in which he had a purely marginal interest took to wabbling in a highly erratic way that called for the eternal putting up of more and more margins. A real-estate deal on which he had counted vastly, back at home, fell through.

That ten-thousand-dollar wager with Belden began to look big and bigger to Hogan. Its winning would do much to haul him out of the temporary financial hole wherein he was floundering. But its losing would come unpleasantly close, just now, to wiping him out.

With ever-increasing care and skill he groomed Bandit's splendid coat. With equal care he supervised the collie's meed of daily exercise and of ring-rehearsals. Nervously he watched Bandit's diet.

The feeding of the dogs boarded at the road house was in charge of a slack-jawed youth who was also handy boy around the inn itself. Hogan's liberal tips made the lad's slack mouth gape with joy. But Hogan's eternal nagging as to proper food for his dog made the same slack mouth twist with annoyance.

Man and boy were not on over-friendly terms as the date drew near for the Kingcroft show. Twice or thrice Hogan's chidings at ill-cooked fare for Bandit had slain the memory of the plump tips lavished on the food-preparer.

Three days before the show the climax arrived.

Stung in the finance glands by a fresh demand from his brokers for margins, Hogan strolled out, at breakfast-time, to superintend the feeding of Bandit. At the same instant the youth-of-all-work was starting for the road house's kennels with a pailful of food for the dogs.

He dumped a quantity of the provender into a tin dish and stuck it into Bandit's yard. The collie was hungry, after his long early-morning run. He began eating with avidity. As Hogan came up, the dog was crunching blissfully at a bone. The sound made Hogan spring forward and snatch the bone away from the astonished collie.

The peculiar crunching sound is well known and dreaded by all dogmen. For that especial noise is made only when a poultry bone is champed through. And poultry bones are potential death to all large dogs.

These bones, crushed between strong jaws, break up into needle-like slivers, which are prone to thrust themselves through the stomachs or throats or intestines of the eaters.

The youth-of-all-work had eked out the breakfast pail's contents by dumping into it some of the table scraps from last night's road-house dinners—scraps including a quantity of chicken bones.

Thousands of dogs every year, throughout the land, die in agony from the devouring of chicken or duck or turkey or other poultry bones. Sometimes a dog will eat them with seeming safety. But oftener—and always, soon or late, if the diet be continued—they will kill him.

Almost as safely might a human eat a handful of pins or tacks, as a dog may gorge such bones. The bones of beef, etc., are harmless and even highly beneficial to dogs. These bones do not break into pointed slivers under the eater's powerfully crunching teeth, as do the bones of poultry.

Yet, for thousands of years, wolves and foxes and coyotes have eaten the bones of chickens and of other birds they have caught, and they have felt no known ill-effect therefrom. For those bones are raw and pliable and have not been calcined and rendered brittle by cooking.

The dog-owner who allows a servant to feed his canine pals is risking their lives if he does not inspect the feed dish for traces of sliver-making poultry bones; especially if his dogs be fed on table scraps.

Table scraps are often an ideal diet for a dog, as they are nutritious and contain a well-balanced ration. But it is all too easy for a careless servant or housewife to scrape chicken bones from the plates along with the more healthful scrapings.

All of which information may or may not some day save your own dog from dying in torment.

In any event, it explains the horror of Cassius Malachi Hogan as the sinister crunching smote upon his ears.

Hogan sprang at the collie and caught him deftly by the jaws. Instant action was called for. Even now the dog might perhaps have swallowed some of the deadly stuff.

But by rare luck and swift action Hogan was able to yank the half-crushed mouthful of bone away from his dog before Bandit had time to swallow any of it.

Wheeling, the irate Cassius Malachi flung the unsavory wad of chewed bone full into the slack-jawed face of the youth.

In practically the same set of motions—his temper going to pieces all at once—Hogan drove his thudding left fist into that same slack-jawed face; sending the boy rolling over and over in the muddy yard, and yelling lurid curses at him as the victim crawled to his feet and slunk into the house.

Followed a wrathful dialogue with the road house's proprietor, in which the vials of Hogan's wrath were scattered over the whole establishment.

The scene ended with the proprietor ordering the sobbing and raging handy boy to get his things together and clear out. Then, somewhat mollified, Hogan prepared a new dish of food for Bandit, after which he went indoors to his own breakfast.

He sat long over his meal and over the morning paper whose financial pages brought him scant ease of mind. By the time Hogan finished breakfast and strolled out again to Bandit's kennel-yard, the slack-jawed boy had departed.

But the boy had had a full half-hour in which to do other things—things to ease his aching chin and his loosened teeth and to sate his impotent hatred against the man who had hit him and who had made him lose a good job.

Bandit trotted forward to greet his owner, as usual. But Hogan halted as though stricken to stone, and peered in dumb horror at his collie. The slack-jawed youth had worked fast and to much purpose.

One half of Brightcliff Bandit's shimmering coat was as thick and as long and as magnificent as ever—one half of it, laterally, from head to hips. The other half was shorn as close to the skin as a fast-wielded pair of horse-clippers had been able to shear it.

The left side of the snowy ruff and frill hung heavy and luxuriant. So did the coat all along the left. The right side, from mid-chest to mid-hip, was naked. The finely plumed tail was as hairless as a rat's.

Not for another six months, at very least, could Brightcliff Bandit hope to regain a tithe of his former splendor of coat. For the present—as he must be for months to come—he was unbelievably hideous—a monstrosity.

He could no more appear in a dog-show's judging ring than a legless man could run a Marathon.

Long did Cassius Malachi Hogan stand there, paralyzed and moveless. In front of him was not merely a pitifully disfigured collie, but an irretrievably lost ten thousand dollars.

With numb self-loathing Hogan recalled that it was not Belden, but himself, who craftily had insisted on a clause in their agreement which forbade cancellation of the wager "for illness or for other cause whatsoever."

So calmly certain had Hogan been of Bandit's sturdy good health and steady nerves and prime condition that he had believed this clause gave his dog a strong advantage over the fragile and temperamental Sahib. Sahib was likely to sicken from the sudden change of climate or to go out of condition from any of a half-dozen causes, before the Kingcroft show. And now——!

Hogan turned about, at last, and went to his own room, moving like a man in a dream. He locked the door behind him and sat down facing the wall—the wall that was no blanker than his own palsied brain. There he sat for two full hours.

Bit by bit, as he stared unseeingly, his mind began to function anew. Faster and more clearly its thoughts sped. The numbness had passed.

Brought to bay, Hogan was making ready to fight. His wits were waxing nimbler. Ratlike, those wits raced hither and thither in quest of a hole for escape from this black dilemma. After two hours' racing they had found the hole they sought.

The scheme sprang full-grown into Hogan's brain, dazing him with its audacious simplicity. He tried out section after section of it. It was failure-proof. True, it entailed risky and fast work, but the prize was certain. This was not the first time Cassius Malachi Hogan's tricky twist of mind had ripped triumph for him out of surest defeat.

He went into action.

First he took the landlord to the kennel-yards and showed him the havoc wrought by the discharged helper. Then he said he himself was going away for a week, and he paid in advance for Bandit's keep during that time.

Then, getting into his car, he drove to a village

eight miles beyond Kingcroft and engaged lodgings at an inn on its outskirts for himself and for his dog—a dog he had entered for the Kingcroft show. Next, he stopped at two shops in the village and made simple purchases.

At dusk he drove to Sunnybank. The evening was cold and rainy for so early in the autumn. Thus, the superintendent of The Place did not happen to be sitting on his porch, as usual, at the lodge gates. Instead, he and his family were indoors. Their radio was going. Their blinds were closed, barring out the inclement night.

Down the sinuous oak-lined driveway rolled the car. No lights appeared in Sunnybank House, not even in the kitchen wing. The maids were at the movies, over in the mile-distant village.

Luck was with the intruder. The simplest and the safest of his several projected modes of procedure could be carried through without need for a second or third visit to The Place.

From the kennels came a swirl of barks as the dogs saw and heard the approaching car.

Wolf, the fiery little collie whose life job it was to serve as The Place's official watchdog, had been shut into one of the kennel runs by the maids, lest he follow them to the village. Gray Dawn had been shut into another yard, for the same reason. Treve and Bruce were dozing on the floor of the lodge's living-room, having accompanied the superintendent up the hill when he went to supper.

Sunnybank Lad alone lay majestically on the front-door mat, he who never deigned to follow anyone away from the grounds, except only the Mistress or the Master, and who preferred to mope alone on this dear veranda, rather than to cadge titbits from the superintendent's supper table.

As the car halted and as Hogan stepped out from it, Lad arose from his resting-place on the mat. Hogan spoke to him cheerily, calling him by name, and advanced up the steps toward him with the assured air of one who had every right to be there.

By voice and by scent Lad recognized the invader. This was a human the Mistress and Master had accepted as a guest and who had been welcomed by them at least twice in the past few months. Thus, by Guest Law, he was not to be attacked at sight or driven away, but must be tolerated.

With no hint of welcome, Lad stood at the top of the steps as Hogan ascended toward him.

Again the man called him by name, in friendly fashion, and stretched out a thick-gloved hand to pat his head. As before, Lad moved quietly aside, to avoid the caress. He did not like this man. Moreover, he was becoming aware of an odor he did not like—an odor new to him and emanating either from the visitor himself or else from a bundle which Hogan was carrying under his left arm.

With no haste at all, but in self-evident aversion, Lad drew away from the outstretched hand. With sudden snakelike swiftness the hand darted forward when it was within an inch or two of the unsuspicious dog. Its gloved fingers seized Lad tightly by the throat.

With practiced speed Hogan had made his grab, catching the collie just behind the right jawbone and holding him with iron grip.

Lad snarled furiously, at this painful familiarity. He snapped with murderous intent at the gloved hand and wrist. But Hogan had caught him just where the collie's rending jaws could not reach him. A dog's jaws are his one weapon of attack. Once they are made helpless, he is the least formidable animal of his size on earth.

While Lad snarled and snapped and struggled wildly, Hogan slipped a canvas bag over the helplessly writhing head. In the bottom of the bag was a double-handful of absorbent cotton, newly drenched with chloroform. The bag's drawstring was pulled tight behind Lad's ears.

Lifting the struggling animal in his arms, Hogan deposited him in the rumble seat of the car, shutting the top.

Out through the driveway and to the highroad sped the machine. By the time it reached the gates, Lad was ceasing his futile writhings to get free. He was growing weak and drowsy. It seemed all at once too much trouble to go on battling for freedom or even to stay awake.

A mile down the road, Hogan stopped the car and got out to look at his captive. The chloroform had done its work. He removed the bag and fastened a stout muzzle over the sleeper's flaccid jaws.

Then, leaving the rumble top a little open, for air, he drove onward up the valley to the inn where, that day, he had taken up his new quarters.

The Mistress and the Master finished their Canada motor run, as guests at a jolly house party at a mountain-lake camp. The house party was to have lasted for a week. On the fifth day the hostess was stricken with appendicitis and was rushed to a Montreal hospital. The party came to an abrupt end two days early.

Thus it was that the Sunnybank folk returned homeward forty-eight hours before they had planned to. Thus it was, too, that they drove through Kingcroft late on the morning of the loudly heralded dog-show.

There seemed no hurry about getting back to Sunnybank. Accordingly, they decided to stop at the show for an hour or two—if possible, long enough to watch the judging of the collies.

An inquiry at the gate made them speed their car through the half-mile which intervened between the park entrance and the shaded meadow where the show was in progress. For they were told the collie-judging already was due to begin.

The Kingcroft Kennel Club had spent much money, and more than money, to make its first annual show a mammoth success.

Seven hundred dogs, of standard breeds, were benched under gayly striped marquee tents. The green stretch of turf in front of the tents was cut off by ropes and stakes into ten ample show-rings; each ring with its judging-block and blackboard and table and chair, and surrounded by a double row of camp stools for spectators. From somewhere in the near-by woods a band was playing noisily.

The tweed-clad English collie judge was making quick and accurate work of his various classes.

Cap tugged down over his eyebrows, black pipe in a corner of his mouth, his florid face inscrutable, he was according expert care to the recurrent groups of collies led into the ring for inspection.

From almost the first, the critical "railbirds" nodded approval of the Englishman's judgment. Here was a man who knew collies, inside and out, and who made his awards wisely and without taint of favor. Moreover, he insisted on soundness as well as on beauty.

More than one flashy and highly groomed dog was "gated" mercilessly by him as his puckered eyes and sensitive fingers explored its anatomy and found (under the artistically-piled wealth of coat) a narrow chest or weak quarters or a swayed spine or a receding back skull or some other cunningly disguised defect.

Class after class was judged—Puppy, Novice, American-bred, Limit; and so on to the several "Open" classes, the toughest competitions in any show. At last, the runner announced the "Open, Any Color, Males" class.

The Master glanced at his catalogue and pointed out the entries to his wife.

"Here comes our ten-thousand-dollar contest," he remarked. "See—Brightcliff Bandit, Beldencroft Sahib—and only two more dogs. I don't know what quality those two others have, but they'll have to step fast if they're as good as Bandit's picture makes him out. . . . Hello! There's Sahib, now—that slim golden sable just coming in. I know, because that's Belden's little old Scotch kennel manager, Jamie Mackellar, leading him. Grand dog, all right, but I like them a little huskier in build. And he's too high strung. His nerves are raw, too. See how Mackellar is trying to quiet him? The long journey and the new climate must have gotten hold of him. Hogan was wise to bring Bandit here a month early, to get him used to it all. He——"

Two more dogs were led into the ring—both of good type, but both easily inferior to the showy golden Sahib. Mackellar had taken Sahib to one end of the ring and was seeking to soothe the trembling and over-excited collie by word and by caress.

The judge sat back in his corner chair beside the ribbon-strewn table, chatting with the ring steward and seeming to take no note of the several entrants as they were brought in.

But, from his own experience as a dog-judge, the Master knew the Englishman's puckered eyes were studying surreptitiously every line and every motion of every dog as it stood or moved at its ease, before it should be braced up by its handler for exhibition.

It is at this prejudging moment that an expert often can get his best line on the actual quality of the dogs before him.

There was a pause. Then through the mass of standees at the gate Cassius Malachi Hogan pushed his way.

He was leading—half dragging—a huge mahogany-and-snow collie that protested fiercely every step of the short journey.

There was a mutter of amazement among the railbirds. For this glorious and perfectly groomed dog was disfigured by a steel muzzle fastened tightly about his foam-flecked jaws. Also, Hogan carried under one arm a short and thick rawhide quirt.

At the entrance to the ring the steward met Hogan and slipped a numbered brassard over his left cuff. Then the steward turned toward the judge and announced:

"They are all here, sir."

But the judge no longer was sitting idly in his corner. At the sight of the newcomer he had jumped to his feet as though there were hornets in his chair. Down he bore upon Hogan, demanding, sharply:

"What do you mean by bringing your dog into the ring muzzled? And what is that rawhide for?"

Hogan smiled in conciliation as he made answer:

"Bandit is ugly with strangers, Judge. I don't want him biting you when you get to handling his head and to looking into his mouth. So I thought I'd ——"

"Take that muzzle off him!" ordered the judge. "And throw that rawhide out of the ring, too. As for his biting me—that is a chance every dog-judge takes. If you haven't been able to teach him better ring manners than to need a whip and a steel muzzle, you ought not to bring him to a show. Get rid of them!"

In the ring, a judge's word is absolute law. For the time, he is as much of a tyrant or martinet as he may choose to be. There is no appeal from his commands.

Cassius Malachi Hogan drew forth and donned a pair of thick gauntlets. Then, in gingerly fashion, he bent to undo the straps of the muzzle. Either the padded glove fingers or else his stark nervousness made him fumble.

Impatiently the judge pushed the awkward hands aside and unfastened the muzzle, tossing it across the ring.

Relieved of the hurt and the cruel discomfort of the unaccustomed steel springs about his sensitive mouth, the collie looked up gratefully at his benefactor, even making shift to wave his unhappily drooped tail as he laid his head against the Englishman's gnarled hand in a gesture of dumb thanks.

"H'm!" grunted the judge. "You said he was vicious with strangers. If I know anything about collies, there isn't one drop of vicious or mean blood in this dog. He ——"

The judge broke off with an exclamation of surprise. An unconscious tug given to the leash reminded the collie that Hogan was at the other end of that same leash. With a yell of blind fury, the dog whirled about and sprang roaring at his handler.

Hogan was a veteran dog-man. He had taken the precaution to hold the leash a bare twelve inches from the dog's neck. As the collie sprang, Hogan tightened his own hold on the shortened leash and held his arm out straight.

As a result, the dog's feet left the ground with a jerk. The leathern leash-noose tightened unbearably about his throat as he bit uselessly at the unreachable man who held him. For an instant there was much commotion in the ring. The judge rasped out:

"Behaves civilly to everyone but his owner, hey? That's a new one to me!"

Hogan lowered the raging and choking collie

to the ground, still holding him on short leash-way and as far from him as might be.

At the same time, another diversion occurred in the ring.

Jamie Mackellar had been soothing and quieting the nerve-tortured Beldencroft Sahib as best he could in a far corner, doing his best to allay the spasmodic trembling which shook the golden dog ever more and more convulsively.

The sudden mad fury of Hogan's collie was more or less infectious to the taut nerves of every other dog in the ring. But to Sahib the shock furnished the very little impetus needed to change his sick tremors into a decidedly spectacular convulsion.

To the ground Sahib hurled himself, foaming, kicking, gurgling.

Now this is no unusual sight at a summer dog-show. Like "running fits" (of which it is a phase), it is a recognized risk which is entailed in taking a high-strung and none-too-healthy dog to a show in hot weather. No fewer than four such fits marred a single outdoor exhibition a year or two ago.

Mackellar picked up his fit-ridden dog in his arms as tenderly as though the stricken collie had been a sick child. To the judge he said, with respectful firmness:

"By your leave, sir, I'm taking this poor chap from the ring. You can see he is in no condition to be shown. When he comes out of this attack he must have bromide and rest and quiet. It might kill him to put him through his paces. I ask leave to withdraw him."

"Certainly," assented the Englishman; adding, "I'd gate any dog whose handler made him show after a fit like that. Carry him to the vet. He——"

"You understand, Mackellar," spoke up Hogan, excitedly, barring the way to the gate and still holding his own snarling and struggling collie at arm's-length—"you understand you're forfeiting this match by withdrawing your dog from the ring? You realize Mr. Belden loses his wager with me if Sahib doesn't enter into regular competition with my Bandit, here? I want it clearly understood that he forfeits our——"

"If Mr. Belden was the kind of a man to want me to show a half-dead dog that had just come out of a fit," retorted Mackellar, "I'd leave his service tomorrow. It don't matter whether there's ten thousand dollars at stake or ten times ten thousand dollars. Sahib isn't going to be tortured. And if you're a poor enough sportsman to claim the wager—why, that's up to you."

"I claim it," declared Hogan. "Bandit is here, ready to be judged. Sahib isn't. By the forfeit clause, I win. I ——"

The giant mahogany-and-snow collie had ceased his useless efforts to reach any part of Hogan's anatomy into which he could sink his teeth. Now, panting and with head and tail adroop, he stood listless.

It was then that Hogan shifted his own position, in calling his final words to Mackellar as the latter carried Sahib from the ring.

For the first time, the thick bodies of the judge and Hogan no longer obstructed a full view of the dog from the side of the ring where sat the Mistress and the Master. They had had only a fleeting rear view of the collie as he was led in. After that, both Hogan and the Englishman had been between them and him.

"Poor cuss!" commented the Master. "He looks as wretched as Lad looks when we go away from home, and he's even more like Laddie than his picture was. Bandit's the living image of ——"

"It *is* Laddie!" cried the Mistress, finding her voice after the bewilderment of that first full sight of the dog. "*Laddie!* LAD!"

Her clear voice cut through the looser volume of ringside noise. The judge had just given the order, "Walk your dogs, please," when she called to the comrade she loved.

The droopingly miserable mahogany-and-snow collie was galvanized to wildly eager life. His deep-set dark eyes with their "look of eagles," swept the ring, then focused on a woman just outside the rope barrier—a woman who had sprung to her feet and was calling to him.

With one tremendous bound Lad ripped loose Hogan's slightly slackened hold on the leash. Across the ring flashed the collie, whimpering and sobbing with crazy delight as he flung himself upon the adored Mistress.

The judge turned, just in time to see the dog tear free from his handler and, it seemed, launch himself murderously at a ringside spectator—on a woman, at that!

He rushed forward to avert the seeming disaster. By the time he and the steward and one or two more volunteers reached the rope, the maniac collie was flinging himself screamingly not only at the woman, but at a man who stood beside her.

The two supposed victims were so far from resenting the assault that they both were petting and talking to the great brute whose flying white paws smote them alternately and smeared mud impartially upon their sports clothes.

The rescuers paused in uncertainty, a bit ashamed of their needless gestures of heroism. The judge shouted to Hogan:

"Get your dog! He's holding up the judging. We can't wait all day while he recognizes friends of his at the rail. Get ——"

"Yes!" indorsed the Master. "Get him, Hogan. Here he is."

Hogan stood in mid-ring, face blank, knees shaking.

"No?" jeered the Master. "Won't you even take the trouble to get your own dog? Then he'll save you that trouble. Get *him*, Laddie!"

In the wink of an eye Lad turned from his hysterical greeting of his two deities. Ever obedient, and remembering suddenly his own black wrongs, he flew at the terrified Hogan. The man spun about and fled. Before he could reach the safety of the railbird crowd Lad was upon him.

Down crashed Hogan on his face, under the eighty-pound blow that smashed against his shoulders and his back as he ran. He fell as, long ago, Horace Dilver had fallen under a like impact of Lad's whalebone muscular weight on his back. With ferocious relish Lad bored in at him.

Then, at the very outset of the collie's punitive spree, the Mistress's voice recalled him to her.

Unwillingly Lad deserted his howling prey and strode meekly back to where the Mistress stood.

By this time the ring and the ringside were in an uproar. From other rings and from the tents people were running.

Briefly, yet with startling accuracy, the Mistress was explaining to the judge and to the superintendent of the show that Mr. Cassius Malachi Hogan had somehow contrived to "borrow" her collie and to foist him off as a "ringer" for his own inexplicably absent Brightcliff Bandit.

The news traveled on wings. But it did not travel fast enough to overtake Hogan himself. The instant Lad was called away from him, Hogan scrambled to his feet and ran at top speed to his parked car.

Out of the park whizzed the car; nor did it stop until it reached the road house where the half-shorn Brightcliff Bandit was lodged. Stopping there only long enough to annex his dog and his luggage, Cassius Malachi Hogan turned the nose of his car westward toward his far-distant home.

As the Mistress made her way to her own car, with Lad dancing joyously about her, the Master sought out Rufus G. Belden's kennel manager. He found Mackellar still ministering to the slowly recovering Beldencroft Sahib, and he told him what had happened in the ring.

"The ten-thousand-dollar bet is off," concluded the Master. "Neither dog competed. But I think the American Kennel Club is due to disqualify Hogan, for life, for the dirty fraud he tried to work. So his career as a dog-man is over."

"I congratulate his dogs!" answered Mackellar, tersely; adding:

"But, if I may make so free as to ask, why did a fine wise lady like your wife ever call Laddie away from the man, just as the good old dog was beginning to even up the score?"

"I don't know," said the Master. "Women are queer that way, sometimes. She——"

"They are!" solemnly affirmed Jamie Mackellar, "I thank the good Lord they are! That's how they come pretty close to making this crooked old world a straight place to live in. Long may they stay 'queer,' God bless 'em!"

Chapter Seven

LAD AND LOHENGRIN

THERE was to be a wedding at The Place, the first in many years.

The time was mid-June. Sunnybank was aglow with a million roses and with all the lush glory of the coming summer. An ideal time and an ideal scene for such a festivity.

The ceremony itself was to be in the pre-Revolutionary white church on the edge of the mile-distant village. But the reception was to be on the rose-girt and oak-shaded green lawns of Sunnybank itself. For weeks, with increasing impetus, the marriage preparations had been in progress.

Consultations with caterers' men, with florist assistants, with demure dressmakers, all of them arriving by motor from New York, at any and every time of day; one station wagon after another delivering big and small wedding gifts from the express office; the two telephones buzzing their horrible bells incessantly; the Place's laborers toiling mightily, under the commands of Robert Friend, the English superintendent of Sunnybank, to get the grounds in shimmering condition; the house servants on tiptoe (and sometimes on edge) with the manifold extra duties and the excitement thrill—all that kind of thing.

Fifty cars came down the long winding driveway where of old one had come. The kennel collies hailed the fitfully incessant procession with vibrant spasms of barking. The house dogs were more sedate at first. But presently the noise and the constant bustle and the incursion of hordes of strangers began to get on their nerves and to lure them into joining the salvos of barks from the kennel dogs.

"I used to call this 'The House Of Peace!'" grumbled the Master, right sourly. "I can look back, with an effort, to a dim long-ago era when Sunnybank was girt with its forty beautiful acres of sweet solitude and by the lake, as a barrier against the outer world. Those were the days when I got some work done and when the collies weren't barking their fool heads off every minute, and when the only strangers who butted in were the army of measly motor-trippers who had read my third-rate yarns and who wanted to meet me and to see the dogs. They could be staved off by locking the lodge gates. But now they're only a fraction of the crowd that horns in on us, and the gates have to stand open day and night."

"It's only for a little while, dear!" soothed the Mistress, "Then everything will be exactly as it was. Can't you get just a tiny bit of fun out of it? It's all so—so wonderful and so beautiful and ——"

"What is?" snarled the Master in dire ill-temper. "What is 'so beautiful'? The mass of trades people who are fixing things for the wedding and are trampling all over my writing hours and all over the grounds? The express wagons that bring seventy-nine bridge lamps and ninety-eight silver vases and a thousand and three boxes of china that have to be unpacked and then duly shrieked over, amid a cloud of jute and wrapping-paper? The phone calls from newspapers that want a photo of the bride and a full list of 'distinguished guests?' My secretary is knee-deep in the ads and circulars and photographers' letters that flood my mail, and prospectuses from jewelers and from clipping bureaus and ——"

"It's only for a *very* little while," repeated his wife. "And ——"

"So is the pulling of a back tooth," complained the Master. "But it's no merry sport while it lasts. A 'very little while' more of this will earn me a season ticket to the foolish house. Why, it's beginning even to get old Laddie! He's psychic, as all collies are. This silly atmosphere of day-after-day rumpus, over nothing, has got his hair-trigger nerves going. He doesn't know what's up. And for a while he was content to stay out in the woods most of the time. But now it's infecting him. He barks at the line of cars and delivery trucks, like any unbroke puppy. He ——"

Around the corner of the rambling old gray stucco house, toward the vine-green veranda shade where the Mistress and the Master sat at lunch, lurched a bicycle.

"Lurched" is the correct word. It hopped spasmodically and jerkily, to the accompaniment of treble squawks. On the machine's swaying saddle careened and yelped a buck-toothed delivery boy who had brought a sheaf of wedding telegrams to The Place from the Western Union office in the village.

As a rule, telegraph delivery at Sunnybank was a sought-for errand by the village youths, for it meant a tip and a chance to look at the collies. But there was scant pleasance and vast malaise in the demeanor of today's visitant.

Close behind the messenger, as the bicycle rounded the house corner, trotted Lad.

The collie's mighty body and head were vibrant

with mischief. At every alternate stride he reached forward and nipped gently the shrinking heels of the lad's pedaling feet.

The nips were not true bites, nor was there wrath in the demeanor of the biter.

Sunnybank Lad had been asleep in the sun when the cyclist coasted cockily down the long drive from the highway above. With rollicking pleasure the dog had sprung into life, as the bicycle whizzed close past him.

As a result, the last fifty yards of the trip had been minor anguish and major fright to the rider, and puppy-like delight to the pursuing collie.

"See?" expounded the Master, when the yellow telegrams had been delivered and the terrified boy had gone, and when the Mistress could release her hold on Lad's furry neck to prevent him from following the departing youth. "That cost me a double tip. And the news will go around the village that Laddie has turned savage. The next important telegram that comes for me will wait at the office till it is gray with dust, before anyone can be found who has the nerve to deliver it. Lad, you old fool, haven't you any sense at all?"

"He has more sense than any dog that ever lived!" declared the Mistress. "But it's just as you said. He is psychic. All the excitement of The Place, this past week or two, has gotten into his blood. And he wants to do his part, in enhancing it. He has never behaved like that, even when he was a puppy. Laddie, I'm mortified at you!"

At the stern words, spoken in anything but a stern voice, the great collie came over to the Mistress, making hideous faces in mock remorse as he came.

It was Lad's life-long habit to show all his teeth and to wrinkle his classic foreface into a mask of puckered imbecility when he felt he had done wrong and wanted to sue for pardon from the adored Mistress. Now he positively outdid himself in the way of facial contortions as he ran up to her.

"Lad is due to make some extra kind of idiot of himself on the day of the wedding," commented the Master. "I've arranged to have all the other dogs locked in the stables that day—all except Bruce, who couldn't misbehave if he tried. And I think I'll have Laddie sent over to Doctor Hopper's kennels in the morning, and kept there till the whole thing is over. Something tells me he is going to make trouble. What do you think of the idea?"

The Mistress's face, of a sudden, went sober.

"Lad stayed here all that terrible time when you thought I was dying from pneumonia," she said, softly. "He lay outside my door, night and day, without eating or drinking, till I was out of danger. He pulled me out of the lake when my canoe upset. He has been with us for nine years, in every joy and sorrow we have known—in every crisis and in every good time. He is going to stay here for the wedding, Laddie is. He—he *belongs*."

"All right!" agreed the Master. "He belongs. That settles that. On your head be anything he may pull down to spoil the whole show!"

"He won't! He won't spoil anything. He——"

"Something tells me he is going to," prophesied the Master, gloomily. "Lad and the 'Lohengrin Wedding March,' somehow, don't go together. But we'll chance it. You say he 'belongs.' Perhaps he does, though I have my doubts. But *I* don't belong. You women all love weddings. You weep blissfully at them. I can't see where the rapture comes in. No he-man does. You're looking forward to this wedding like a kid to his first revolver. That's the woman of it. I'm looking forward to it like the same kid to his first licking. That's the man of it."

"But——"

"You're going to revel in lovely filmy clothes and a big bouquet," he insisted. "You'll look almost as young as the bride and twice as pretty. I've got to shed my disreputable khaki-and-leather clothes and get into a top-hat and a morning suit, and 'give away' the bride at the altar. It'll be a hot day and my high collar will be a wreck and I'll look like a red-faced longshoreman at a funeral."

"No!" loyally denied the Mistress. "You'll look ——"

"That's the difference between us," grumbled the Master, unheeding. "Every normal woman adores big weddings. Every normal man loathes them. A good lively ten-round prize-fight is better worth watching than all the weddings since the one at Cana. I've a good mind to quit, cold, and go fishing off our point that afternoon in a scow, and sit there with a pipe and a torn flannel suit and a straw hat with a hole in it, and watch the sweating guests up here on the lawn and —— What's the joke?" he broke off.

"The joke," she explained, swallowing her laughter with difficulty—"the joke is that you said exactly the same thing before our own wedding, nearly twenty-five years ago. I told you then that nobody ever looks at the groom—as long as he's there. I tell you now that nobody ever yet looked at the man who gives the bride away. And a few hours after that we'll both settle down to our dear old-time routine of country life, here. So you and Laddie can have years and years to quiet your ruffled nerves in. . . . *Please* try to be just a little happy about it, won't you, dear?"

On an evening, two days later, several cars journeyed from The Place to the white little church. In them were the wedding party, on their way to rehearse the next day's ceremony. The Mistress and the Master drove over in the former's coupé.

As the Master leaned out to close the car's door, Lad stepped gravely into the machine and snuggled down at the Mistress's feet.

Thus did the big collie dispose himself on practically every drive taken by these two human deities of his. There seemed no reason why he should not go along with them tonight, as usual. Often he had even driven to church in this way, lying on guard in the coupé until the service was over.

Arrived at the church door, the Master snapped his fingers to Lad, in invitation to jump out. The dog had just settled himself resignedly to the usual hour-and-a-half of dull waiting which had been his whenever the car had stopped here.

Overjoyed at permission to follow, he capered

up the flagged walk to the doorway, where a knot of the wedding party's members were chatting.

He was hailed with much cordiality by the group. The maid of honor, who was an old friend of Laddie's, unlimbered a candy box from under her arm and offered the collie a large and mushy and delectable bonbon.

With outward gravity, but inward bliss, he accepted the gift daintily, and fell to munching it with infinite epicurean relish. Sweets were taboo for dogs, at The Place, as a rule. Lad loved them the more for their rarity.

As the party drifted into the dim-lit sacred edifice, Lad fell into step at the Mistress's side. The acting sexton interfered.

"Sorry, ma'am," said he, "but dogs aren't allowed here. That big collie of yours will have to stay out in your car, at the service. He——"

"This isn't a service," snapped the Master, nettled at the man's rebuking tone. "And there is no law of any church forbidding a well-behaved dog from coming into it with his owner. In Scotland, a score of times, I have seen collies lying in the aisles, alongside their masters' pews, through a two-hour service. Worse Christians than old Sunnybank Lad have been coming to church all their lives. Some of them even get to be sextons' assistants. But if you want to put him out, you are welcome to do it."

The man took advantage of the permission by grabbing Lad harshly by the scruff of his neck and giving him a sharp yank toward the door. From nobody, save only the Mistress or the Master, would this treatment have been permissible, with Lad. In a single lightning-swift motion he had broken free from his captor's grip. In what seemed the same motion he had slashed the man's wrist, deep and raggedly.

"Lad!" reproved the Master.

Obediently, the collie dropped into step once more beside his two owners, while the bitten man shrank back into the vestibule, nursing his injured wrist and sputtering forth lurid threats of vengeance.

The Mistress was deeply distressed at the incongruous scene which had marred the holy serenity of the consecrated spot. The Master himself had the grace to be sorry for what he had brought about. But the wedding party were in high glee over it.

The Master motioned the growlingly wrathful Lad into a pew and bade him lie there and be quiet. The maid of honor surreptitiously fed him two more fat candies while the procession was waiting to form and while the organist fiddled with the keys and stops.

The church's regular sexton came in, almost colliding with his assistant, who had carried his imprecations and his hurt wrist out of the vestibule into the churchyard.

"What's happened, sir?" asked the sexton, of the Master, whom he had known from boyhood. "That feller was cursing something terrible."

The Master explained, adding the query:

"Who is he, anyhow? I don't know him. He can't be anyone from around here. He told me he was in charge of the church till you got back from your supper. I can't compliment you on your new deputy. He is ——"

"He's no deputy of mine, sir," disclaimed the sexton. "He's working for *you*. At least, you're paying him."

"I never saw him before. You're mistak ——"

"He's one of the caterer's men, for the wedding reception at your place tomorrow," went on the sexton. "He was sent up from New York to be at the station first thing in the morning, to look after some of the caterer's things that are coming up by express. He's spending the night here at a boarding-house. I s'pose he wants to turn an extra penny while he's waiting; because he dropped in here late this afternoon, and said he'd heard at the boarding-house that my assistant was took sick, and he asked me did I want to give him a dollar to be handy around here this evening and help me out."

"I see."

"I took him on for the evening, and I left him on watch while I ate. There wasn't anything but decorations he could steal. Besides, a big New York caterer's men are pretty generally proved to be honest. That's all I know about him. He hadn't any call to tell you what you could or couldn't bring in here. I'll give him a stiff call-down for it, too."

The procession formed and the music cue was given.

Lad was keenly interested in his new surroundings. He was a prey to what Victorian novelists used to call "mingled emotions."

It was monstrous pleasant to be allowed inside the building, instead of being left on guard in the car, as usual. It was nice to have been hailed so affectionately by the group of young people whom he knew so well at home. It was heavenly to be fed one luscious candy after another.

So much for the credit side. But there was a most decided debit side to it, as well.

He had been grabbed and yanked and man-handled, he who would suffer no one's touch save that of the Mistress and the Master. A slimy stranger had laid violent grip on him and had subjected him to public and painful humiliation.

True, Lad had been able to pay off a fraction of the debt by that single punitive slash. But the slash had been no more than a deep scratch, and before he could follow it up with something more drastic the Master had ordered him to desist.

The hackles on Lad's shoulder bristled, and his eyeteeth glinted, as he glared back through the near-by doorway, every few moments, in quest of the man who had insulted him. His nostrils were aquiver, isolating and tabulating the assailant's scent, for future use. For a dog does his recognizing by scent, rather than by sight. The smell of the man's perspiring hand was still rank on Lad's neck fur.

The dog would not forget. If ever the occasion should arise, he would not fail to pay the rest of the account. A collie has a queer power of remembering both good and ill—save only toward those he loves. With those he shows a divine forgetfulness of past bad treatment.

Out in the dark churchyard, the waiter was binding his scratched wrist and breathing threats against the savage dog. In the bottom of the pew, the dog was brooding with equal rancor on the punishment due the waiter.

Then something happened that swept anger and even the candy-hunger far into the back of Lad's mind, to be brought forth at some less immediately thrilling time.

Of a sudden the faint-lit church was pulsing and reverberating and throbbing with a mighty rhythmic noise. The organist had broken into the opening bars of the "Lohengrin Wedding March." The bridal rehearsal was beginning.

Never before had Lad heard organ music—save muffled and far off as he had lain in the car during services. Now it was surging all around him, beating against his super-sensitive eardrums in recurrent waves and billows of deep sound.

It stirred the dog to his very marrow, filling him with strange, joyous excitement. He yearned to leap to his feet with a thunderous fanfare of barking. Only the memory of the Master's stern command to lie down and to be quiet held him tremblingly moveless.

Many dogs are queerly affected by music. The high notes of violin or of cornet or mandolin are cruel torture to their delicate tympana. But there are dogs by the dozen to which a piano's music is a real pleasure. There are others to which the organ's lower notes are almost rapture.

Lad was having one of the biggest and most stirring experiences of his life. Music, candy, a human jollification of some kind! The combination was matchless. But for the clash with the grabbing and yanking waiter it would have been a sublimely happy hour for him.

Again and again the procession formed, and marched to the Lohengrin strains. Again and again the bride and groom met at the altar and practiced the exact angle at which they were to stand. Again and again the sulky Master paraded up the aisle with the bride on his arm.

In brief, the party went through all the usual endless repetitions incident to rehearsing the simplest set of evolutions ever devised.

Lad was reveling in it all. Impatiently he waited for the recurrence of that thunder and throb of organ music. When at last—a long and boresome last—the rehearsal ended, the dog wished it might have continued all night.

But now, as the humans flocked out through the doorway, Laddie had scope to remember his bitter feud and grievance. He glanced around, sniffing inquiringly. But his enemy had left the scene of conflict a full hour earlier.

Disappointed, Lad stepped into the car and curled up at the Mistress's feet. The Master stooped to pat the dog's classic head, saying in sorry triumph to his wife:

"Remember what I prophesied about Lad and 'Lohengrin' not going well together and about his being sure to start something before this pesky wedding was over? He came near giving that fool waiter a nasty bite this evening. And he came nearer turning the rehearsal into a fight, by flying at the man as he did."

"It wasn't Laddie's fault!" declared the Mistress. "You gave the man leave to try to drag him out of the church. You knew what would happen. Dear, it was—it was *horrible* of you! Honestly it was. In a church, too! I——"

"You're right!" sighed her husband. "It *was* my fault. But all at once I couldn't resist the craving to give that impudent cuss something to remember me by. I couldn't very well slug him in the jaw, there in church. So—so I put the job up to Laddie. It was rotten of me. I'm sorry."

"Don't let's think any more about it," counseled the Mistress. "You were tired and hot, and the wedding plans had been getting on your nerves. It's all right. Besides, it's over, now."

Seldom was the wise and gentle Mistress mistaken. But this was to be one of those very few times. It was not "over, now." It had not really begun.

The church ceremony was set for four, the next afternoon; the reception at Sunnybank to begin a half-hour later.

All the dogs except Lad and Bruce were banished to the "winter kennels" in the stables, lest they deafen the guests by tumultuous and multiple barking at every arriving car. Lad and Bruce were called into the study, after lunch, to be shut in there until after the services should be finished and the reception begun.

Both dogs were loved by guests of The Place. Their presence at the reception would be that of two dignified and stately old gentlemen. At least, so the Mistress foretold, from recollection of many earlier social appearances of these favorite collies.

Bruce accepted philosophically his incarceration in the study. Gracefully he stretched himself on a rug and went to sleep.

But Lad was anything but sleepy. The noise of bustling feet and of gay voices, the faint and distant scent once or twice of the waiter who had throttled him at the church door, the indefinable atmosphere of excitement—all these bit deep into Lad's taut nerves. Sleep was not for him. He stood at the study window, peering interestedly out onto the driveway and the lawn.

Then, at a little before four, he saw a short

procession of cars set forth up the drive. In one of them rode the bride, strangely enveloped in fluffs and glisters of white. Lad's friend, the candy-giving maid of honor, was with her. In another car rode the Mistress and the Master, also oddly clad. Other cars bore still others of his acquaintances.

Lad whined softly. Thus, the night before, had the same procession started out, and he had gone with it to a most entertaining performance. As the last of the cars turned into the highroad at the lodge gates, Lad left the window and lay down with a thump, close to the study door.

He had been put into this stuffy prison, but he had not been bidden to stay here. He felt himself under no moral obligation to remain, if he could get free.

The caterer's manager in the hallway outside called an order. Somebody hurried to obey it.

"Not in there!" said the manager. "That's the study. The room beyond."

The study door was half opened, then pushed shut as the subordinate moved on to the next room. The door swung to its latch, but the push was too light for the latch to snap.

On the instant, Lad was nosing the door open. In another brace of seconds he was out in the driveway, casting about for the scent of the Master's car; for, like many another dog, he could follow the seemingly scentless trail of a set of familiar tires as easily as the trail of a rabbit. Up the drive toward the highroad he went, at a dead run.

In the vestibule of the church stood the bridal procession, waiting for the organ cue. The first strains of the "Lohengrin March" blared out. The crowded assemblage arose to its feet. The groom and his best man stepped shamefacedly out from the organ-room and took their places beside the clergyman at the altar. The procession paced slowly up the endless aisle.

The Master was pinchingly aware that the bride's fingers were digging deep into his arm, though her face was as serene as the summer day itself. All but noiselessly she whispered to him, in response to his side glance of inquiry:

"I'm—I *think* I'm scared!"

"Steady!" whispered back the Master, reassuringly. "It's all right, kid. Think of all the other women in the world! And you're looking gorgeous. I ——"

He got no further. The bridesmaids and ushers had come to the altar and had taken their appointed places at either side of it. The bride and the Master were at the altar steps. The groom moved forward to meet them. The ceremony began.

Then, through the hushed silence of the spectators which underlay the clergyman's first words, came a raucous snicker.

It came from the gallery. It was taken up, if more decorously, from every corner of the church. The bride started as if she had been stung. Involuntarily the Master glanced around.

"*Who giveth this woman to be married to this man?*" intoned the clergyman.

Before the Master could reply, something pushed vehemently between the bride and himself—something large and shaggy and drippingly wet and dust-smeared.

Laddie had had no trouble at all in following the scent of the car. When at last he became certain whither it was bound, he was thrilled with delight. There might be more of that stirring rhythmic thunder; perhaps even more candy; assuredly more gay excitement.

No longer did he follow the somewhat winding road at its wider twists. Instead, at one point, he took a short cut which involved his swimming a hundred-foot creek at some distance below its bridge. Then, taking to the road again, he acquired a nicely abundant blanket of dust from its powdery surface.

As he reached the church the door stood open. He could see the Master standing with the bride at the far end of the aisle. Close by sat the Mistress, in one of the frontmost pews.

Closer stood the girl who had fed him all that delicious candy and who perhaps might be relied on now to give him some more. He trotted eagerly toward her, pushing through the narrow space between the bride and the Master.

It was the Mistress who saved the day. Her sweet voice was pitched so low that it barely reached the dog's acute ears. But it held a note of almost fierce authority as she called, softly:

"*Lad!!!*"

At that all-compelling undernote the collie wheeled swiftly toward her. Her gloved finger made one slight imperative gesture. Obedient to it, Lad crouched on the aisle floor, as near to her feet as he could get.

There, statue-still, he lay throughout the rest of the service. Once and again he looked up worriedly into the Mistress's face, trying to read there the cause for the stark urgency that had been in her loved voice.

The clergyman had held field services in France when the shells were dropping all about his khaki congregation. Thus, the advent of a huge and muddily shaggy dog did not throw him off his mental balance in the mere reading of a marriage service.

Presently it was all over. The organ struck up the "Mendelssohn March." The bridal party formed in new alignment and started down the aisle again, its leaders skirting carefully a big collie which shrank as close as he could to the edge of the pew where sat the Mistress. Then, she and the Master and others were moving down the aisle.

Crestfallen and wondering, the dog obeyed the Mistress's covert signal to fall in behind her and her husband, and to follow. As they passed the filled ranks of pews, hundreds of faces were wreathed in smiles somewhat more jovially amused than ordinarily are lavished on a recessant bridal party. Seldom in civilized circles has a wet and worried collie been a part of such a procession in a church.

Truly, the Master had been right in his glum foreboding that Lad and "Lohengrin"—and in this instance "Mendelssohn's March"—would not "go well together." They did not.

As Lad reached the church steps, the Master turned to him. In no affectionate accents at all, and with a murderous glower, the Master snarled out the command:

"Home, Lad! Get *home!*"

There was no mistaking the meaning of the ire of the mandate. Lad wheeled about and made for Sunnybank at a choppy wolf-trot. He was in disgrace. He did not know why, but he was. He had not disobeyed any orders or done anything he knew to be wrong. If he had erred in coming thus into the church, had not the Master himself bidden him enter it, only last evening? Yet the Master was ragingly angry at him for some unknown reason.

Faster and faster went Lad; his trot merging into a hand gallop, his plumed tail adroop, every inch of his magnificent body dejected and miserable.

As he came into the grounds of The Place and down the driveway, he did not go indoors at once. Instead, he slunk into the garage and lay down there to brood.

He was abnormally sensitive, and disgrace ever made him heartsick. There he lay while car after car came down the driveway from the distant church and disgorged the reception guests at the house's wide-swung front doors. From somewhere came the crooning of an orchestra. The reception had begun. Not that Laddie knew or cared.

Time went on as he lay there, his head between his white little forepaws, his dark eyes troubled and pathetic. Then a waiter came out from the kitchen end of the house and went to a caterer's van behind a shed, and took something therefrom and carried it indoors.

Lad started up. A hated and familiar scent was wafted to him on the afternoon breeze. He was just in time to see the waiter vanish into the house. At once the dog's unhappiness was lost in the gust of rage that swept him at scent and sight of the man who had had the audacity to mistreat him the night before.

Head down and body flying, Lad charged in pursuit. He dashed into the laundry and thence through the kitchen and areaway and butler's pantry, toward the dining-room, whose door was swinging shut behind his foe.

The guests were on the lawns and on the verandas, some of them in the house. The waiters were toiling manfully from group to group, laden with plates or cups.

The dining-room was the source and center whence radiated the flying squadron of waiters. Its elongated table ran almost the full length of the room. It was covered today with an enormous antique Florentine lace tablecloth, on which were platters of food and piles of dishes and the like, as well as silver and a wide centerpiece of flowers.

A waiter had just returned from fetching some forgotten article from the caterer-van and was laying it on a corner of the crowded table. Something leaped in through the ajar door behind him and bore him down.

Thrown off his balance, the waiter crashed forward across the middle of the table, his clawing hands instinctively closing on the lace. Lad was driving punitively for any part of his victim he could reach. His impact sent the waiter rolling from the table, still clutching spasmodically the double handful of lace tablecloth he had grasped.

Waiter and dog smote the floor together, in a right unloving embrace. The man was screaming in terror. The collie was growling and mauling.

Down upon their prostrate and writhing bodies avalanched the entire high-piled contents of the table. Tiers of plates, cascades of salad and coffee, a rainstorm of flowers, a myriad fragments of thin glass; silver table ornaments that thudded clashingly and dentingly to the hardwood floor—these and an unbelievable assortment of other things heaped themselves upon the struggling man and dog, as though seeking mercifully to bury from sight the spectacle of their ungodly strife.

Other waiters and attendants shouted. Some one bawled, "Mad dog!" (that being ever the remark deemed appropriate to any scene of violence in which a dog happens to be concerned), and somewhere a woman shrieked.

Ten seconds earlier, the soft afternoon June sun had smiled down on a tranquilly festive scene. People had been talking and eating and drinking happily together on the emerald lawns above the fire-blue lake or on the vine-shaded porches. Music from a hidden orchestra had served as a gently sweet undertone accompaniment to their talk.

Then, in a trice, Bedlam had cut loose.

Guests thronged to the impromptu field of battle. The Master arrived just in time to see Lad wriggle free from the mountain of glass and food and crockery and torn lace under which he and the waiter had been interred, and make a fresh dive at his squirming and screeching adversary. A yelled word from the Master turned the collie instantly if reluctantly from the fray, while men helped the jarred and panic-stricken victim to his feet.

The whole encounter had lasted but an atom of time. Lad had been so thoroughly bombarded by the table's cataract of falling contents that he had been able to make practically no use of his brief opportunity for mayhem.

Twice he had struck for the fallen and fighting man's throat. Once the frantically shoving hands had thrust him back. The second time, his jaws had missed the jugular, but they had cloven through the neckband of the waiter's shirt and had rent the collar away.

The ravening teeth had rent away something else from the skinny neck of the man—something which came loose along with the collar and inside of it; something that had entangled itself with one of Lad's curved eyeteeth and would not be shaken free as he had shaken free the collar itself.

"Lad!" exploded the Master, as the salad-smeared and coffee-dripping and glass-strewn collie faced him at the first cry of his name. "Lad, you filthy cur! You've never been thrashed, but you're sure due to be now! Gray Dawn, at his worst, never ——"

The Master's voice trailed away. He was blinking at something that swung to and fro glitteringly from the collie's panting jaws.

He looked from it to the rent collar, then to the spindly bare throat of the waiter. He removed the shining thing from the eyetooth around which a loop of it had been wedged. Then he turned to the caterer's manager, who was supporting in his arms the half-swooning waiter.

"I hired a plain-clothes man, through your firm," said he, "to keep an eye on the presents, today. Some of them are rather too good to risk being stolen. This pearl-and-aquamarine necklace, for instance. 'Gift of the groom,' you know. Just before we left for the church, it was lying in its open case, among the other presents. Of course, I know how it came to be hanging, now, from this dog's teeth. I saw him pull it from around that waiter's neck, where it was neatly hidden inside of a 'trick' collar. But what I don't understand is how your man happened to have it around his neck, unless ——"

With an incredibly swift motion the seemingly swooning waiter tore himself from the manager's supporting arms. In a single bound he had cleared the sill of the nearest open window and the veranda beyond it. Sprinting with all the skilled speed of a professional athlete, he was dashing for the nearest stretch of woodland.

The Master, with one sharp word, quieted the outburst of tumult about him. Then, pointing to the fast-running and fast-receding man, he said to the collie:

"After him, Laddie!"

The order was but half-uttered when the collie flashed through the open window in merrily ferocious pursuit. As he sped at express-train speed, he showered behind him a trail of mayonnaise and coffee and punch and particles of glass and china.

"No human on earth can hope to escape, with a good collie at his heels," remarked the Master to the flustered and gabbling manager. "And Lad is the best of them. Better send some one on the run, though, to drag him off when he overhauls your talented thief-waiter. . . . No, never mind!" he finished. "The man's safe."

As he talked he had been following the progress of the chase.

The waiter had glanced back over his shoulder, in mid-flight. That glance was his salvation. For it had shown him the murderously pursuing dog, almost at his very heels. With a howl, the man had made for a lawn oak whose wide lower limbs hung within eight feet of the turf.

With a spring as agile as had been his leap from the window, the fugitive hurled himself aloft, grasping the nearest limb and hauling himself up to a perch on it.

Fast as he was, he reached his haven barely in time. Lad sprang after him. High in air bounded the collie. His jaws found a wildly waving goal in the calf of the waiter's thin leg. There, his teeth all but met.

The waiter shrieked to high heaven. The dog dropped back to earth, his mouth full of bloody trouser-cloth.

"Apparently," said the Master, still addressing the jabbering manager, "your bright young friend prefers capture and jail to chancing a free-for-all race with Laddie, on the lawn or in the woods. Better send upstairs, to the present-room, for that plain-clothes man of yours. Here's one chance for him to earn his pay. When he gets under the tree, I'll call Lad off. Tell him not to get heart-trouble by hurrying. That thief will stay up there till Judgment Day, sooner than come down and 'shoot it out' with Lad."

It was two hours after midnight. Long ago the reception had ended. A few minutes ago, the last house guest had gone to bed.

The Mistress came out onto the veranda. She sat there in the waning moonlight, thinking over the day's varied and vehement events. To her appeared two dim-seen figures.

One was old Sunnybank Lad, newly washed and brushed and combed free of the salad and other edibles which had gummed his beautiful mahogany coat. The other was a bulky giant, clad from head to foot in disreputable khaki-and-leather, a vile-smelling pipe between his teeth.

The Master had reverted to type.

"Tired, dear?" he asked. "If you aren't, let's sit here quietly together a few minutes before we turn in—you and Laddie and I. Let's try to forget there are a bunch of house guests asleep upstairs, who won't be out of the way till tomorrow.

Let's try to imagine that we three are here alone together, at our own glorious Sunnybank, as we used to be in the days before the gruesome wedding-preparations began to wreck us."

He slumped into a big porch-chair that creaked with his vast weight, and he stretched out his puttee-girt legs and puffed long and lovingly at his smelly old pipe. His eyes roamed drowsily across the moon-bathed lawn and flower-borders, through the trees to the shimmering lake blow.

"The only place that's better than Sunnybank," he mused, his hand on Lad's silken head, his eyes ceasing to rove over his moonlit acres and resting happily on his wife—"the only place that's better than Sunnybank is heaven. And that's only because in heaven, according to the Bible, '*there is no marrying or giving in marriage*.' "

He fell silent. Presently he spoke again, more briskly:

"By the way, three newspapers have called me up, in the past hour, to ask me if it is true that Laddie discovered a thief stealing the wedding presents and killed him in defense of them. And the caterer people phoned that it turns out the fake waiter was a crook who picked the pocket of some one a reliable agency was sending them as an 'emergency man,' and stole his credentials, and got here on the strength of them. He has a prison record, the police say. The plain-clothes man remembers his passing through the present-room just after four o'clock, on some alleged errand. But as he was one of the regular force, the detective didn't watch him closely. They're all horribly sorry, they say, and they hope we won't make any of it public."

"We won't!" fervidly declared the Mistress. "I'm too ashamed of it all, to want to tell. It's the first time I've ever been ashamed of dear old Laddie. But I *was!*"

"Why?" argued the Master. "Everyone was praising him for his 'psychic skill' in knowing the waiter had stolen the necklace and just where he had hidden it. I didn't set them right. What was the use? Anyhow, it's the only interesting wedding I ever went to. And, after all, Laddie has a right to be hailed as a hero. Columbus blundered upon America, when he was looking for India. So he is immortal. Laddie blundered on a necklace, when he was looking for a jugular. Why shouldn't Laddie deserve just as much credit, in his way, as Columbus?"

Chapter Eight

DOG DAYS

FROM somewhere up the valley, one parching summer day, a little mongrel dog padded southward—driven by the restless urge of fretted nerves or by adventure or merely for a day's outing.

As he neared the village of Hampton, a speeding motor car grazed him. The dog was not killed, nor even dangerously hurt, but he was badly bruised, and his nerves, for the time, were wrecked. The impact flung him into a wayside ditch, where he was rolled over and over by sheer momentum, before he could tuck his legs under him again.

To his feet he reeled, breathless, mud-smeared, half delirious with terror. His lip had been scratched by a ditch stone. Ki-yi-ing, he fled blindly down the main street of the village.

Instantly there was more commotion than if a meteorite had crashed into the middle of the street. The sight of the frantically fleeing and yelping dog, bespattered with mud and with bloody tongue lolling, sent the villagers ascatter into the nearest doorways.

The street rang with the multiple bellow of "Mad dog!"—a cry which lurks ever in the fear swamps at the back of the human brain. There were shouts and screeches. One woman improved the opportunity by fainting, in the very middle of the roadway, as the mongrel galloped dazedly toward her.

Too near to skirt her plump and prostrate body, the dog cleared the fleshy obstacle in a single scrambling leap, and continued his flight.

To the end of her days, that woman will regard her escape from death as a heaven-sent miracle. On scampered the dog, intent only on getting away from the clamorous throng and as far as possible from the car that had struck him.

Ahead, perhaps a half-mile off, hills arose—hills covered with forest and underbrush and doubtless traversed by a cool brook or two—hills where a panic-tortured and hurt and thirsty and overheated little dog might hope to burrow into the green coolness, there to lie panting and unpestered until he should have rallied enough from pain and shock to make his way home.

The mongrel scampered for the hills at top speed.

A man rushed into a shop, and emerged brandishing a double-barreled shotgun. As the mongrel dashed past him, the man took snap-aim and loosed both barrels at the fugitive.

It would have seemed there could be no missing, at that point-blank range. Moreover, the man was a veteran hunter. But it is one thing to hit a bouncily galloping rabbit or a rocketing pheasant, and quite another thing to keep brain and muscles steady in face of the hideous peril of rabies.

One birdshot scratched the speeding dog's flank. The rest of the pellets smote the concrete roadbed at an angle which sent many of them ricocheting destructively against glass shop fronts on the other side of the street or whizzing around the running legs of such pedestrians as had not yet succeeded in diving to cover.

The roar of the dual report, the tinkling of glass, and the shrieks of two people whom the pellets had dusted in passing—these formed a momentary diversion and gave the poor mongrel a few seconds' leeway.

He fled the faster for the augmented racket behind him, reaching the railroad tracks a few jumps ahead of the fast-following hue-and-cry. A train was pulling into the station. The dog darted under it, and so onward, the cars blocking the roadway to his pursuers. In another five minutes he was safe among the hillside underbrush and was drinking long and deep from a brook-trickle between two rocks.

So he passes out of our story.

But he left behind him one of the recurrent mad-dog scares which scourge nearly every suburban community at least once in two or three years.

The local paper that week described graphically the perilous passage through Hampton's fair Main Street of a rabid dog, and told how he snapped to right and left at all that came in his path. Any one of those snaps, said the newspaper account, would have spelled death to such luckless person as the death-dealing teeth might have touched.

The woman who had fainted found she had grazed her left knee in falling. To be on the safe side, she took Pasteur treatment for the graze, lest it might be a bite.

In short, the conventional and time-dishonored mad-dog scare was on. The mayor and council passed resolutions. Life, for the next few months, was made all but unbearable for the village's dogs, all of which were on the suspected list until such time as sanity and continued immunity should wear away the dire memory of the horrendous danger. Then folk would calm down—till the next time.

Sunnybank drowsed among its green lawns and ancient oaks, a mile or more away from the village, and separated from it by meadows and by the lake. Few of Hampton's occasional excitements seeped to The Place across the intervening mile of water. Thus, news of the mad-dog scare caused not a ripple in that quiet abode of humans and of collies.

The Master saw the village council's warning notice stuck up in front of the post office, one day. He read its flaring-typed commands.

"It is the same kind of warning that is sent out in a thousand towns and villages," he commented. "It orders dogs to be leashed and muzzled and kept at home and all the rest of the usual rigmarole. But it doesn't say a word about having shallow dishes kept full of cool water, at shady spots, here and there, for thirsty dogs to drink from in hot weather. It would cost a lot less to supply cheap earthen dishes and to keep them filled, than to buy muzzles and leashes and to hold town meetings. Besides, it would do fifty times as much to solve the problem of dogs in hot weather. It's such a sanely simple plan that no council, anywhere, seems to have thought of adopting it."

The Mistress made sad reply:

"I'm sorry for the throng of harmless and friendly chum-dogs that will be shot before this scare dies down. We'd better not take any of our collies out in the car, till then. Some zealous citizen's bullet might find its way to one of them. People who are sane about everything else lose their heads about mad dogs. Laddie, you'll have to give up your motoring for a while."

The big collie was stretched luxuriously on the car's rear seat. At sound of his name, he smote the cushion with his plumed tail. But the note of worry in the Mistress's voice made him peer anxiously up at her. Lad could read voices and moods as readily as humans read books.

As the car drove through the village's neat main street on its way homeward, more than one passer-by glanced with frowning apprehension at the great collie lolling there on the rear seat. The rabies fear was abroad and all dogs were eyed askance.

Lad was quick to note the attitude of these people, even as a collie is ever swift to observe a sharp change of emotion in the humans around him.

Not that it interested Lad to any extent, this lowering aspect of folk who were wont to chirp friendlily at him as he passed. To him, the Mistress and the Master, in the order named, were his whole world. Outsiders did not mean anything to him.

If there were continents or oceans or giant mountain ranges scattered here and there over the surface of the earth, Lad did not know it. His world was bounded by the Ramapo hills which clustered around the sweet valley wherein lay Sunnybank. If there were other hills and valleys beyond that green circle, they meant nothing to him, nor were they any concern of his.

Lad's life, from puppyhood, had centered upon The Place—on its background of forest; on its soft lawns, oak shaded, that billowed downward to the lake; on the gray old vine-covered house wherein dwelt his two deities, the Mistress and the Master. Nothing else mattered.

True, he was on pleasant terms with all the people at Sunnybank. Also, he liked one or two guests who came thither. Incidentally, he had a gift-begotten esteem for the local butcher, at whose shop the car was even then halting.

It was Lad's habit to go into this shop with the Mistress when she did her marketing. The scent of such a vast quantity and variety of raw meat was an æsthetic delight to the dog. Also, the butcher had a most engaging way of shaving off a thin and wondrously appetizing slice from some loin of beef and of handing it to Lad.

The first time this had happened, the dog had drawn back in reluctant refusal as he stood statue-like beside the Mistress; and he had raised his eyes to her in mute appeal. For he had been taught from puppyhood to accept no food from strangers. But the Mistress had laughed and patted his classic head and had said to him:

"It's all right, Laddie."

Thus the collie had feasted joyously on the gift. Pleased with Lad's obedience and by the fact that he would stand for ten minutes at a time at the counter by the Mistress's side without so much as looking at the galaxy of meat displayed all around him, the butcher, thenceforward, had shaved off a thinly luscious slice of raw beef and had fed it to him whenever the dog happened to come into the shop with either of his owners.

Today, when the car stopped, the Master got out at the far side, to attend to an errand in a store across the street. The Mistress, studying her market memorandum, dismounted in front of the butcher's and went inside.

The day was cool and the shop's spring door was shut. She opened it and passed in. The door swung shut in Lad's very face as he trotted after her. He was barred out of this beloved stopping-place where gifts of beef were dispensed.

Moreover, the slamming door had hit and stung his sensitive nostrils. The Mistress, still studying an undecipherable item on the memorandum, had forgotten him.

Left alone on the sidewalk, Lad peered wistfully at the shut door and pondered in sadness on the joys he was missing. Then, as he could not hope to get in, he turned about to follow the Master into the shop on the far side of the roadway.

As he was halfway across the wide street, a child came trotting toward him from the other direction—a fluffy wisp of a girl, little more than a baby.

The youngster evidently had been warned to be careful in crossing thoroughfares, for she had paused at the curb, looking up and down the highway for possible traffic. Seeing the way clear, she started across, in a pattering dash of speed.

She swerved rather wide, to avoid the big brown dog which she saw approaching her from in front of the butcher shop. Both of her parents had talked to her, long and dramatically, at breakfast, about the untold horrors of danger from rabies, and had cautioned her not to go near any dog she might see in the street.

Ordinarily it would have been great fun for her to run up to this huge and gentle-looking collie and pat him. But the terrors of her parents' lecture were still fresh in her baby mind. Wherefore, with a pringling of dread, she made a swinging détour which should keep her far out of the way of the presumably dangerous beast.

The swerve from a wholly imaginary peril brought her into the track of a very real menace—a Thing that crushes out and mutilates more human lives in a single year than have all the real or supposedly rabid dogs in the past three centuries.

From an intersecting by-road whizzed a motor car guided by a speed-mad boy who was still driving with a "learner's license" and who had had but three ill-assimilated lessons at the steering-wheel. Out of the by-road and into the broader Main Street he drove, at a pace which tilted his car dangerously. Stepping on the gas, he prepared to take full advantage of the smooth concrete roadbed he had come out onto.

Then and only then did the fool catch sight of a wisp of a white-clad child directly in front of him.

As she saw the car swing into the apparently empty street the tiny girl stopped dead short in mid-road, dazed and uncertain.

But she was no more palsied of brain than was the novice motorist when he saw her. He stamped with all his might on what he thought was the footbrake.

It was the accelerator.

To save his soul he could not remember which way to twitch the steering-wheel. His icy hands clung to it impotently. He screeched in ear-splitting panic horror.

All this in the space of a single breath.

Then it was that Lad did what a thousand other wise and fearless dogs have done in like crises.

With the swiftness of light he launched himself forward bearing down upon the dizzy child with express-train speed.

Snatching her by one baby shoulder—firmly, yet with a grip that did not so much as bruise her —he continued his thunderbolt dash; even as once he had bolted across the track in front of a locomotive, with the unsainted Massoud between his jaws. Dog and child were all but grazed by the left fender of the car as it flashed past them.

Nearly everywhere, the carrying of a pistol or other lethal weapon is a felony punishable by imprisonment. It is a wise and just law which ordains this, although it has been computed that not one pistol-shot in five reaches its human target and not one in twelve causes death. Still, the criminal law steps in right sternly to avert that slight off-chance of murder; by banning the carrying or even the possession of such weapons.

Yet any reckless half-wit may drive a motor car if he has barely sense enough to pass a very simple examination to prove he knows how to handle it. In other words, there is no legal barrier against the use of a weapon more deadly than fifty revolvers or knives.

People who are not mentally fit to drive an ox-wagon are permitted to handle an engine of destruction weighing from a ton to four tons—an irresistible monster with a possible speed of nearly a hundred miles an hour.

A heedless high-school boy—a feather-brained flapper—a drunkard—a degenerate speed-maniac—any or all of these are allowed to drive a gigantic metal projectile of death, through crowded streets or along peaceful country roads. The examination they have taken in order to get a driver's license has made no test of their reliability or even of their sanity. They are turned loose with full chance to kill or to maim.

Pistols must be paid for with spot-cash. But expensive cars may be bought by all but penniless folk, who thereafter remain in continuous financial bondage in order to pay the various instalments on the purchase they cannot afford; and who are given power of life and death over the rest of mankind. Folk of ampler means receive the same killing power, plus an added recklessness engendered by their greater ability to pay any fine their bad driving may incur.

When a motorist is arrested for speeding or for making a wrong turn or for passing traffic signals —any of which faults might readily cause loss of life to one or more pedestrians or to other drivers —he is fined from $1 up. When a timid householder is caught carrying a pistol for self-defense, he faces a prison term.

One-hundred-and-twenty-thousand Americans lost their lives in the World War. One-hundred-and-ninety-thousand Americans during the past ten years have been killed by motor cars. Each year's motor death-list is appallingly larger than was the previous year's.

Solemnly ineffective editorials and other preachments are written every day, deploring wonderingly the fast-increasing list of motor-casualties and suggesting that somebody do something about it. (Like this digressive little preachment of mine, if you like.)

But "somebody" does *not* "do something about it." Meantime, the number of pleasure cars is increasing incredibly fast, and with it the motor killings and the crop of hare-brained potential killers.

The Juggernaut crushed out a few lives—lives of Hindus who were eager to die beneath its wheels and thus enter a Higher Life. Yet throughout the centuries, the Juggernaut has thus been regarded as the symbol of destruction. The motor car's red record makes the Juggernaut's feeble exploits look like those of a baby-carriage.

And so back to our story:

Lad had done his work. He had thrust the little girl out of the path of death. He and she had been missed by the merciless car by scarcely a hair's-breadth as it roared over the spot where, an instant earlier, the child had been crouching.

Somebody from an upper window screamed loud and repeatedly.

Immediately the quiet morning street was filled with people. Everyone was talking at once. The child was sprawling in the gutter, unhurt, but crying in fright, while above her a great dog stood; trying to lick her tear-blotched little face in a frantic effort to comfort her.

The man who had been screaming so industriously from the upper window now bawled down to the gathering crowd:

"She was crossing the street. That big cur

jumped out and bit her, something terrible, right in the shoulder, and then he slung her into the gutter. I saw it all. A feller going past in a car must have seen it, too. He drove right past the two of them. He could bear witness to it, only he never stopped."

The crowd shrank back from Lad. The child's mother pushed her way through the receding group, brandishing an axe-handle she had seized as she ran.

Made fearless by her love for her baby, she snatched up the weeping child, apparently from between the very jaws of the rabid monster. Made fiercely vengeful by that same mother-love, she swung the axe-handle aloft and brought it down crashingly, if awkwardly, at the dog's head.

With the incredible quickness and self-protective instinct of a collie, Lad shifted sidewise, wolf-fashion. The axe-handle, which might well have brained him, merely glanced painfully from the edge of his shoulder and broke in two as it smote the curbing.

Had a strange man—or indeed any man save only the Master—struck thus at him, Lad would have been at the assailant before the latter could brace himself for the counter-attack. But this was a woman. The dog showed all his formidable white teeth in a snarl of utter loathing. Then, wheeling, he trotted toward the shop into which the Master had vanished.

But Lad was not to escape so easily from the results of having risked his life that a human child might not be crushed to death.

A fist-size stone sang close to his ear and smashed the nearest shop window. A stick grazed his hip, hurting cruelly. In hot anger, the dog spun about to face his pursuers.

So sudden was the whirl and so threatening was his aspect that the chorus of "Mad dog!" shouters recoiled for an instant with ridiculous suddenness.

One of them was leveling a pistol, as Lad stood at bay, when the Mistress forced her way through the press to her dog's side and placed her own fragile body between him and the avengers.

Turning back, at the counter, when a query of the butcher's had reminded her that Lad was not in the shop with her, she had reached the glass door in time to see her collie snatch the child from under the very wheels of the speeding car and deposit her gently in the gutter. The door was jammed, and the Mistress had to wrestle with it for several seconds before she could get it open and could make her way through the ever-larger crowd to Lad's rescue.

Something of this she was trying to explain, when the Master came out of the shop on the opposite side of the road from the butcher's. He had heard the multiple outcry, and he reached the sidewalk in time to see an angrily gesturing clump of people surrounding his wife and his dog.

Through the human pack he clove his charging way, with more rough vigor and manhandling than ever in his earlier days he had displayed on the football field.

Ensued a most painful and noisy scene, in which the Mistress and Lad were the only participants to keep their tempers and their voices within bounds. It ended with the Master picking up the dog, bodily, and carrying him through the bunch of muttering and milling men to the car, the Mistress following close behind.

"All our lives here," grumbled the Master, as they set off for home, "we've been on mighty pleasant terms with our neighbors. They are as white and fine a lot of people as ever were born—or they were till they got this scare about every animal that moves on four legs. But in the past five minutes I suppose I've made enemies of half of them. That's the rotten part of it: One can spend thirty years in building up friendships that can be wrecked forever in thirty seconds."

"I never heard *anyone* use such utterly horrible language as you used to them!" exclaimed the Mistress, almost in awe. "Luckily, I couldn't understand what most of it meant, but I understood enough to make me wonder where you have been keeping it all these years. If I hadn't been so furiously indignant about dear old Laddie here ——"

"I'm sorry!" said the Master, ashamed of his crazy burst of temper. "And I'm sorry if I upset and stepped on one or two men while I was trying to butt my way through to you. But when I saw them crowding around you and Lad, all yelling and ——"

"Did you hear that woman—the baby's mother—saying over and over again that she is going to get a warrant to have Laddie shot?" asked the Mistress, with an involuntary shudder and a whitening of face. "She ——"

"Yes!" grunted the Master. "And I couldn't do or say anything to her. For the same reason that Lad let her alone when she tried to brain him. I wish her husband had been there. But don't let her threat bother you. Sunnybank is outside the borough limits. Besides, the borough police are mighty good fellows. I'll phone the chief, when we get home, and I'll tell him the whole story. He'll understand, and he'll see nothing is done. Just the same, Lad will have to stay on our own side of the lake for the next month or two. So will the other Sunnybank collies. The dog days are not the time of year when a dog has his day."

Lad heard, but, being only a real-life collie, of course Lad did not understand. Motoring was a joy to him, as it is to nine collies out of ten.

He was destined to innumerable disappointments during the weeks to come, when he would dance out to the car as it came up from the garage, only to be met by a curt:

"Not today, Laddie. Go back."

The summer had begun, hot and dry. It waxed hotter and drier. Drouth lay over the land like a blight. Streams dried. The lake sank several inches, and was weedy and warm and all but stagnant.

The once-shaven turf of the lawns was allowed to grow long and uneven, lest the cutting of the grass should cause its sun-exposed roots to die. It changed from emerald to a dirty brownish gray.

The sun hung like a copper ball in a sickly copper sky. The nights were breathless, while heat lightning played and flickered all along the western heavens—a false lightning that brought no blessèd rain in its wake. Not for years had the North Jersey hinterland known such drouth and such unending heat.

The humans of The Place made themselves as nearly comfortable as they might and drew upon their philosophy to withstand the ordeal. Sunnybank's superintendent, Robert Friend, mourned keenly the drying up of the flower roots and of almost the entire vegetable garden. The laborers sweated sullenly over their hopeless tasks of keeping alive the gardens and garnering shriveled crops.

But it was the collies which suffered most. And it was Lad that suffered most, of all the collies.

Nature arranges that the average long-haired dog shall begin shedding his coat in springtime, and shall be all but coatless during the hot months. With the coming of the autumn coolness, the thick winter coat begins to grow luxuriantly. Yet once in a while, for some reason, a collie will hold his winter coat until September before he begins to shed it.

Such a collie was Lad. At a time when Bruce and Wolf and Bobby and Lady and young Gray Dawn were half naked, Lad was still carrying the enormous outer and under coat which by rights should have been his in January. Not for another month or more would he begin to shed in real earnest—and to strew the floors and rugs and furniture, and the trousers legs and skirts of the household, with tufts and strands of dead hair.

As a result, he weltered and panted under such a burden as might a human who, in hottest midsummer, should undertake to wear a fifteen-pound coonskin overcoat above a suit of winter clothing.

Wise was the big dog, and philosophical withal. He did not let the heat and the flies and the drouth get on his nerves and scourge him to irritability and quarrelsomeness; as did some of the younger collies, whose tempers were assuming a razor edge as the torrid summer swooned on.

One of the coolest spots at Sunnybank was Laddie's "cave" under the piano in the music-room. Here he lay, for the most part, throughout the hottest hours of the day, leaving that semi-comfortable nook only to sally out occasionally to the five-gallon jardinière which always stood in a corner of the music-room and which was filled twice a day with fresh cold water for the house dogs. Lad would drink long and deeply, then return to his cave.

At meal-times he came always into the dining-room, to his place on the floor to the left of the Master's chair, and in the evenings he strolled with his two human deities in their tour of the stricken lawns and gardens. Early in the mornings, too, he would swim and wallow in the lake, before the pitiless sun could dissipate the tinge of coolness which night had brought to the water.

Yet, ever, in the hottest part of the day, he was on his feet, ready and eager, if the Mistress or the Master went outdoors. The heat and discomfort meant nothing to Lad, compared with the privilege of accompanying one or both of them on the longest or most broiling walk. Fortunately, neither of them would permit him to go along when they were forced to brave the midday heat; but ordered him back to his cave.

The kennel dogs dug deep holes in the earth beneath their raised houses; and lay there, panting, in the shade, while the sun scorched the world. Before sunrise and after sunset, nowadays, the Master gave them their daily cross-country runs. And even then the runs were shortened. In spite of all that could be done for their comfort, they suffered cruelly from the eternal hot drouth.

With grim care the Master and the superintendent watched them. It is at such times of climatic stress that dogs occasionally become sick or half crazed with the heat, unless they are kept quiet and as cool as may be. Hence the superstition that rabies walks rampant during the so-called dog days. Almost never is it true rabies. Nearly always it is some malady or other due to exposure or over-exertion or wrong feeding, on the part of the humans in charge.

Lad bore it all like the calm thoroughbred that he was. As long as he could be near the Mistress and the Master, he was happy, in spite of weather or of any other discomfort. But at last even that solace was to be taken from him. On a morning in August the Master said to his wife:

"This is getting on your nerves, just as it's getting on mine. Let's drop everything and motor up to the Berkshires. If it isn't comfortable there, we'll keep on till we find some region that is. But Vanderslice wrote me from Stockbridge that there is a spell of cool weather up there, just now. I'm going to wire for reservations at the Red Lion. Can you clear things away so as to be able to start at daylight tomorrow? A week in the Berkshires will brace you more than anything else could."

Accordingly, to his dismay, at dawn next morning Lad saw suitcases and other luggage loaded into one of the cars, and saw the Mistress and the Master come down to breakfast dressed for traveling. Seldom did they leave the collie that loved them; and these few periods of loneliness were a mental anguish to him. Being only a dog, Lad had no way of knowing his vanished deities ever would come back to him.

Pitifully he followed the Mistress upstairs and down and everywhere she moved, as she prepared for the departure. He refused to be consoled when she patted him and when she said she and the Master would be back in a few days. His classic head drooped. His plumed tail hung disconsolate. He was the picture of utter misery.

"Oh, I hate to see anything as unhappy as Laddie is!" mourned the Mistress. "I do wish we could take him along!"

"We can't," said the Master. "Don't worry about him. He'll be all right. Everyone here is devoted to him. They'll spoil him and pet him and overfeed him, the way they always do when our backs are turned. He'll get on splendidly. Won't you, Laddie?"

For once, Lad gave no sign of having heard his own name. Forlorn and desolate he stood on the porch, watching the car chug its way up the drive to the main road above. Then, sighing, he slouched back to his cave under the piano, and lay down with a dull thump of his heavy body, stretched there with his head between his absurdly small white forepaws, his deep-set eyes full of sorrow.

The Master had been right. Everyone on The Place liked Lad, above all the other dogs. During that first day of his owners' absence, the house servants made excuse, one after another, to drop into the music-room to pat him and to bring him forbidden lumps of sugar and other dainties. When he strolled out to the stables in the afternoon, one of the laborers gave him a hunk of cold pork saved out for this purpose from the man's own dinner pail.

Robert Friend took him for a long walk in the comparative cool of the moonlit evening. This after the superintendent had been toiling from dawn to dusk, with the men, in the torrid hayfield.

With grave courtesy Lad accepted these attentions. But his heart was heavy within him. The heat, during the next day or two, seemed to strike deeper than ever before into his very heart. He was tired and listless and morbidly unhappy. He was grieving for his absent gods. Nor did the contraband diet, showered on him by everyone in sight, contribute to his general health.

Then, on the fourth evening, he was not hungry for the regulation evening-feed dish which formed his one daily meal.

The superintendent had been feeding him, personally, since the Mistress and the Master had gone away, instead of leaving the task to one of the men. On this evening, seeing how little appetite the dog had—and unaware of the many dainties slipped surreptitiously to him that day by the maids—the superintendent went up to his own house and took from its refrigerator a dish of cold mutton stew.

This he brought down to the stables and gave

to Lad in place of the almost untouched dish of break-and-milk.

The dog was not hungry, but he was egregiously fond of cooked mutton. Wherefore, he began mincingly to pick out various morsels from the plate of stew, and to eat them with more epicurean relish than hunger. He rolled the food slowly about his mouth, instead of bolting it.

Of a sudden he drew back from the plate with something like a shiver, his eyes roving worriedly toward the superintendent as if in sudden pain.

Robert Friend bent over him, and noted that the powerful jaws no longer closed, but were held half open. Nor would they come together again. They remained fixed, at that impossible angle from each other, the upper and lower jaw, as if carven into immobility.

Friend jumped to the telephone and called up three veterinaries in succession. All three, by some black chance, were out of town. He riffled the pages of the telephone book for the names of other veterinaries than these three who were familiar to The Place and its dogs. At last he found one—a stranger—who was at home and who promised to drive over at once.

"That's the way with vets," the superintendent complained as he hung up the receiver. "Those of them that are any good are always kept too busy to be home when you want them. The ones that are sitting around their offices waiting for calls are mostly no good."

Back he went to the stricken dog. Lad had turned away from his dinner and was standing above a water-pail. Vainly he was trying to drink. But a dog cannot drink when his jaws are fixed wide apart. Already his pink tongue was darkening, from thirst and dryness.

The veterinary—a spruce young man with a sprucely new college diploma—drove into the grounds with gratifying promptness.

Gravely and expertly he examined the stricken collie, first donning a pair of padded leather gloves with long sleeve protectors. He pulled back Lad's eyelids and peered into the painfully exposed eyes. He took his temperature and found him feverish. Glumly he noted the swelling tongue and the posture of the parted jaws. Then, turning to the anxiously waiting superintendent, the vet made known his verdict.

"Rabies!" he announced. "Dumb rabies."

"*No!*" shouted Friend. "The Boss says not one dog in a million has rabies. He says ——"

"This is dumb rabies," repeated the vet. "A pronounced case. The collie must be shot, at once."

"He'll be shot when the Boss says to have him

shot!" declared the superintendent. "And not till then. Not if you get all the court orders in New Jersey. And if the Boss says he's got to be shot, he'll have to get somebody else than me to do it. I'd rather shoot a dozen vets than shoot the big dog here. He's—he's a pal of mine, Laddie is. And nobody's going to shoot him, either."

Followed two days of stark anguish for Sunnybank Lad, and stark unhappiness for The Place's humans.

The Master had not left any address whence he and the Mistress might be summoned. Friend could only wait. He locked Lad in the largest box stall, and did for him all that any mortal could do—which was nothing.

Daily, the vet called, with renewed demand that the dumb-rabies victim be slain. Daily, Robert Friend refused, with growing vehemence. The superintendent's heart was sick for the sufferings of the great collie.

By no flinching or frantic struggle did Lad give sign of the torment that was his. Hour after hour he paced restlessly about the box stall, pausing every few minutes to lean over the water pail in fruitless effort to drink. His spirit was dead within him, and he was racked by awful thirst-throes throughout the hot days and nights,

The pain added to the heat in making his slake-less thirst unbearable.

His two gods were gone. They had left him to his torture alone, forsaken. All he could do was to bear it all as a thoroughbred should, and to keep iron-firm grip on his jangled nerves and to resist the mad longing to hurl himself about in writhing hysteria.

The Mistress and the Master were on their way home. As they passed through the village, on their way to The Place, they stopped at the post office for the afternoon mail.

Out from the office came a woman, who promptly forgot her wrapped-up weekly newspaper and her two circulars, at sight of the car's occupants. She scuttled across to them, her face reddening and her eyes growing smaller.

The Mistress recognized her as the mother of the little girl whom Lad had shoved from the motor's path—the mother who had sought to repay the mighty service by braining the collie with an axe handle.

"*Well!*" shrilled the woman. "Maybe you folks won't be turning up your noses so hard at rabies, now that your own dog has got it! I said to my husband, I said, 'It's a judgment on him for trying to bite our baby!' I said. I said to him ——"

The Mistress heard no more. The car was in flying motion with a suddenness that jarred every atom of its machinery. With unwonted disregard for every speed law, the Mistress drove homeward at a pace which consumed the intervening mile in something short of record time. Down the driveway flashed the machine, swaying perilously at the curves.

From the stables, at sound of its approach, came the superintendent. The veterinary and another man were with him. Friend left them and came running forward.

"That vet's here again!" he called out. "And this time he's got some kind of state official with him. I've been staving them off for half an hour. I wouldn't unlock the stable and let them in to Laddie. They say they'll have me arrested for ——"

The car was racing to the stable, taking scant account of the two strangers who had to hop nimbly out of its path. In another five seconds Friend was unlocking the door and the Mistress and the Master were hurrying to the box stall.

Lad had heard the coming of their motor before it had passed the lodge gates. To his feet he had staggered; from the sick lethargy in which he had lain all day except when pain and thirst had goaded him into action. To the box-stall door he lurched; feebly trying to wave his sagging tail and to catch sight of his deities through fast-dimming eyes.

Concisely, and speaking fast, Friend was telling what had befallen. Brushing past the excited vet and the state official, the Mistress ran into the stall, the Master at her heels.

Lad stumbled toward her, his deep eyes rapturously happy through their veil of suffering, his blackened tongue hanging limp from between his parted jaws.

The Mistress did not waste the fraction of an instant, after her first swiftly appraising glance at the tortured dog. She dropped on her knees beside him, thrusting her white fingers exploratively in between the transfixed jaws.

"Careful, there!" bawled the vet, pushing forward and clawing the kneeling woman's shoulder. "If you've any tiniest abrasion on your hand, it's death to touch his mouth. Besides, he may bite——"

The Master spun the babbling veterinary to a far corner of the stall, snarling at him:

"If the dog can't get his jaws shut, how is he going to bite her? Keep your slimy hands off her! She——"

"Here it is!" broke in the Mistress, excitedly. "I knew it would be on one side or the other. It's on the left side. But I haven't strength enough in my fingers to ——"

"Let me try it," said the Master, taking her place beside the patiently quiescent collie. "Left side, you said? I —— Here it is."

He gave a sharp wrench, exerting all his force. Then he withdrew his hand from between the jaws that fell shut behind it. Between his thumb and forefinger the Master held a piece of mutton knucklebone, oblong and perhaps a half inch thick and an inch long.

"This was jammed in the hinge of his jaws, on the left," he reported to the superintendent. "It held them apart as securely as if a wedge had been driven there. No wonder he couldn't get his mouth shut! He —— Hold on there, old chap!" he interrupted himself, catching Lad by the ruff. "That's enough for now. In five minutes you can have a little more."

For the dog had reeled over to the water-pail and was drinking in mad zest, plunging his foreface far into the cool liquid and lapping with all the slight power remaining to his swelled and blackened tongue.

"Too much of that, all at once, after three days of thirst, would be about as bad for him as the dumb rabies he didn't have," the Master explained to Friend, adding: "Will you warm a quart of milk and bring it here? Beat some raw eggs in it. I can give it to him, little by little, instead of the water. It will be time enough for him to drink his fill when he's more braced up."

"I don't understand this!" began the discomfited vet, importantly. "I still maintain he has ——"

"Both of us knew it couldn't be dumb rabies, or any other kind of rabies, as soon as we heard it came upon him while he was eating," explained the Mistress. "No dog would be eating a single mouthful, with a dangerous disease setting in. Then Robert said it was mutton stew, and this isn't the first or the second time we've known of mutton-bone chunks getting wedged into the hinge of a dog's jaw. It used to happen every now and then to Jean, and she'd always run straight to my husband or myself to have us pry it loose."

"Yes," growled the Master, letting Lad dip his nose in the pail again for one more exasperatingly brief drink, "and it isn't the first or the hundredth time a callow vet has seen that same condition and said it was dumb rabies and ordered a dog shot. Keep on as you've begun, and most likely you'll get on a town council, some day, and have a chance to frame nice rules for mad-dog scares. In the meantime, don't let me detain you from bungling some other case you may have been called in on. Clear out. Take your boy friend with the tin badge along with you.

"That's enough, Laddie!" continued the Master. "You can have some warm milk in a minute. Here it comes now. And there go your two would-be executioners. Three solid days and nights of no water or food, in red-hot weather, and with no chance to swallow or to close your aching jaws! Any other dog would have gone to smash under it. How about some of this milk? It's food and drink together."

The coppery sun had been blotted from the coppery sky by a fast-forming bank of ink-dark clouds. A splitting roar of thunder shook the stable to its foundation. A gust of almost chilly breeze swept over the parched ground. With it came a drumming downpour of rain that swelled into a sluicing torrent.

The drouth was broken and with it was broken the hideous spell of torrid heat.

Lad lifted his head from the half-emptied bowl of eggs and milk. Deep into his lungs he drew the cool and damp air. Life was seeping back into him. Once more he could breathe and eat and drink. Once more his adored Mistress and

Master were at home with him. The reaction was too much for the dog's habitual stateliness.

Growling in terrific menace, he stooped and caught the Mistress's little foot between his mighty jaws, exerting not a tenth-of-an-ounce's pressure as he pretended to shake it viciously to and fro.

In his weakened state the effort was almost too much for him. But, as ever, it made the Mistress laugh. And that was precisely what Laddie had sought to make her do. For there had been tears in her dear voice, try as she would to steady it. Lad would have undergone fiftyfold the exertion of this feeble romp with her, for the sake of driving away her unhappiness.

Chapter Nine

"HOW'S ZAT?"

THERE had been a whipping gale from the forty-mile distant Atlantic Ocean—a gale which had roared and rioted all night, at airplane speed, across the lawns and woods of The Place; strewing the turf and driveways and paths with riven branches and windrows of leafy twigs.

Now and again a seeming stanch big tree fell with a swish and then a rending crash, leaving a gap it would take fifty years to fill.

The hurricane yelled across the lake, whipping it to white froth and sending torrents of spray high over the green-clad banks. It shook the stanch old vine-bowered gray stucco house—the house that had withstood gallantly seventy-odd years of tempest.

At the tremor of the stout oaken beams and the creak of joist and sill, Sunnybank Lad got up from a rug at the stair foot—the rug whereon Gray Dawn later kept his nightly indoor vigil—and he made a tour of the whole interior of the house, padding noiselessly from room to room, alert, on guard against any possible menace to this loved home of his or to the Mistress and the Master who were his deities.

Wolf, The Place's official watchdog, lay serenely on his front-porch mat, throughout the storm.

In all weathers this was Wolf's sentry box. He feared nothing on earth. Tough of body and thick of coat, he cared little for wind or for cold. Only once did he start up, in watchful interest, while the gale was at its worst. That was when something smote the side of the veranda with a crash and tumbled to the porch floor with a heavy flapping which presently ceased.

Wolf strolled over to investigate. There, white wings asprawl, lay a dead sea gull, its head bashed in by contact with the side of the house, against which the tempest had slammed it.

Wolf smelled at the alien thing, in sad inquisitiveness. He had not the bird-lore to know that at this season there were no sea gulls within twenty-odd miles of The Place; and that the storm must indeed have been overwhelming, to drive this strong fowl, as helpless as a sheet of paper, before it, all that distance.

Then, just before daybreak, there was a dull, yet abrupt boom, far off. Immediately thereafter the whole earth rocked and every windowpane in Sunnybank House danced in its setting.

Fifteen miles away, a powder factory had had one of the semi-occasional explosions which make the powder-works-dotted hinterland of northern New Jersey less popular as a region of homes than otherwise so lovely a region might be.

Bits of explosion-wreckage—some of it in the form of seven-pound boards—fluttered noisily into the lake or on the lawns. One of them knocked down a policeman in the mile-distant village. Truly, this was a night of violence and of phenomena!

At dawn, the gale dropped to a softly caressing breeze. The sun came up over a peaceful summer world. Nature seemed thoroughly ashamed of herself for last night's gust of wild temper; and, by smiling appealingly on her children, to be seeking to make amends or to win forgiveness for the crazy outburst.

The Mistress and the Master were at breakfast, as usual, in a vine-shaded corner of the veranda; with Lad lying at the Master's left side, as ever, on the stone-flagged floor.

Lad had accompanied him on a before-breakfast tour of the grounds, during a rueful examination of the storm-wrought damage to tree and vine and shrub and outbuildings.

Together they had watched one of the men bury the crushed sea gull, in the course of "redding up" after the gale. Together they had come to the waiting breakfast. The Mistress and her husband talked much of the storm, during the meal, lamenting its wanton destruction of flowers and of age-honored oak and elm branches.

"I lay awake for hours, listening to it," the Mistress was saying. "It sounded as if a whole worldful of mischief-sprites were let loose and were trying to see how much harm they could do us mortals. All manner of black spirits seemed to be abroad! I was wide awake when that powder-blast roused you. . . . I wonder how soon we can find how many people it killed or maimed. I telephoned, but ——"

A sharp growl, as of protest, from Lad, interrupted her.

Subconsciously, for several minutes, the Mistress had heard an ever-louder cawing among the upper branches of one of the hundred-year-old giant oaks down near the lake. Apparently, a battalion of crows were holding a conference there, as sometimes they did. But this conference was more like a wholesale rackety dispute.

At last, it had attracted even lofty old Lad's attention and had brought from his furry throat a disapproving growl. Lad hated noise and confusion. Confusion and noise were rife, up there in the tree-top, and the din was swelling louder and louder. The Mistress and the Master turned to look.

Twenty or twenty-five crows were flapping about hysterically, or were lighting on branch after branch. All their attention was centered on a single crow which perched crouchingly on the dead tip of an upper limb. He clung feebly to the swaying perch, and seemed either injured or exhausted. The other crows were cawing wrathfully at him and making threatful swoops toward his limb-tip.

Then they all flung themselves upon him; pecking, clawing, beating him with their black pinions. Under that multiple onslaught, the victim tumbled from his perch, thudding to the earth far below. The cloud of crows flocked down to the slaughter.

The Mistress caught up a table napkin. Waving this futile weapon, she ran toward the scene of assassination, followed by the Master. But Sunnybank Lad was far ahead, before they had traveled a dozen steps.

The dog's chivalrous heart may have been stirred at sight of one weakling fighting against such desperate odds; or he may have sensed the

Mistress's wish to save the luckless crow. In any case, he sped toward the assailants at top speed.

As he swept across the lawn and down the slope, others of the Sunnybank dogs caught sight of him. Noting his speed and his evident excitement, they joined in the run—Bruce, Wolf, Bobby, and big young Gray Dawn.

Down the hill swept the five dogs, like a cavalry charge, Laddie well in the lead.

Behind the canine quintet hurried the Mistress and the Master. At sight of the rescue party, the punitive crows drew away, fluttering reluctantly from their prey and either perching on the lowest branches of the near-by trees or continuing to fly low in preparation for another swoop.

The crow they had been trying to kill had put up the best possible fight, considering his exhaustion. Now he was half sitting, half lying backward, supported by his spread tail and by his outstretched wings. He was bleeding. Many of his feathers were lost. He was a wobegone spectacle.

Yet he did not flinch as the dogs galloped up. Instead, he braced himself on the supporting tail-and-wing quills, and smote feebly at them with his once-formidable black beak.

The collies circled him, nosing, in mild curiosity and with no rancor at all, at the stricken creature. All except young Sunnybank Gray Dawn.

Dawn was little more than a puppy and he had a genius for getting into trouble. This, plus an unquenchable curiosity, often led him forward when the other dogs had sense enough to pause. Now, with playfully clownish interest, he nosed the panting and bleeding crow.

As reward he received a peck on the nostrils which wrung a snarl of wrathful pain and astonishment from him. Before he could carry the matter further, old Laddie stepped authoritatively between him and the crow. Then the Mistress and the Master came up.

The crows, just overhead, continued to circle low, angrily and with deafening caws. The dogs were pressing close around the stricken victim. The hapless creature glared up at the two approaching humans with not one shred of fear.

Then a wholly impossible thing happened.

The wounded bird let his eyes roll defiantly around the circle of dogs and up to the swooping crows. After which his gaze returned, almost twinklingly, to the man and woman. Bracing himself afresh on his sagging quills, he ceased panting long enough to say with startling distinctness:

"Well, *well*, WELL! How's zat?"

The effect of the miracle was electric. The dogs shrank back, trembling, on their haunches. The cloud of crows, overhead, burst into terrified squalls and flew wildly away in every direction, as if trying to put as much distance as possible between themselves and this demon in guise of a bird which spoke with human voice.

The Master stared with mouth ajar. The Mistress only laughed. She went forward without a trace of hesitation and picked the wounded thing up and held it lightly between her hands.

The crow seemed to recognize her sure touch and to know she was an inspired handler of all manner of animals. For his terrible beak made no move to resent the clasp of her little hands.

The dogs, as one, moved forward, though with visible reluctance; as if to guard their adored Mistress against hurt from the talking bird. Lad, as ever, reached her side first. He stood with upcurled lip, showing a glint of his terrible fangs, ready to snatch and crush the bird if it should seek to harm her.

Turning to her open-mouthed husband, the Mistress said:

"Don't you see? It's a talking crow. We used to have one up at Hampden, when I was a girl. (It used to say perfectly horrible things. But that was all right, for it didn't know what they meant.) People do something to their tongues—I don't know just what, and I wouldn't do it if I knew—to make them able to talk. Then they teach them words. There's almost nothing a pet crow can't be taught, if it is taught early enough and if it will take the bother to learn."

"But——"

"This one may have been a pet, somewhere over at the powder works," she went on. "Or it may have been blown here from somewhere even farther, by the hurricane. It got away or it was blown away from its owner. It landed on that tree, up there, all tired out. Then, either because it was a stranger or because it was a pet, these wild crows all attacked it. I'm going to take it up to the house and wash those cuts on its head and breast and give it something to eat and drink and a place to rest. Then we'll let it loose again, to fly home if it wants to. . . . Witch hazel and some warm water and soft rags, please, Tino," she broke off to hail one of The Place's day laborers who had drawn near. "Bring them to the veranda as quickly as you can. I——"

"Well, *well*, WELL!" hailed the crow as the laborer came closer. "How's zat?"

The man crossed himself and fled.

"Your crow friend has cost us a fairly good workman, I'm afraid," commented the Master.

"Unless I'm mistaken, Tino has started on a dead run, to Robert, for his money. Down in the Italian settlement we'll be looked on, after this, as sorcerers or as something else that superstitious folk won't work for. I suppose you will be wanting to keep the miserable creature as a pet! We've had about everything except a crow and a rhinoceros, and each was worse than the last. Do you think there's anything else the creature can say? Try him."

"Zat!" croaked the crow, from between the Mistress's gentle hands. "How's zat? Well, *well*, WELL! How's *zat?*"

"He means, 'How is that?' " translated the Mistress. "He was taught by some one whose English wasn't at all like Cæsar's wife. It isn't the crow's fault he talks like a tough. I'm going to call him, 'Zat,' I think. It's one of the words he knows, so he ought to answer to it more easily than to a strange name. He ——"

"That means you've made up your mind to keep him!" fumed the Master, in despair. "I knew it! I knew it by the way you picked him up. We've had a raccoon and a fox and a flea-some monkey, and a kind Providence has removed them, one by one, from us. But they say crows live to be a hundred years old. This one is wished on us for keeps."

"We won't keep him if you don't want us to," said the Mistress. "Honestly we won't, dear. I'll just dress his hurts and feed him and let him rest and then set him free. He must be pretty young. Because the only way to train crows and teach them to talk is to take them from the nest. And if they live to be a hundred ——"

"A thought for the day!" grumbled the Master. "He may be ten or eleven years old, even now. That means he can't have more than ninety years longer to live, at most. I'll be rather an old man by that time, of course. But it gives me something to live for and to look forward to. . . . Edgar Allan Poe had one of the pesky things, too, didn't he?" the man continued, as he and the Mistress started back toward the house; the ill-at-ease collies trooping uncomfortably along behind them.

"A raven," corrected the Mistress, adding:

" '*Doubtless,' said I, 'what it utters is its only stock and store,*
Caught from some unhappy master whom unmerciful disaster
Followed fast and followed faster; till his songs one burden bore
Of "Never—nevermore"!'

"Perhaps, after all," she suggested, "we'd better advertise Zat. His owner may ——"

"No," contradicted her husband. "Let's give his 'unhappy master' one chance of happiness by getting rid of him."

Thus Zat became a member of The Place's group of Little People—a pathetic group for the most part, in that they had but a handful of years to live and only so much life-joy as their human gods might be pleased to impart to them.

(Sunnybank Gray Dawn outlived all the Little People I have spoken of—except Tippy—in this book. Dawn was the last of the *great* Sunnybank collies. He died on May 30, 1929, leaving bitter heartaches behind him. Peace to his white soul!)

The bird ate and drank ravenously when the Mistress had tended his superficial hurts. Then, huddled in the corner of an impromptu packing-box coop, he slept the clock around.

For this is Nature's cure for her exhausted children, though the so-called lower animals alone seem wise enough to avail themselves of it to the full.

A day later, Zat emerged from his slumber orgy, hungry and full of gay spirit. He showed no desire to fly back whence he had come—nor did the Mistress's advertisements in four different papers bring to light his owner.

Within a week, Zat was as much at home at

Sunnybank as though he had been born there. It had been a week of humorously solemn exploration and of acquaintance-making. By the end of that time he was familiar with the grounds and the buildings and had tried to become equally familiar with The Place's human and animal population.

The humans greeted him as an amusing novelty. The various animals differed in their reception of him.

From that first moment of involuntary shrinking at sound of Zat's articulate speech, not one of the dogs, except only Laddie, would consent to have anything at all to do with the crow.

If Zat landed on the porch floor where Bruce was dozing, the stately collie would get up with contemptuous dignity and move far away. Wolf met Zat's merry advances with a growl and a flash of teeth whose threat even the insolently gay newcomer could not ignore. Bobby and Dawn regarded the crow with frank aversion.

Tippy, the Mistress's temperamental gray Persian cat, spat virulently and fluffed her fur to the size of an old-fashioned muff when he drew near. Once, indeed, the cat crouched, in vibrant preparation to launch herself at him. But, as she was about to spring, his debonair cry of, "Well, *well*, WELL! How's zat?" sent her scuttling up the side of a steep bookcase for safety from the creature she could not classify.

Either Laddie remembered his own first defense of the wounded bird or else he was too philosophical and too used to every vagary of human speech to take fright or umbrage at Zat's utterances. He showed no affection for the eerie black fowl, but he showed no aversion; and he even displayed a certain benign civility toward Zat, such as Lad lavished on all weak or bullied Little People that drifted into the great dog's life.

Encouraged at this tolerance, Zat warmed to the one canine which treated him well. He developed an evident fondness for the mahogany-and-snow collie; riding sometimes on the dog's haunches during Lad's lordly march through the grounds, or else hopping or fluttering along at Lad's side on these walks; or cuddling to sleep in the sun, close against the collie's shaggy side.

If Lad did not care overmuch for these demonstrations, at least he did not resent them. He seemed to gain a mild amusement from the crow's flattering companionship.

The humans judged that the enigmatic black creature must be genuinely fond of Lad, because the latter was the only animal on The Place on which Zat did not at some time or at many times try to play impish tricks.

The crow had a positive genius for mischief.

For example, he would swoop down with unbelievable speed upon the feed dish from which one of the collies was about to gobble some particularly tempting morsel. This morsel Zat would snap up; and would fly with it to the very lowest perch, where he was safe from the springing body and angry jaws of the defrauded dog.

After listening joyously for a time to the dog's harrowing barks, the crow would deposit the bit of stolen food on some tree trunk or bush-fork, just out of the other's reach, and would leave it there. Or else he would flap away in quest of Lad, and would drop the morsel at his collie chum's feet as a gift.

Similarly, just as Tippy was settling herself in dainty contentment to the lapping of her saucer of milk, there would be an indescribably swift beat of wings from nowhere in particular. Before she could guess what was impending, a strong beak would smite the saucer edge, upsetting its contents all over the cat or smashing the china in bits.

One of the workmen had a new felt hat, fawn-colored and jaunty, of which he was proud. He laid it on a rock while he wiped his sweating forehead. Then he turned to find his costly new headgear soaring clumsily and slowly through the air, gripped by Zat's beak and claws. The crow abandoned his plunder far out on the weakest bough of a high elm, under which the despoiled laborer danced in impotent wrath.

At theft, Zat had not his equal. He learned the whereabouts of every hidden hen's nest in loft or shed corner. He would emerge from a foray into such a nest, carrying a pilfered egg dexterously between his prehensile claws and flying low; while he sought some stone on which to drop his plunder. Dropping it, he would land beside the sloppy mass and devour it with zest. It was his favorite way of breaking an egg.

But when he fished the lake edge for mussels, he broke them open by holding them steady under one of his feet, while his stabbing beak hammered or ripped wide the shell.

Once, he found the superintendent's vest hanging on a nail where it had been left during the heat of the day. Zat drew gingerly a watch from the waistcoat pocket, and proceeded to try to open it as if it had been a mussel. The watch was a total loss, and the Master had to make up its value to the irate loser.

Wearying of these petty forms of entertainment, Zat developed a habit of chasing delivery boys—especially those on bicycles—who came to The Place with telegrams and the like. He would fly at them from the rear, pecking their ears, snatching off their caps, putting them to panic rout, following their retreat with his pagan triumph-yell of "Well, *well*, WELL! How's zat?"

As a result there was no competition whatever in the village, for the privilege of delivering telegrams and parcels and special-delivery letters at The Place. The fierceness of the ordeal outweighed tenfold any pleasure to be derived from possible tips.

Then, one morning, Lad was missing.

The big collie had sauntered forth, just after breakfast, on one of his stately tours of The Place's boundaries—a progress which always reminded the Mistress of some Old World squire inspecting his ancestral acres.

But he did not come back; nor had he returned at nightfall. Quite often his stroll would wind up with a desultory rabbit-hunt in the farther woods. But always he had been at home again by lunch-time. Today, he was not.

In crossing the highroad which split in two the grounds of Sunnybank, Lad had learned extreme caution—as befits any dog which may desire to stay alive in this era of crazily reckless motorists.

Yet, the Master made a tour of the road for a half-mile in either direction, in dread of finding his best-loved collie lying somewhere in a wayside ditch. There was no sign of Lad. The Master worried no longer. Since he was not run over, the wise collie could be trusted to come home again when he was ready to come. While Lad never had stayed away so long before, of his own accord, yet in all probability he was safe.

But when, at bedtime, and the next morning, he had not come back, both the Mistress and the Master were keenly distressed. They and the superintendent and the laborers dropped all other forms of employment, and they spent the day ranging the woods, for an area of perhaps ten miles. They trooped home, tired and miserable, at nightfall.

There the Mistress must listen to a vehement complaint from the cook.

It seemed, the day having been warm, the cook had carried out onto the breezy and vine-bowered kitchen piazza a piece of beef, two or three pounds in weight, which she was going to cut up for a savoury French ragoût of her own devising. She had cut the beef into four or five lengthwise strips, and was about to dice these, when she had to hurry back into the kitchen because a preserving-kettle boiled over.

By the time she set the kettle on a less torrid part of the range and wiped up the sticky overflow and washed her hands, several minutes had gone by. She returned to the piazza to see Zat flapping away with the last of the lengthwise strips of beef.

She screeched at the crow and even threw a knife at him. But these demonstrations failed to waken his conscience to the point of restitution. Off he flew, in a bee line, for parts unknown, carrying with him the strip of meat whose several predecessors presumably he had already borne to some unfindable cache.

"That settles it!" stormed the Master, glad to find some legitimate vent for the sick worry which was his at the absence of Lad. "First thing in the morning—even before I start out again to look for Laddie—I'm going to shoot that pest. He's gotten the whole Place on edge with his abominable thefts and mischief. One man has left and another is threatening to go; I had to buy Robert a watch to make up for the one Zat destroyed; the dogs' nerves are raw, from him; and now the cook is talking about leaving. That's rather a high price to pay for the pleasure of hearing a crow jabber one silly speech at us all day and every day. He's not any use and he ——"

"Zat is a little use, dear," timidly protested the Mistress. "Those crows, down in the oak trees by the lake, that used to wake us with their cawing every morning before daybreak. There isn't one of them within a half mile of here, any more. Zat has frightened them all away, just by his voice. If he had spoken to them that first morning, instead of trying to fight back when they attacked him, he would have scared them off at a single word. They skirt all around The Place, now, and they never dare come within a furlong of the lake trees. That's *one* good thing Zat has done by being here. He ——"

"It's a case where thirty crows are better than one," the Master declared. "I'm going to shoot him as soon as it's light enough to take aim. We aren't running a zoo, here, or an insane asylum for freak beasts and birds. . . . Lord! but I'd give a year's income to know Laddie is all right!"

Next morning, at first dawn, the Master ceased trying to go to sleep. He got up silently and dressed; then tiptoed downstairs. It was best to get the execution over with before his wife should have a chance to be unhappy over the dread of it. He found his shotgun, slipped a couple of No. 6 shells into it, and fared forth from the house.

But fifteen minutes of diligent searching of Zat's favorite roosting-places—the rooftree, a house-side oak limb, the clothes-posts, the kennel ridgepoles, and elsewhere—failed to disclose the miscreant bird.

Breakfast would not be ready for another two

hours. The Master resolved to put in the time in one more forlorn-hope beating of the forests for Lad.

With no great optimism and with heart heavy with worry he set out for the still woodlands, beyond The Place. He had traveled more than a quarter-mile before he realized the gun was still tucked absent-mindedly under his right arm. On he tramped, aimlessly, now and then pausing to shout Lad's name. There was no responsive bark.

Back into Pancake Hollow, behind the nearer woods, he made his way, and toward the rise of tree-thick broken ground which sloped with jut and dip toward the wildness of the mountains.

Over the thickest clump of underbrush—carpeted second-growth timber—some distance ahead of the Master and far to one side, a flock of crows were circling. Their caws reached the man clearly through the still dawn-air. There was excitement in the clangorous sound—excitement and greed.

Again and again the Master had heard that sinister note in the cawing of crows above some wilderness carcass. His heart beat thick at thought that it might readily be Lad they were cawing over—Lad killed or made helpless by some accident, perhaps.

He pushed forward as fast as he could go, over the uneven slope, heading for the distant copse,

Old Sunnybank Lad had finished his stroll ot the grounds, the preceding day. Then, as often he did, he ranged back into the farther woods in quest of a rabbit-chase. He cast about vainly for nearly a mile before he caught so much as a hopeful scent. Then he struck a trail he followed to a windfall. From under the windfall burst a cottontail, bumping over the rough ground ahead of the dog in most alluring fashion.

Lad gave chase, following hotly and with all the speed and vigor of his vanished youth. There is something vastly intriguing in the chase of a fast-running rabbit. All modern grayhound-racing is based on that overwhelming canine trait.

Along bumped the bunny, like a furry jumping-jack. Along, hot on his trail, flashed one of the fleetest and most powerful dogs of his generation. It was always a privilege to see Lad in such a pursuit.

Up a low slope whizzed the rabbit and into a spinney of second-growth trees whose boles were swathed in lush bushes and briars. Through bush stem and bramble tangle the cottontail writhed his way. Close behind him, straight and swift as a flung spear, dashed Lad, cleaving the undergrowth as if it had been a fog.

Into a thicket dived the rabbit. Midway he saw or sensed something which made him swerve sharply. Lad, too close behind to swerve, made a snap at the dodging rabbit.

His head lunged forward and close to earth as he struck for his shifting quarry. Then something snapped at him even as he snapped at the bunny. There was a red-hot sting in his left cheek, just back of his lip corner. He crashed to the stony and brambly ground with a force which knocked the breath out of him and all but stunned him.

There he lay, his neck wrenched, his body cruelly bruised, as he fought to draw air back into his shock-deflated lungs. He was caught fast by the cheek, his classic head held helpless and close to earth.

Here, a week agone, a farm hand had set a fox trap, right craftily, covering its merciless spread of steel jaws with dead leaves. The same night the farm hand had gotten drunk at a Pompton speakeasy. He had tried later to thrash a policeman, and had been sent to jail for a month.

It was the reek of man scent as well as a shiningly exposed corner of the trap which had made the rabbit swerve in mid-flight. Lad, his head low as he struck for the elusive prey, had grazed with his chin the delicately adjusted "platform" of the trap. The serrated steel jaws had snapped shut on his cheek, throwing him and holding him there.

So, in some part of their bodies, have many hundred questing dogs been caught, in a woodland steel trap, in every state of the Union. Hundreds and thousands of dogs have died in such imprisonment, from thirst and starvation. Hundreds and thousands of fine dogs will continue to die thus as long as the laws permit an irresponsible fool to set a trap at will and then neglect to revisit it daily.

More than once during the torture hours which followed, Lad heard the voices of the Master and the other searchers, sometimes muffled by distance, sometimes maddeningly near.

He could not bark, with his nose kept so close to the ground by the trap grip. A dog must lift his head to bark with any effectiveness. Such low gurgling sounds as he was able to make, between his side-twisted jaws, did not penetrate to the humans who were stamping noisily through the bushes in quest of him.

So, for more than twenty hours he lay, tortured by thirst and by the unnatural twisting of his muscles and by the ever-pinching trap. But he was not left to lie there wholly alone and deserted.

Just at sunset there was a soft winnowing of

wings overhead. A large and glossy crow came to earth a yard or so away and stalked gravely up to him. In the bird's beak was a strip of fresh beef. Silently Zat laid the gift on the ground, a bare six inches from Lad's moveless head. Then, silently, he flew away again.

During the next hour the crow returned three times, each time bearing a strip of the beef he had filched from the Sunnybank cook for his afflicted chum.

Yes, that sounds like a fairy-story. But, next day, when Lad was found, all four of the beef strips still lay within what Zat presumably had thought was easy reach of the collie's mouth.

How the crow had traced him to the hidden spot no human ever was to know. Perhaps by smell—which draws carrion birds to a feast through dozens of miles of upper air. In any case—or so the Mistress afterward deduced—he had followed Lad to the woods and had seen his hopeless plight, and then had flown to The Place for food for him.

At first hint of daylight, Zat was back again on the ground beside Lad. But the two did not long remain alone together. The scent of fresh meat, or perhaps the scent of blood from Lad's torn cheek, brought from every quarter a hungry flock of crows. They alighted in the treetops above the trap; cawing, fluttering downward, and then returning to their perches.

More and more of them gathered. Bolder and bolder they waxed as their numbers increased and as the hard-held dog showed no ability to move in his own defense. Moreover, an alien crow was crouched in front of the collie, his blazing black eyes glaring up at the sable horde in hot defiance.

At last, as if at some secret signal, the whole mass of winged marauders swooped downward. But for Zat, they would have had Laddie's eyes out in an instant, and their rending beaks would have been busy with the rest of his numbed body.

It was then that Zat shouted his battle cry—the cry he had not had the wit to use when crows assailed him on his arrival at The Place, but which he had grown mightily proud of since then, as he had noted its startling effect on strange humans and animals and birds.

"Well, *well*, WELL!" he challenged, harshly. "How's zat?"

As he croaked the defiance, he launched himself upward, into the thick of the down-swooping inky murderers, prepared with beak and claws and wings to fight them back from the mutilation of his collie pal.

The single body precipitating itself at them would have had pitifully small effect in stemming their charge. But, at the human words which preceded it, the flock of descending crows faltered, wavered motionless in air with a deafening beat of pinions, then flew upward raggedly and in terror.

Up after them and among them dashed Zat, the valiant, madly and suicidally bent on driving them far away from his helpless friend.

It was at that instant the Master fired.

Both barrels of his gun he emptied into the thick of the swirling crows. So intent had they been upon the feast and the victory which awaited them just below, that they had not observed his covertly fast approach, against the wind. He was in fair range when he let fly the double volley.

The crow flock scattered to the four points of the compass as the rain of No. 6 pellets whizzed like angry hornets through their ragged formation. To the ground plumped five of them, stone dead or beating futilely against the reddened grass with their wings.

Running forward through the maze of impeding underbrush, the Master came to the little handkerchief-sized clearing in the copse, in whose center lay Sunnybank Lad with an irregular ring of dead or wounded crows around him.

The Master dropped his gun and knelt over the

dog, prying apart the grim trap-jaws and lifting the numbed head in his arms.

Lad lay panting for breath, in stark relief at the cessation of his twenty-hour torment. He was sick and strangely weak and benumbed, and he was still in dire pain from the wrench of his muscles and the anguish in his cheek.

In another week or so he was to be as well as ever, except for the fast-healing face wound.

But, for the moment it was good—oh, it was passing *good!*—to lie thus inert, with the Master holding him and telling him what a splendid old dog he was. There was a break, too, in the man's rough voice, that made Lad lick the nearer hand with his swollen and parched tongue.

The Master made quick examination of the cheek gouges. Then he laid the dog's head tenderly back on the ground and started for the brook, a hundred yards below, to fill his cap with water for Lad to drink.

As he took the first step, his eyes fell on the five crows. One or two of them were still beating their wings, if more and more feebly, against the ground.

The Master paused in his rescue mission, long enough to pick up his gun and to swing it club-wise. These carrion murderers might better be put out of their misery, with a blow or two, before he went to the brook.

The gun but descended on the head of one flutterer. The beating wings lay moveless.

Then, almost at the Master's very feet, another crow stirred—a crow that had seemed to be dead, but which now began to quiver all over and then flutter its glossy black wings.

The Master glanced down at the bird. He saw that a pellet of shot had inflicted on it the merest light graze in whizzing past. The tap from the bit of lead had stunned it. Now the crow was coming to its senses, little the worse for the brief concussion. The Master swung his gun butt aloft.

But, before the butt could descend on its death mission, something pushed, staggeringly, between the man and the fast-recovering bird.

Lad had seen the peril to Zat—to the creature which had sought to save him from starvation and which had been prepared to cast away its own worthless life in his defense.

Weak and sick as he was, the collie lurched to his feet, reeling forward, covering Zat with his own body, staring at the Master with an appeal that went to the man's heart.

"Lad!" exclaimed the Master, in amaze.

Then his eye fell on the four strips of beef lying

ranged just in front of where the dog had been held captive. His mind went back to the cook's loud complaint of the stolen ragôut meat she had been cutting into strips for dicing.

He peered more closely at the crow. Zat was squatting on the ground, blinking drunkenly from side to side as his sharp wits began to return to him. His hurt had been as trivial as is that of a pugilist who suffers a two-minute knockout.

On the bird's right wing was a splash of white —memento of the time he had upset the white-wash bucket, a week ago, from its precarious position on a shed top, over the head and shoulders of a workman at The Place, who was reaching up for it. The prank had been one of Zat's most successful and most blasphemy-evoking. But he had not escaped without a generous daub of the white stuff on his shining black wing.

By it, as well as otherwise, the Master recognized him now. His eye ranged from the meat strips to the sheltering body of the collie, then to the boozily leering crow.

All at once the Master understood. The gun butt sank harmless to the ground. Gently the crow was lifted in two hands whose owner no longer had a cranky yearning to wring the bird's glossy neck.

"Zat," said the Master, stroking the ruffled

plumage smooth again, "you're coming back home with us. And you're coming back alive. You've won your welcome, you miserable old scoundrel!"

"Well, *well*, WELL!" gurgled the dizzy bird. "How's zat?"

Chapter Ten

"OUT OF THE DEPTHS"

I HAVE said that visitors to The Place found scant favor in Lad's eyes. For the most part, these guests tried in all friendliness to pet him or to take other undue familiarities on short acquaintance. Besides, they tended to upset the big dog's daily routine—which was the routine of The Place itself.

More and more was this so as the first subtly advancing tendrils of old age began to creep about Lad—unseen and insidious tendrils which, all too soon, were to become fetters to bind his gloriously sweeping gallop to a heavy canter and to stiffen the lithely powerful limbs by their ever-tightening grip, and were to bring heavy flesh to the once compactly slender body and a silvering to the classic muzzle and a slight dimness to the deep-set, sorrowful eyes.

All of that was still a few years off. But imperceptibly, Lad was aging. Not yet had come the day when unwieldy bulk and shortness of breath were to rouse his puzzled resentment and to score his abnormally sensitive feelings to the point of making him seek laboriously to romp and gallop as of yore, in order to hide his infirmity from the two humans he loved.

But he was beginning to grow old. He slept more than had been his wont, and bit by bit his long daily runs were shortening.

As with some fastidious elderly bachelor or spinster, the approach of age made Lad fussily averse to any disturbing change in the routine of his placid daily life. Strangers and guests were increasingly unwelcome to him.

Thus, when the Mistress and the Master returned from the railway station one day, with three visitors in the car, the big collie peered up the driveway with a ludicrous air of annoyance.

He had not been permitted to go, as usual, on the brief ride. That, by itself, had jarred his touchy feelings. But to have them come home with this load of intruders ——!

At sound of the car turning into the drive from the highroad, Lad had cantered gayly out from his cave under the piano, preparing, as always, to dash up the driveway to welcome the returning deities and to escort them to the house.

But the scent of the car's other occupants made him come to a shuffling halt, today, in mid-stride, and to turn about with head and tail disgustedly adroop. Back he plodded to the piano cave. There, with a half-human mutter of vexation, he lay down heavily, his head between his white little forepaws, his sorrowful eyes sullen.

He heard the car stop at the veranda. He heard voices and laughter, and steps on the porch —steps which were approaching the front door.

One of the maids had come forward from the kitchen wing, to admit the guests and to take their hand-luggage. As the maid passed the music-room she chirped to Lad as he lay sulking in his cave.

Lad was mildly fond of the maids and more than mildly fond of the surreptitious bits of food they used to give him. Ordinarily, he would have responded to the chirp by a thumping of his plumed tail on the floor. But now he was in no mood for friendliness or even for civility. He turned his head coldly away from the maid and flattened back his ears.

The guests were a boyhood friend of the Master's, and the friend's wife and their four-year-old son.

It was long since a child had played and laughed at Sunnybank. Wherefore the Mistress and the Master had looked forward happily to this ten-day visit of the Morvens. Both of them were tremendously fond of little Bobby Morven and had been fond of him ever since he was born.

Bobby was an elfin child, small for his age, and with a rare sweetness and magnetism that won its way to everyone's heart. Always he had been the chum and hourly comrade of his parents. Thus he was far more mature than the average four-year-old youngster. He spoke with no hint of lisp or of baby talk, and he had the mind of the average child of seven.

(There are children like that, though not over-many of them. Perhaps it is as well they are so few. For, too often, they do not live long enough for smug and stodgy maturity to blur their strange loveliness. I think in most people's lives there has been at least one such child—a child who has become a radiant memory instead of slumping into commonplace grown-upness.)

Now, as his parents came into the house, Bobby caught sight of the white-bear rug in the adjoining music-room. He trotted in, fearlessly, to stare in wide-eyed interest at the monster's fiercely gaping red plaster jaws and at the gigantic stuffed head.

To Bobby it was a right awesome, if fascinating, sight. Who could tell at what moment the flat-lying white giant with the ferocious face might stop being a rug and become a boy-eating bear again? Already his head was very much more like a live bear's than like a rug. If the rest of him——

Not in rout, but in very orderly retreat, Bobby trotted out of the music-room to rejoin his parents in the hall beyond. There was something wondrous protecting about his mother's skirts; and he knew his father could be relied on to destroy a whole army of white bears, if need be.

It might be just as well to go back where they were. Not that there was any danger, of course. But if the rest of the rug *should* decide to become a bear again, and if the bear should decide to follow him——

And, sure enough, the bear did follow him!

Lad, from his piano cave, had lifted suddenly interested eyes at first sound of the child's voice. At sight of Bobby himself, Lad had gotten to his feet, his tail awag in welcome, his sulks forgotten.

He adored children. He would suffer willingly any ill-treatment from them. The few youngsters who nowadays came to The Place were shining exceptions to the unwelcomeness of other guests.

Bobby had turned around and started from the room. Laddie followed him, in glad good-fellowship, catching up with him at the threshold and touching the round little cheek affectionately with his own cold nose.

Yes, the bear had followed! Bobby could feel its furry bulk against his hand and its cold muzzle sniffing exploratively at his face as if seeking the most appetizing spot for a bite.

There was a gallant soul in the child's undersized body. Instead of roaring in terror and hurling himself on his mother for refuge, he turned valiantly to face the awful peril. He didn't want to. He wanted to screech for help and to get behind his mother's skirts. But men didn't do such things. Daddy had said so.

Wherefore, he wheeled about to meet his fate. Then, with a little gurgle of reassurance he saw the bear was still stretched ruglike on the floor, and that nothing more murderous than a huge and shaggy brown dog had accosted him on his way to safety.

Moreover, looking deep into the collie's eyes that were almost on a level with his own, Bobby knew all at once that he had found a chum, yes, and a protector as mighty as Daddy himself—a dog that could put to flight every fur rug on earth that might take a notion to turn back into a bear.

In sheer relief Bobby flung both his thin arms around Lad's shaggy neck, hugging the dog's head close to his breast.

From no grown human, save the Mistress and the Master, would Lad have permitted such a gross familiarity. He hated to be pawed over or so much as touched. But the child's discomfitingly tight squeezing was a delight to him. Instead of drawing away in disgusted aloofness, Lad wagged his tail faster and sought to lick the joyous little face just above him.

Glancing in from the hallway, Morven said to the Master:

"I suppose that's all right, isn't it? I've tried to teach the kid not to be afraid of anything. Just the same, dogs are apt to snap, aren't they, if strangers haul them around or handle them roughly? I wouldn't want Bobby to get a fear of animals or ——"

"You can have a thousand dollars of mine," laughed the Master, "for every bite Lad gives Bobby—or any other child. Let them alone. Neither of them could have a better pal than the other. With Lad to tag around with him, Bobby is safer than if you hired three private detectives to guard him."

The Mistress and Mrs. Morven had turned to watch the pretty picture framed in the doorway—the great dog and the tiny child standing together in a shaft of May sunlight, glad in their new-made friendship, already well past the barrier of mere preliminary acquaintance.

The first glance at the pair disarmed any uneasiness Mrs. Morven might have had as to her boy's safety in the company of Sunnybank Lad.

"I was a bit worried," she said, "when I remembered the lake at the foot of your lawn. But I'm sure that beautiful collie of yours would live up to dog-story exploits by rescuing Bobby. He ——"

"Not unless he had to," corrected the Mistress. "Laddie never does melodramatic things when he can get his results in a simpler way. Watch."

She took Bobby's hand and led him out on the veranda and down to the lawn. Lad followed closely.

"Would you like to play out here on the grass with Laddie, till it's time to get ready for lunch?" she asked.

"Yes, thank you," Bobby made eager answer, adding: "What's the name of that little ocean down there?"

"That's the lake," said the Mistress. "Perhaps by and by we'll all go out rowing on it, to watch the sunset. Shall we?"

"Yes, please. And we'll take Laddie. Come along, Laddie."

Down the billowed slope of the lawn Bobby trudged; lured, as is every child, by sight of the sparkling lake beyond. Lad walked close alongside. The Mistress turned back to the others, who were standing on the veranda.

"Don't be frightened," she urged the Morvens. "He's heading straight for the water. I knew he would. But it's shallow, just down there. He'd have to wade out ever so far before he would be in any danger. Not that he'll get a chance to set foot in the water, at all. Lad will see to that. But I wanted you to see how safe he is, so you won't worry if he goes down along the lake shore again with Lad. Watch."

"It's all very well to stand still and say 'watch,' " answered Mrs. Morven. "But he's our baby and——"

"And Laddie is our dog," returned the Mistress. "Watch. If Bobby steps an inch into the water it will be time enough for these men to sprint down the hill and pull him out. But he won't. I'm only trying to ease your minds about his safety when Lad is along. And Lad will be wherever Bobby is, as long as you stay at Sunnybank. He——"

Bobby had come to the foot of the lawn and was running, fascinated, toward the lake. Lad was trotting gayly beside him. Then, as the child was within a yard or two of the shallow water at the shore, and as Morven had taken a hurried step forward from the veranda, Lad stepped calmly between Bobby and the brink.

There was nothing hasty or violent about the collie's action. Simply he moved in front of the youngster and stood sidewise, interposing his own huge furry body as an impassable barrier between Bobby and the lake.

Surprised and a little impatient, Bobby ran around the dog and made for the bank once more. Again to his amaze, before he could take a single forward step, Lad's barrier-like body was in his way.

Four times the child tried to push the dog aside or to skirt around him in order to get to the water. But, every time, with no roughness or seeming haste, Lad stepped between, solidly immovable, impervious to Bobby's commands and shoves.

Presently, the little boy gave up the utterly vain attempt and turned back to the house, toiling up the hilly lawn with Lad at his side.

"I don't think this nice dog likes the lake very much," he announced to the Mistress. "He kept pushing me back when I wanted to go to it. Is he afraid of the lake?"

"If he is," suggested Mrs. Morven, "don't you think it would be nicer for you to keep away from it when you and he are alone, so he won't be frightened? It isn't kind to frighten poor dogs.

you know. Why, I'm sure Laddie would never want to frighten *you!* So you must be just as polite and not frighten him by going near the water unless some of us grown people are along."

Bobby considered the problem an instant, his head on one side. Then he caught the drift of his mother's argument.

"Yes," he assented, with a sigh of renunciation. "I mustn't make him afraid. But—when I met him I hoped he was a very brave dog and not afraid of things. Do—do you suppose he is afraid of bears, too?"

"No," spoke up the Mistress, with solemn certainty. "Laddie isn't one single bit afraid of bears. He wouldn't let one of them hurt you for the world. I promise you that. Besides, there isn't a live bear within a great many miles of here. But if there was, Laddie wouldn't let it hurt you."

They drifted into the house, passing through the living-room. There, the spring day having a hint of chill in its bracing air, a goodly hearth fire was burning. Bobby went over to it, stretching out his cold little hands for warmth.

Instantly and unobtrusively, Lad was between him and the hearth; standing so close, himself, to the blaze, that his coat all but singed.

"You were right," said Morven to the Mistress. "I owe you all kinds of apologies for not trusting him when you said he'd keep Bobby out of harm. If he stands between him and fire and water, he'll stand between him and any other dangers. He's a grand old dog."

He laid his hand caressingly on Lad's silken head as he spoke. With an outward show of displeasure, Lad shifted quietly beyond the hand's reach. The act was significant. Morven did not try to pat him again.

"Laddie doesn't mean to be rude," explained the Mistress. "But he never cares for strangers. It isn't personal to you, at all. There are two extra laborers helping our men dig a foundation for a new wing for the stable, and a new root-cellar. Lad used to go down, two or three times a day, to watch the digging. But when these two new men came and tried to pat him and make friends with him, he stopped going there at all. He's queer and sensitive that way. But he's a glorious old fellow."

Thus began a time of unalloyed happiness for Lad; a continuous holiday.

All day and every day, he and Bobby were together, ranging the nearer woods, romping gently on the lawns, playing queer little imaginative games of the child's devising, lying side by side on the disreputable fur rug in front of the living-room fire on rainy days. At night, deserting his piano cave, Lad slept on guard beside Bobby's cot.

The only part of The Place whither Lad did not enjoy faring with his tiny comrade was to the rear of the stable where the new wing and the root-cellar were under construction.

Not that Lad had any objection to going there with the child, after work hours or on Sunday. But, while the laborers were busy he felt and showed strong reluctance to follow Bobby to the scene of their toil.

The two new men had noticed the dog's cold distaste for them. Thus, whenever he came in sight they amused themselves by whistling to him or calling him, then laughing at his lofty contempt as he turned his back on them and stalked away with flattened ears.

Lad hated to be laughed at. Most high-strung dogs hate it. (Humans themselves are not over-fond of it.)

One of the two men carried the joke so far as to try, one day, with vehement good-nature, to pull the collie's sensitive ears. But that phase of the jest was not repeated.

This because the laborer recoiled, staring foolishly at a thin slash on the fleshy part of his hand, a light but effective reminder from Lad that he did not want to be pawed.

The slash was delivered with unbelievable swiftness and with a mere turn of the head. Nor did the dog follow up his punitive efforts. He had no feud with this stranger who had sought to tease him. But it had been highly needful to rebuke the rough familiarity with much firmness, which he had done.

The laborer stared only for an instant at his lacerated thumb. Then, with a yell of blind anger, he caught up one of the bricks which were to serve as lining for the root-cellar.

This missile he prepared to hurl at the coldly uninterested dog. But before the brick could leave his grasp the man was spun around to face the superintendent, Robert Friend, who was bossing the excavation job.

With one strong hand the superintendent had twisted the laborer around. With the other he tore the brick from him.

"Get back to your work," he ordered, quietly, "or else take your pay and clear out. You've been pestering the Big Dog, right along, by guying him and whistling to him. I didn't stop you, because I knew he'd never come around here of his own accord while you two chaps are on the job. But when it comes to heaving bricks ——"

"The cur bit me!" fumed the man, striving to

wrench free from Friend's iron shoulder-grasp. "He ——"

"If you had let him alone, he'd have let you alone," retorted Friend. "When you laid hands on him he got back at you. I don't blame him. Any human would have done the same if he'd been mauled by a stranger he didn't like. You can't expect a dog to act more civilized than a human, can you? (Not so very much more civilized, anyhow.) And while we're talking about it, I'll ask you not to call the Big Dog a 'cur' any more. He's a thoroughbred. And he's more of a gentleman than ever you'll be in a hundred years. Now get back to your work."

Bobby had stood open-mouthed during the short encounter. Now, as the laborer bound up his hand in a dirty rag and slouched surlily back to his task, the child said conciliatingly to Friend:

"Maybe if Laddie would kiss the place and make it well ——"

A guffaw from the second laborer cut him short. Bobby gazed in mild surprise at the mirthful worker. Friend scowled blackly at the man. Then the superintendent stooped and picked Bobby up, tenderly, and seated the youngster on his broad shoulder.

"You and I know what a grand dog Lad is, Bobby-boy," he said. "But lots of folks don't.

I think that chap wouldn't much want to have the Big Dog kiss him. And I know Laddie'd hate it even worse. Lad gave him what was coming to him. But I wish you hadn't been here, to be scared by it. . . . How would you like me to take you up to the loft and show you the kittens? There's four of them, and they weren't born till last night."

"Where did they come from?" eagerly inquired Bobby, overjoyed at the prospect of seeing the new-born wonders.

"They're the old stable cat's babies," explained Friend as they mounted the loft steps. "The old brown cat that lives down here in the barn. The one I brought out for you to pat, the other day. They're hers."

"Did God send them to her?"

"Of course He did," Friend assured him.

"God is awfully good to cats, that way," mused Bobby. "I —— Oh!" he broke off his theological discourse at sight of four sprawly mites cuddled in the soft hay at the bottom of a box at the far end of the loft. "They're—they're so *noble!* What are we going to call them, do you suppose? Could we name one of them after Laddie, and another ——?"

Again he was interrupted. Lad was standing above the box-nest, gravely viewing the four kittens. Just then the mother cat returned from lapping the saucer of milk that had been left on the barn floor for her.

Ordinarily she and Lad were on comfortable terms of mutual tolerance. Now, seeing the huge collie towering above her precious brood, she flew at him, and scratched his nose with quite unnecessary virulence, arching her back and caterwauling most horribly.

Lad drew back, deeply offended, and went down the stairs to the ground.

"She didn't mean to hurt him," said Friend. "She was just afraid he might eat her babies. He wouldn't, of course. Suppose we go, now, and let her get over being cross at him. I've got to get back to work, and it's almost your lunch-time."

Lad was waiting for his little chum at the foot of the steps. Together they started toward the house. As they passed by the root-cellar excavation, Bobby halted and pointed dramatically to something that caught his eye.

A tall heap of dirt was at the edge of the unfinished cellar pit. The pit itself had not yet been lined with the waiting bricks. Its sides were shored up here and there by a board or two. Up one of these slightly slanting boards a large gray rat was climbing. Bobby squealed with excitement.

Either hearing the squeal or else seeing the child for the first time, the rat scuttled for safety. It dived between two shoring boards which had been left at the top of the hole. The boards touched each other at their far ends. Thus, the fleeing rat found itself caught in a corner, with a pile of loose earth above it. It jumped upward and essayed to climb the mound. The dirt slithered under the clawing feet, dropping the rat back into the corner again.

"Let's go and pet him, Laddie!" suggested Bobby, hurrying toward the cornered creature and holding out his hand in friendly greeting, the while cooing wordlessly to reassure it.

A rat in the open is a furtive and fleeing thing. A rat cornered can be excessively nasty to his cornerer. Unable to escape, the animal crouched, facing the oncoming Bobby.

"See!" exulted Bobby. "He isn't one single bit afraid of me. He ——"

The ingratiatingly out-thrust little hand was barely six inches from the rat's quivering nose. All unaware of the poisonous danger lurking in the creature's half-exposed long tushes, Bobby cooed caressingly at him again. The coo broke off in a cry of dismay.

The rat sprang at the friendly little hand.

But he sprang a fraction of an instant too late. Lad had come alongside. Perhaps from experience, perhaps from instinct, the collie seemed to know the ways of large and cornered rats. For he flashed past Bobby just as the rat leaped at the hand that now was all but touching it.

There was a snarling squeak and Lad tossed the evil creature high in air. Its back broken, the rat fell into the excavation.

"Oh, Laddie!" wailed Bobby. "How *could* you! And just when he was getting to be friends with me! You're a wicked, *wicked* ——"

The child disappeared over the verge of the six-foot drop into the cellar.

Looking over to find the tossed rat, Bobby had lost his balance. He clutched at a wide shoring board as he fell, jerking it out of place, but failing to break his own fall. He landed, quite unhurt, on a soft pile of earth at the cellar's bottom.

Worried, Lad gathered himself for a plunge down into the hole to the rescue of his playmate.

Then a terrible thing happened.

The crumbling top of the pit had been jarred by Bobby's pounding feet. The impact of his body against the ill-shored sides, and the yanking away of the widest piece of shoring, and the final jar of the boy's fall into the bottom of the cellar

—all these combined to start a really spectacular miniature avalanche.

A foot or two of surface earth crumbled. A cascade of dirt and sand and loose boards descended pellmell into the hole.

Lad was tobogganed down on the summit of the sample-sized avalanche that half filled the pit's floor. He scrambled to his feet.

His comrade was nowhere to be seen.

The spot where Bobby had landed was piled two or three feet deep with earth. Under that mass, somewhere, lay the child, pinned down by a suffocating weight and unable to stir hand or foot.

For the merest fraction of a second the dog gazed in moveless horror. Then he seemed to realize that this was a matter for human aid. Gathering himself together, he made a mighty upward leap.

His hind claws dug into the soft dirt just below the brink. A final wriggle that tested all his sinewy strength and agility, and he was on open ground again, racing for the group of men who had been working on the stable wing's foundation, only a few rods distant.

The superintendent had ordered them to go with him to a pile of lumber behind the barn, thence to carry back a load of shoring boards. He had gone along, to oversee the carrying.

One man only was left where last Lad had seen the group. This was the laborer who had teased him. The man had loitered behind, to wrap a fresh rag on his hurt thumb.

Up to him dashed Lad. This was no time to remember personal grievances. Bobby's life was at stake. The job of saving him seemed to call for human skill and power. There was but one human in sight. Lad ran to him, barking frantically.

The man shrank back. In desperate need to bring him to the child's aid, Laddie caught the hem of the worker's overalls between his teeth and attempted to tug him along toward the pit.

Believing himself attacked once more by a fiercely homicidal dog, the laborer hammered furiously at Lad's head with his thick fist. Then he planted a breath-taking kick in the collie's short-ribs.

The pain was sharp. The humiliation was fiftyfold sharper. But this was not the moment to think of pain or of insult. Bobby must be saved.

Heedless of his own injuries, Lad continued to yank at the overalls and to use all his muscular strength in the fruitless effort to draw his assailant toward the caved-in cellar.

The man tore loose and scurried up a barnside

ladder, out of reach. Then and only then did Lad give up hope of bringing him to the rescue. No other human was near.

Lad, and Lad alone, must try to get Bobby out from under that suffocating mountain of earth and boards if the child were not to strangle to death.

There was no time to cruise around in quest of humans more understanding than the panic-stricken laborer.

In two bounds Lad was back at the cellar brink. Then he plunged to its bottom once more. Scarce had his feet touched ground when he was at the half-cone of dirt that buried the child for whose safety Lad had made himself so proudly responsible.

From under the onslaught of his fast-plying forepaws, the soft earth flew in clouds. Lad was digging with all his frantic might and with all the speed his aging limbs could compass. An easy task this, compared with digging into the solid ground to open a rabbit-burrow. Here was no packed soil or unstirrable boulder.

Wide and deep grew the hollow he dug, straight toward the heart of the mound. The pit was dim with dust and with floating particles of earth from the masses flung up by the madly tearing forepaws. Those forepaws no longer were foppishly white, as ever it was Lad's pride to keep them. They were red-brown to the shoulders.

Twice, as he dug, the dog worked his way down to bits of shoring, too big or too tightly jammed for his paws to dislodge them. Then and then only did he cease to dig, and tackled the obstinate wood-slabs with his teeth. He bit deep into them, wrenching and tugging and shaking them until they came free. Then, barely waiting to let them drop from his bleeding jaws, he was back at his crazed digging once more.

Lad's heart was bothering him, an old heart that had not known such a strain for many a day and which was no longer resilient enough to bear it unprotesting. The pain from the laborer's rib-kick was like a red-hot stab. The dog was panting hard—or was trying to—to suck air down into his anguished lungs. But the dust and dirt had filled his nostrils and his throat, even as it was blinding him.

It did not so much as occur to him to cease or even to slacken his terrific exertions. That was Lad's way, ever, from first to last, throughout his shining life. He had never learned the meaning of fear or of failure.

Presently he jerked back one of his fast-flashing forepaws just in time to keep its sharp claws from raking a limp little arm. A much larger shoring plank than any he had encountered barred his further progress. It was much too cumbrous and broad to be torn away by his teeth. From one side of this protruded the arm he had uncovered.

Scarce pausing to shift his position, Lad began to dig from a new angle, to get around to the side of that impeding slab. Here the dirt was lighter in weight and volume. In a few seconds he was thrusting his nose behind the slab. His jaws closed with firm gentleness on Bobby's jacket.

Bracing himself, he began to pull, not with the fierce yanking he had accorded to the piece of plank that had been in his way, but with a steady and unhurtful leverage.

From behind the plank he drew the weeping and half-suffocated child.

It was that wide plank which had saved Bobby from death. It was the shoring board his fingers had clutched at as he fell. It had toppled over, atop him, one end of it still against the crumbled side of the wall.

Thus he had lain under it, as under a low tent, protected by it from the mountain of dirt which otherwise must have choked him. Also, in that tiny space there still had been enough—if barely enough—imprisoned air to keep him conscious.

Out onto the earth-strewn floor of the cellar Lad drew the boy, letting him lie there gasping, fresh air into his lungs. Over him stood the great collie, stooping once to lick the dirty little tear-stained face.

Bobby opened his eyes. He was still too weak to rub the dust out of them. He had not been unconscious. Well did he know everything that had befallen, from the instant of his backward tumble into the pit to the moment Lad had brought him out from under the débris. He wanted to thank the dog, to pat him, to tell him how wonderful he was.

But, for the moment, he was too weak and spent to summon energy for a single word or motion.

So he lay there, panting, and above him stood the frightfully worried Lad, at a loss what to do next for his chum.

Lad knew the boy was in no further danger of smothering. But Bobby was lying so still and so helpless! Wiser aid than the collie's must be summoned, now that there was more time to summon it.

Licking the dirty little cheek again reassuringly, Lad turned about and gauged the distance to the top of the excavation.

The dog was tired. Every muscle and every bone throbbed with painful exhaustion. There was fire in the rib the laborer's kick had broken.

He could not hope to reach the summit in a single mighty bound, as he had done a minute or two ago. He must pick out the most sloping side of the earthy wall and try to clear it in a rush and a scramble. Then to find the nearest human—some human with more sense than had that strange laborer who had buffeted and kicked him.

Now that he had time to remember it, the pain of the kick was beginning to grow worse, burning and searing, sapping such strength as remained to him.

But all of that could wait. Just now he must get out of the pit and summon any available human to his stricken chum.

Lad gauged the distance and the angle at the side of the pit whence the avalanche had descended on Bobby. Here there was much more slope than anywhere else, except for about two feet from the top where part of the surface earth still jutted out, with a hollow just below it.

Had his brain and his eyes been clearer, instinct might have told Lad that that irregularly outjutting shelf of soil, hollow beneath, did not promise the surest and soundest footing for an eighty-pound collie to land on.

Also, instinct might have warned him that where a considerable body of earth has fallen inward from the top of a hole, there is often a quantity of additional earth waiting only for a jar of some kind to make it cave in.

But his eyes were still dim with dust. His wild anxiety for the child's safety made him heedless of his own. Backing to the farthest side of the hole, he went into action.

Calling on his every tired sinew, he rushed across the floor of the pit and up the slope.

Under his feet the mounded dirt gave way, robbing him of much of his impetus. Yet his forepaws reached the overhang of top-soil, and he dug his claws into it, heaving himself upward.

The next second he was falling. The top-soil had given away. Nearly a ton of it, and the loosened ground behind, crashed slitheringly down into the cellar.

Lad landed on his back on the dirt floor. Before he could force his worn-out body to turn over so that his feet could be gotten under him for leverage, the torrent of earth and sticks and stones had smitten him; burying him deep and rendering him as pitifully helpless to escape, or even to move, as had been Bobby himself.

The new avalanche barely missed the child. The sound and sight of it freed him partly from the dazed reaction that had been his.

Bobby sat up and tried to struggle to his feet. But the effort was too much for him. He sank back, against the far side of the pit, viewing in dumb horror the fate that had overtaken his adored collie comrade—and powerless to move hand or foot to help the buried dog.

Around the corner of the barn, convoyed by Robert Friend, came the procession bearing the first planks of shoring from the stack. Two men carried them. They arrived at the former site of their labors just in time to see their hand-slashed colleague descending cautiously from the ladder.

"What were you doing up there?" demanded Friend. "I told you to bear a hand with these boards. We——"

"That savage collie dog chased me up," declared the accused man, wrathfully. "He comes over here and he goes for me like he's a tiger. I got away from him. Then he goes and dives into that cellar, head first, and——"

Involuntarily the superintendent glanced toward the near-by root-cellar excavation at which the speaker was waving an explanatory arm.

As he looked, Friend saw a pair of earth-smeared forepaws grasp the treacherous strip of ground. He had a momentary glimpse of a soiled and bleeding head—classically beautiful despite its caked dirt—above the edge of the cellar. Then head and paws vanished. Down after them caved a section of the bank.

"All hands!" shouted the superintendent, snatching up a spade. "Grab spades and come on the run!"

He himself was running as he spoke. He came to the edge of the cave-in and saw Bobby Morven crouching in its far corner.

The child was ghastly pale under his coating of dirt. He was pointing a palsied finger at a new-fallen half-cone of earth, across the pit from him.

Of Sunnybank Lad there was no sign.

All this the superintendent noted as he jumped down into the pit and drove his spade mightily into the heap of dirt. Before he had cast forth three shovelfuls, other men were down there beside him, digging as frantically as he, though not at all understanding why they were bidden to do so.

Far under the mound Lad lay pinioned, powerless to move, strangling from total lack of air.

He had fought the good fight. He had saved from this hideous death the child that he loved. He was tired—tired out and dizzy. But he was not too weary or too dazed to be aware of the lung-bursting agony that was his.

Instead of giving himself up, sheeplike, to his

fate, he fought on, striving valiantly to force his way through the dead weight, enough to turn over on his stomach, where the leverage of his legs might or might not be of some help to him.

The fight was vain, and Lad knew it. Still he struggled, unafraid, with no thought of surrender. Which, also, was Lad's way.

Then, his reeling senses became aware of hands seizing him, lifting him clear of the grave which had closed over him. Through his clogged nostrils and throat seeped a trickle of fresh air. Then some one was clearing the dog's throat and nostrils so that he might really breathe; he who scarce had life enough left to draw a long breath.

Two weeks later the bandages were taken off Lad's kick-broken rib. Strength had crept back to the half-dead collie. The rib had mended quickly, thanks to Lad's gorgeous health. Once more he could breathe without that cruel stab of pain in his side.

He was himself again; perhaps a bit stiffer and less gayly active than before his stark minutes in the cellar-pit. But there were years of glad life ahead of him; before the September day in 1918 when, as I have told elsewhere, the sixteen-year-old collie should fall asleep in the cool angle under the back-veranda hammock and should fail to wake again.

Yet the dog seemed to have lost some of his buoyant spirit.

Bobby and Bobby's parents had ended their ten-day visit at The Place. Lad was piningly homesick for his little human comrade. He moped for the child, despite his olden joy in the companionship of the Mistress and the Master.

Then, of a late May morning, the Mistress got into the coupé and whistled to Lad. The dog ran forward, eager for a motor ride. Over to the railroad station they drove. There, Lad at her side, the Mistress got out of the car and stood near the tracks.

Presently the train from New York drew in. From it descended Mrs. Morven. Lad wagged his tail with more civility than ardor at sight of the returning guest. Mrs. Morven turned to lift somebody down from the platform.

It was Bobby!

With a trumpeting bark of welcome—the bark he reserved usually for one or both of his deities—Lad galloped forward.

Bobby met him half-way, flinging both thin arms about the great shaggy throat of the dog and squealing with joy, while Lad alternated his fanfare of barks with arduous efforts to lick the glowingly happy little face.

"I knew that would lift you out of your blues, Laddie!" said the Mistress. "Bobby's visit here did him so much good that he has come back to spend the whole long glorious summer at Sunnybank, with us. He has been grieving for you, too, his mother says, just as much as you've grieved for him."

"Only, you must promise not to bite any more nice friendly rats and work-gentlemen, Laddie!" ordained the child, his arms still around the great dog. "If you really *must* bite something, wait till there's a bear that tries to get into my room."

"Say!" drawled one smoking-car passenger to another, as the train moved on. "I wouldn't own a dog like that; not if you gave him to me. Did you hear how he kept up his silly barking all the time we were at the station? That purp hasn't got any sense."

But Lad, just then, was too gorgeously happy to care whether he had sense or not.

THE END

AFTERWORD

About eleven years ago my earliest stories of Sunnybank Lad appeared in book form. It is more than fifteen years since the first of these was published in the *Red Book Magazine*.

The stories themselves had no claim to greatness, nor even to literary merit. I know that as well as you do. But Laddie was great enough to counterbalance any defects of his chronicler, and to bring unlooked-for success to my tales of his adventures and of his strange personality.

Better than that, the stories won for the grand old collie a host of friends, both here and in Europe, friends to whom he was as real as though they had known him in the flesh.

Many of those friends have written to me, again and again, asking to hear more about Lad.

So I have ventured to write this latest book, hoping to please Lad's old-time admirers and perhaps to gain other friends for him, by making our long-dead collie chum live anew in its pages.

ALBERT PAYSON TERHUNE.

"Sunnybank"
Pompton Lakes
New Jersey